D1121580

**L &
OD**

Books by Josef Skvorecky include:

The Cowards

The Legend of Emoke

The Mournful Demeanor of Lieutenant Boruvka

The Bass Saxophone

Miss Silver's Past

The Republic of Whores

The Miracle Game

The Swell Season

The End of Lieutenant Boruvka

The Engineer of Human Souls

The Return of Lieutenant Boruvka

Dvorak In Love

Talkin' Moscow Blues

The Bride of Texas

Two Murders in My Double Life

When Eve Was Naked

ORDINARY
LIVES

ORDINARY LIVES

JOSEF SKVORECKY

TRANSLATED FROM THE CZECH BY

PAUL WILSON

KEY PORTER BOOKS

Published in Czech under the title Obyejné životy by Ivo Železný Publisher, Prague.

Library and Archives Canada Cataloguing in Publication

Škvorecký, Josef, 1924–
[Obyejné životy. English]
    Ordinary lives: a novel / Josef Škvorecký; translated from the Czech by
Paul Wilson.

Translation of: Obyejné životy.
ISBN: 978-0-88619-443-7

    I. Title. II. Title: Obyejné životy. English.

PS8537.K86O2913 2008   C891.8'6354   C2008-902398-6

The publisher gratefully acknowledges the support of the Canada Council for the Arts
and the Ontario Arts Council for its publishing program. We acknowledge the support
of the Government of Ontario through the Ontario Media Development Corporation's
Ontario Book Initiative.

We acknowledge the financial support of the Government of Canada through the Book
Publishing Industry Development Program (BPIDP) for our publishing activities.

L&OD is an imprint of
Key Porter Books Limited
Six Adelaide Street East, Tenth Floor
Toronto, Ontario
Canada M5C 1H6

www.keyporter.com

Text design: Marijke Friesen
Electronic formatting: Alison Carr

Printed and bound in Canada

08 09 10 11 5 4 3 2 1

To Zdena, the girl I met in Prague,
for the fifty good years that followed

AUTHOR'S NOTE

I finished this novel in my eightieth year. To some degree it is a summation, because eighty is when old age really begins. Most of the characters and events in it have their origins in life, but they are neither portraits of real people, nor is this report based on fact.

In the beginning, there was a group of classmates. It was their fate to graduate from high school in 1943, in the fourth year of the German occupation, in a time and place we referred to as the Protectorate of Bohemia and Moravia. The group was torn apart and the lives of its members uprooted by some questionable social engineering, first by the Nazi race laws, which were the first step toward the Final Solution, and then, after the Communist putsch in 1948, by the class-based laws of the new regime, underpinning the brutal "class struggle" that raged on, in various forms, until the late 1980s. Finally, after communism collapsed in 1989, the classmates, or those who remained, found their lives once more flowing back into the common stream of everything that lives.

I have carried this tale around in my head for many years, putting it off from year to year. It's only now that I have finally written it down. Not because I thought it couldn't be done any better, but because I don't know how much more time the Almighty will grant me.

Since my books have been coming out for half a century, my constant readers may welcome the notes I've provided to remind them of some of the characters and events in my novels that make fleeting appearances here, or to bring to mind some of the lesser-known historical facts that figure in the story. Readers who are coming to my work for the first time will perhaps welcome them as well.

The notes appear at the end of the book, together with a list of Danny's classmates, and are indicated throughout by asterisks.

JŠ
Toronto, June 2008

CLASS
REUNION
1963

Twilight. Honey and blood. Indifferent to the historical situation of nation and town, it spoke to me, aged thirty-nine.*

I stood here once, a long, long time ago, in a room papered in purple and gold. The bass saxophonist lay on the brass bed while I held his saxophone in my hands, his asthmatic breathing behind me.

As it had then, the room glowed like a coloured lantern as the golden rays of the Indian summer sunlight reached in through the drapes.

I pulled one of the curtains aside and, hidden behind the golden fabric, looked down on the square. From the bus stop on the far side of the church, I saw Antonin Jebavy walking toward the hotel, a cap on his head, not because it was part of the proletarian uniform appropriate to the historical situation, but because he'd just come back from the mountains. He was the first to arrive—looking just as he had two decades ago, beyond time, perhaps beyond politics—from a two-room schoolhouse in the Eagle Mountains, a couple of kilometres beyond Cerna Hora, Black Mountain, just north of the town.

The mountain loomed over me now, darkened by the woods that reached almost to the restaurant near the summit. Nadia had been dead for seventeen years.

⊰ ⊱

My journey had, in fact, been a pilgrimage to the shrine of
Saint Nadia.* It was spring break, and I'd returned to a
bitterly cold Kostelec. Mother had died only three weeks
before, and Dad was alone. I felt sorry for him; otherwise,
I'd have stayed in Prague with Lizetka. There was no heat-
ing in the train, perhaps because of some bizarre economies
I couldn't comprehend. The locomotive was a steam engine,
after all; what were they trying to do, save steam? Pointless
thoughts, the pain still with me from that final night when
Mother was apparently alive but merely breathing noisily
and it was a while before I realized that this sound, as if her
lungs were cracking apart, was what, in books, they call the
death rattle. Suddenly it stopped. I listened a while longer,
then walked out into the frigid corridor of the former orphanage, the yellow night lights on the wall so dim they
gave off no illumination. I walked quickly through the
gloom to the nursing station, which was brightly lit, and
tapped on the door. A nurse in a cap with starched wings
looked up from her book, a prayer book, perhaps, and saw
me through the glass panel in the door. It was Sister
Udelina.* I'd met her the year before, when I'd wanted to go
into medicine and had worked in the hospital as a volunteer.
She stood up at once.

"I think Mother has..."

"The Lord's will is done," she replied in a loud, joyful
voice. It was only later, in memory, that I understood her
tone; at that moment, it seemed heartless.

I hurried after Sister Udelina's flowing black habit and,
from a distance through the open door, saw my mother's
sallow face. The nurse stopped at the doctor's office, knocked

*loudly, and called out, "Doctor! Mrs. Smiricky has expired,"
then she hurried on to the room where my mother's face, as
if carved from ivory, lay on the white pillow. Sister Udelina
knelt by the bed and began to pray. I knelt as well, and ungovernable thoughts carried me away to a distant time
when I had knelt at the altar, the Venerable Father Meloun*
in front of me, the laces of his highland underwear showing
beneath his black trouser cuffs as he stood up—and then
back to my dead mother. And to the dead Nadia. An ungovernable torrent, scarcely even thoughts.*

*The doctor came in, took Mother's ivory hand, and felt
no pulse; he murmured something to Sister Udelina and left.
The nurse stood and opened the window, letting icy air, sharp
as a dagger, into the cool room. I knew why she had done
so. But could the soul fly up to its Maker in such frigid
weather?*

*"You must leave now, Danny," Udelina said. "The chapel
is open. Go and pray for your mother." She hadn't expressed
her condolences, perhaps because this had been a beautiful
death. Mother had received the last rites and afterwards, in
the corridor, the young priest had asked me how many had
enrolled in the freshman year at the Faculty of Arts in
Prague, and he seemed sad when I told him of the large
numbers. In the seminary there are only seventeen novitiates,
he sighed.*

AT TEN O'CLOCK *the next morning my father went to the
bank again, leaving me to arrange everything: a coffin of
medium quality, a cross. I told the undertaker the service
would be conducted by Father Meloun, and then I went to
the vicarage.*

*Everything was white; snow had fallen overnight and
it seemed to me that Mother was already an angel. I was*

tormented by a belated regret that nothing I had done could now be atoned for, nothing. I couldn't even remember the ways in which I had actually hurt my mother. In my ears I could hear the silent voice of the dead woman uttering that old Czech saw about posthumous guilt: You'll be digging me up with a needle, Danny! But what sins I had committed against her I no longer knew. Thoughtlessness, yes. My head was full of Irena, Marie, then Lizetka: Mother had already vanished utterly from my mind. Lizetka wasn't even a Catholic anymore, but she was still religious. She had converted to Methodism, and I knew it was because she had wanted to be different—how many Methodists were there in Prague, after all? There was hell to pay at home, but Lizetka was their only daughter. Perhaps she wasn't even that religious. We fooled around every afternoon, until nightfall, when she would look at the clock, pull her skirt down, and announce, "That's it, Danny. It's late. Go home." I'd take the midnight streetcar in the bitter cold, writhing in agony from my glands' unfulfilled expectations. Fortunately, I was almost alone, with just a couple of sleeping workers heading home from a late shift, or more likely from the pub, reeking of drink and prompting the shivering conductor to remark: "Smell that, young man? Like they crawled straight out of the barrel." I could think only of Lizetka; Mother was no longer with us.*

Later, in bed, I felt Nadia climb in with me and lie close, and though I knew the dead weighed nothing, she helped ease my agony. And I didn't even go to confession, not knowing exactly what kind of sin I had committed. Ah, but I did know. I had forgotten my mother. Honour thy father and thy mother. *Then I thought about it no longer.*

⚜ ⚜

From behind the hotel curtain, I watched as the Venerable Father Meloun emerged from the church. Time and history had left their mark on him, and he had fared badly. He had survived Buchenwald and a lot more since then. He'd lost weight, but his face, like a full moon, was the same, though wrinkled now: a melon above a clerical collar encircling a gaunt neck, a moon rising out of the black uniform of his estate, hanging threadbare from his thin shoulders as if from a coat hanger. He was supporting himself with a cane, his other hand resting on the shoulder of a young chaplain I did not know.

In front of the priest and his new chaplain walked a young man who looked like an overage altar boy, a communion robe draped over his arm, just as I had carried it myself once, long, long ago, the Venerable Father striding briskly across the square, chiding me in a loud voice: "Shake a leg, Smiricky, you're late!"

⚔ ⚔

Sometime just after the war began, I knocked on the door of the vicarage, and Father Meloun himself opened it a crack. When he saw it was me, he said quietly, "Smiricky, come by a little later. In about half an hour. I'm ..."

Through the partially open door I could see Tonda Kratochvil and a girl. Her back was to me, then she turned slightly and I recognized her in profile. Dasa—once, but now no longer—Sommernitzova.

"On second thought, go into the church," Father Meloun said. "Into the sacristy. I'll meet you there."

I turned and walked down some worn wooden steps, then looked around and caught a glimpse of that moonlike face just before the door closed on it, a moon at the full, my private symbol for the paradoxical but benign heaven in which I believed. Or did not believe. That's why I would still sometimes go to see the Venerable Father, although he taught us religion only up to Third Form, and by now I was finishing Fifth. I'd just drop in to chat. Father Meloun's chaplain at the time had left on a pilgrimage to Rome a couple of days before the Germans occupied the country, and had never returned. So the Venerable Father remained alone in the vicarage. They hadn't assigned him a new chaplain yet, nor did he have a housekeeper. He took his meals in Soucek's pub, where they gave him a special rate.

I went to the sacristy and began to pray. But my wayward thoughts soon led me to Irena. I heard her voice, always so full of laughter. I saw the field at the Sokol grounds, where the girls were playing a game in which they had to strike the ground with a stick, then drop it and start running while the boy opposite would throw a ball at them. If he hit one of the girls before she made it to home base, she was out of the game. So far the girls had all been eliminated. Then it was Irena's turn. She bent down, swung the stick, but didn't let it touch the ground. The boy didn't notice her trick and threw the ball at her hard, hitting her so sharply on the thigh that she yelped, and the ball bounced off to one side. Only then did she finally strike the ground with the stick and run elegantly to the safety of home base, where she made faces at him. That ploy hadn't occurred to any other girl. Irena was brilliant, one of a kind. I kept on praying, saying the words to myself, but I was preoccupied by visions of this recent, utterly insignificant sporting event. To concentrate on the prayer, I closed my eyes tightly—only to see Nadia standing sheepishly in front of my mother the day Mother practically caught us in flagrante delicto.*

Si cor non orat, in vanum lingua laborat. *If the prayer is not from the heart, the tongue labours in vain.*

THE VENERABLE FATHER entered the sacristy and sat down in a worn armchair intended for episcopal visitors. Well-laundered vestments hung in the closet, pluvials and surplices, altar boy gowns I had long since outgrown. The room was gloomy and would have been dark but for the light coming from a narrow window that was most likely a left-over from the church's earlier Gothic incarnation. The priest stared at me without saying a word; he could see I was out of sorts, as indeed I was. Why couldn't Tonda and Dasa have been satisfied just to have each other, and stayed at home? Why did they have to come sneaking in here to see the Venerable Father, visible to anyone who made it his business to observe that kind of thing?

"What were they doing here, Father?" I said hesitantly. "Isn't it—isn't all this—a bit risky?"

"Have no fear, Smiricky," said the priest. "Even in Germany, for the time being at least, such marriages are quite legal." He was smiling, but his voice was uncertain.

"Yes, but . . ." I stopped, not wanting to add to Father Meloun's troubles. I had wanted to say that it would only take someone who notices such things to notice, and the authorities would send a man to the vicarage, and then . . . I knew how these things worked from my Jewish friend Alex Karpeles, whose cousin got married in the nick of time, just before the Nuremberg Laws kicked in,* to Hilde Schlösser, and though Hilde's Aryan status was backed up by all seven birth certificates required by the Laws, someone took notice all the same. The word got round among her compatriots and, after the fact, their marriage became a criminal act called Rassenschande. Defiling the race.

By this time, the Germans were firmly in charge of the country and I knew the term from our Fifth Form lessons in

Die Deutsche Ideologie, which our teacher, Miss Brunnen-schatten, had to teach us. Having no choice in the matter, she didn't actually teach the subject, but merely read to us from a book of that title. It was a rather slim volume, containing everything Germans were expected to believe, except that Miss Brunnenschatten, who, as my father would say, was as German as a fence post, didn't believe a word of it, and by that time her name wasn't really Brunnenschatten anymore, but Cvancarova. She had married Mr. Cvancara, trading in her beautiful German name for a comic-opera Czech one, and causing the school inspector, Herr Werner, great displeasure. The teacher—that is, Mrs. Cvancarova, though I still thought of her as Miss Brunnenschatten—read to us in a monotonous voice, like an automaton, although when she felt like it, she could recite the poetry of Reiner Maria Rilke by heart with great passion.*

"What happens to Tonda and Dasa is in God's hands," said the Venerable Father Meloun.

In God's hands, or in the hands of someone quite different. Unless God was using the two of them for some kind of experiment that we couldn't really understand. That's how Father Urbanec would have explained it.* He was a professor of dogmatics at the Faculty of Theology in Prague. He knew the Summa Theologiae of St. Thomas Aquinas by heart, and was my Uncle Neumann's confessor. Father Urbanec had an explanation for everything. If only you could believe him.

By now it was eight thirty and nightfall, too late for St. Thomas Aquinas, even though such things are best discussed in the dark.

I went home.

⚐ ⚑

Nina, just off the train from Hermanice, walked out onto the square from Kamenice Street. Her cheeks were moon-like too, though they were hollow with grief, or so it seemed to me. I knew nothing about her, nor was I particularly interested. Highland hiking boots, thin calves, a shabby pale blue overcoat that may have been the same one she wore in Eighth Form during the war, for God's sake. A grey beret atop faded golden curls. She was alone. Then she vanished from my sight under the window ledge.

᛭ ᛭

In the back room of a hotel that belonged to Bara's father, where everything was spinning, Bara had leaned over to me and whispered, "Why are you ignoring her?"

I looked at Bara uncomprehendingly. There were two of her, but it was the booze: the hotelier had supplied us with a small keg of rum for the party. None of us was used to drinking because it was wartime and alcohol was available only by ration card and only to factory workers, and anyone who had a bottle at home saved it for special occasions, which often involved bribing someone from the Imperial Work Office. I looked at the two Baras and tried to bring them into focus, to make a single entity of her. But I couldn't. Both Baras tilted their heads. I turned in the direction they indicated to encounter damp moon-like cheeks and Nina lifting them toward me.

"I—I'm not ignoring her," I stammered, slipping my arm around Nina's neck, for the first time in my life feeling the warm dampness of a girl's mouth on my lips.

So began my first quasi-affair. Against my will. And counter to my Hollywood expectations. As a songster put it years later, "When I'm not near the girl I love, I love the girl I'm near . . ."

I went walking in the woods with her. We would kiss, and then I would take her to the station to catch her train home. My wayward thoughts carried me away to Irena, to Marie. Nadia wasn't yet part of this comedy with a tragicomic ending, only these two, and neither would have me. I kissed Nina, but that was as far as it went. I had had nothing more than a baptism by fire of rouge on my lips; I didn't even venture under her skirt. She wasn't Judy Garland, who at night stood in for those other two who were not forthcoming, though perhaps they might have been had I not been paralyzed by fear in their presence, able to move only the muscles that governed my tongue.

It was always the same: we went from school to the woods. By that time, our classes were held in the afternoon, in the Business Academy, because the high school had been taken over by the Hitlerjungend. *On a bench in the woods, we had nothing to talk about and were mostly silent. Then we walked from the woods to the train station. I had no idea how this was going to end.*

The ungovernable torrent of thoughts ...

I waited for Marie in front of Mr. Skocdopole's house because she walked that way to school. Prema and I had set it up. We pretended to be having a conversation. She showed up in her blue coat, the white hood that normally hung down like a V for Victory covering her head because it was snowing,* and I fell in beside her, but she stuck her nose in the air and wouldn't bring it down the whole way to school. I couldn't hook up with her after class that day, and she got away from me. The end of one of those chapters.*

And Nina, naturally, was wiser than I was.

⚐ ⚑

Nina and Bara Innemanova had been inseparable friends at school, but Bara had long ago stopped travelling on the same train to Kostelec. Bara now lived in Prague. According to the timetable, the express train from Prague was supposed to arrive before Nina's milk train from Hermanice, except that in this historical situation, the trains had stopped running on time. Their girlhood friendship had been destroyed by wedlock. Nina had married a pastor in the church of the Czechoslovak Bretheren from Hermanice nad Ledhuji, and Bara was married to a Mr. Cefelin, an advisor in the Ministry of the Interior, or maybe it was the Ministry of Foreign Trade. Perhaps with some pull from her husband, she'd become a school inspector or something like that, I wasn't sure. But she was definitely a Party member. The hotel no longer belonged to her father, but that didn't matter. Her father was said to have accepted President Gottwald's invitation to join the Party, and evil tongues had it that he'd become thick as thieves with the Kostelec inner Party, the one praised by the president himself for providing exemplary assistance in bringing about the conviction and subsequent hanging of the Slansky gang* just about the time the president started drinking himself to death, perhaps because of what that exemplary assistance had wrought. I don't know. None of this mattered anymore.

⇥ ⇤

Occasionally, when I was in the woods, I would see Miss Brunnenschatten with a man. They were obviously dating, and it took me aback. Despite being as German as a fence post, she was pretty, a slender blonde wearing a dirndl over the white blouse that the upright principal, Mr. Zach, had recently forbidden her to wear to school, or so it was said: I was in First Form at the time and didn't know that Mr. Zach had banned her blouse so that she wouldn't overstimulate the upper-school boys, and perhaps even the Fourth and Third Formers. But by the Second Form I'd figured it out because it was summer and Miss Brunnenschatten wore this blouse around town, without the dirndl. In school, she wore brown dresses, and from time to time the pink hem of her slip would show. It bothered the girls, and so, once, they sent Stazka Anastazova to put a word in her ear at the beginning of German class. As Stazka walked up to the front, I saw that she had a hole in the back of her skirt, and it was clear that underneath she wore not a pink slip but pale blue panties. "Aufstehen! Umdrehen!" Miss Brunnenschatten commanded, and when the whole class stood up and turned their backs, she must have hitched up her slip, because when she commanded us to turn around and sit down again, it was no longer visible.

At that time, I would walk home from school with Stazka, who lived in a cottage in the yard behind our apartment building, and one day I pointed out that she had a hole in her skirt. Her reply was: "So what?" But the next day, when I joined her for the walk home, she held her school bag over her bottom with both hands. Cruelly, I asked her why she was carrying it like that—wasn't it uncomfortable?— and she shot back: "Because, as you were kind enough to point out to me yesterday, I have a hole over my ass, but I had to do my math homework and I had no time to darn it." It was too big to darn anyway.

Miss Brunnenschatten's suitor was a nondescript man slightly shorter than me, with red hair and glasses. I was surprised. Then Kveta, who lived in Babi, announced: "Girls! Brunnenschatten's going out with Cvancara from the District

Office." The news was meant only for the girls, but Kveta had a voice like a bugle, so everyone heard. The boys weren't much interested; I was the exception.

"With that redhead?" Bara said.

"With that little squirt?" Pitasova added, though she was pretty small herself.

Ruda Sepp, who sat behind me and had his feet up on his desk, said, "She'll be in trouble soon enough."*

*The girls fell silent and the boys pricked up their ears. This was February 1939, the time of the Second Republic. Mr. Mrstina had put a sloppy handwritten sign in the window of the Beranek that said "*NO JEWS ALLOWED*," and underneath it, in his tiny scrawl, "With apologies to our valued customers." But what of it? Cvancara wasn't a Jew, nor was the German-as-a-fence-post Miss B. Nor was Ruda Sepp, for that matter. He spoke German pretty badly.*

*"What kind of trouble, my good man?" said Lexa.**

"If she marries him, she's gonna have a problem," said Ruda. "Pop said so yesterday, and he's pretty up on stuff like that."

"Why should should she have a problem?" Lexa persisted.

Ruda spat a stale wad of chewing gum at the map of the country on the wall. The gum landed on Brno, and stuck. "Brunnenschatten is Volksdeutsche.*"*

"What's that?" asked Jebavy.

"A hundred percent German," said Ruda. "They'll treat her just like she lived in the Reich."

"You're a hundred percent too," Nina said. "Allegedly."

*"Pop says that 'cause the Czechs didn't fight back last fall, Der Fewer's gonna order the German army to march out of Sudetenland and occupy us," Ruda said.**

"That's bullshit, man!" shouted Pilous.

"You see me jumping for joy?" Ruda stuffed a fresh stick

of gum into his mouth. They had a stash of this rare commodity at home. "I'm gonna have problems too."

"Why?" said Pilous angrily. "After all, you're Volks-deutsche *too."*

"So they say," said Ruda. "And if I am, it won't be long before I'll be on the parade ground learning the goose step instead of Latin."

The room fell silent.

"It's a serious fuck-up," said Ruda.

Just then Bivoj, the math teacher, burst into the room and looked around in astonishment. He was used to being greeted by a pandemonium that would subside only after he had roared at us like a lion. His first words were usually: "What do you think this is? A Jewish school, or what?" But ever since Mr. Mrstina had put that sign up in the Beranek, where Bivoj went to play chess with Mr. Lewith, he only shouted: "Silence!"

The room was quiet now, for we had a lot to think about. Bivoj growled something under his breath and sat down on his chair so hard it cracked. "Anastazova!" he roared. "Come up here."

In no time, Stazka had been handed a goose egg in math.

⚔ ⚔

A soldier in a shabby uniform walked across the square from the station. A woman emerged from the church and waved at him. The soldier's uniform had the black epaulettes worn by sappers, but I knew he wasn't a real sapper. The woman wore an elegant suede jacket and had the same rich black hair she'd had a long time ago when, based on the evidence of my own eyes, I had first become aware of poverty: climbing up a ladder behind her at the lookout tower on Lipi, I had seen her underpants—mended, laundered, no longer pale blue but grey from the permanent struggle for cleanliness. Anka Pitasova.

Berta Moutelik was still in the army.* It must have been his sixth year by now. When I was called up, the country was still in that interregnum between the end of the war and the beginning of Communism that we were supposed to call the Third Republic but didn't. I got a student deferral, whereas Berta was turned down because he was nearsighted. They issued him his blue booklet, confirming his exemption from military service, but then later, quite a few years after the Communist putsch in 1948, some eager beaver discovered that Berta had failed to discharge the "joyous duty of every young man," as they described military service in that historical situation, and at that point his poor eyesight ceased to be an issue. They withdrew his blue book, and he went off to do his duty.

Though his balding father no longer owned the City of London department store, Mr. Moutelik still worked there, still playing the obliging merchant, serving the ladies of the town, some of them newcomers, some of them old customers, all day long. Given the usual fate of such businessmen in that historical situation, Mr. Moutelik's continued presence in the store he no longer owned was puzzling. Equally puzzling, his good wife still sat at the checkout desk with the same tall hairdo of such solid construction that by afternoon, when the sun was beating into the store, not a hair would have gone astray. And Berta was still in the army after all these years, and still a lowly private.

⚞ ⚟

We all decided to go to the wedding, even Knobloch, whom Miss Brunnenschatten had made to resit the exam, and

Ruda, whose father had apparently forbidden him to go, and Ilse Seligerova,* a real German, unlike Ruda, whom Nina claimed was only a would-be German. The woman in Ilse won out over the part of her that read Vom Kaiserhof zur Reichskanzlei—*From the Kaiser's Court to the Reich's Chancellery—a brown-covered book that she would ostentatiously pore over during breaks instead of gossiping with the other girls. "Why aren't you in tears?" Lexa would tease her. He was the class joker; irony was his element. "Haven't they plighted their troth yet?"*

"I don't read romances," Ilse would retort. "This is by Dr. Josef Goebbels, and it happens to be very interesting."

Lexa would click his heels together and give the Aryan salute, but it didn't bother us. Ilse was Ilse, and she had gone gaga over Der Fewer, but otherwise she was a normal girl, hopelessly in love with Jarek Pila from grade IV B. Not even Der Fewer could come between them. In that regard, she was just as silly as the other girls.

Ruda probably was German, though you couldn't tell by looking at him, but he obviously felt Czech and was not happy about his prospects as a virtual citizen of the Reich. According to a story making the rounds in town, Ruda's grandfather's name was Septal and he had worked as a gravedigger in the Jewish cemetery. When Emperor Franz Josef died—and old Mr. Septal passed away at almost the same time—Ruda's father changed the family name to the German-sounding Sepp, a gesture that made clear his allegiance to the local German minority. I didn't really believe this story, but once, before the war, I was sitting with my mother and father at a banquet in the Sokol pub, and the men around the table were arguing about something I didn't understand. Mr. Sepp, who took no part in the argument but merely listened, suddenly stood up and started singing, in a martial manner, a song the Nazis had taken up, "Fest steht und treu die Wacht am Rhein."* My father leapt to his feet and slapped his face.

So Mr. Sepp was a German, after all, and I came up with a private hypothesis that it was actually Ruda's mother who was the offspring of the gravedigger in the Jewish cemetery. The gravedigger may have been Czech, but he probably spoke German to his Jewish customers. In any case, Ruda's mother spoke German so well that she would occasionally correct her husband, though her Czech was also impeccable. But the person who really spoke the language of "our traditional enemy," as my father would say, was their daughter, Ruda's sister, Hannelore. After the Munich decree annexing the Sudetenland came into force, Hannelore used German even in the stores, though she had always spoken flawless Czech in public before that. The grocer, Mr. Hernajs, who was a Czech fascist, pretended he didn't understand what she wanted, until Hannelore went to the town hall to complain.

Nina insisted that Ruda was a "would-be German," which would help to explain why he spoke German so badly. Lexa claimed Ruda was doing it deliberately to make himself seem more Czech and that at home he could talk the imperial language a blue streak, except that no one had ever visited him at home. They lived in some kind of Aryan ghetto. So we simply didn't know.

Whenever possible, Ruda would get out of the ghetto.

"D'you think I could go to the wedding too?" Gerta Woticka asked shyly.*

"Why not?" said Berta. By that time they had started going out together.

"You know what I mean," said Gerta.

"No, I don't know what you mean," said Vlasak. "Do

you know what she's talking about, Bara?" He turned to the hotelier's daughter, and Nina's best friend, because he was going out with her. Bara shook her head.

"Does anyone know," said Vlasak loudly, "why Gerta shouldn't go to Brunnenschatten's wedding?"

Everyone shook their heads, and Gerta said quietly, "Daddy isn't even allowed to go to the café."

"We're going to church, sweetie!" said Lexa. "You can go to church no matter what your religion. And that includes Seligerova. Not sure about Sepp, though, since I'm not clear on whether no religion can be considered a religion." A smattering of laughter.

"Ish bin ein Toitcher und kenne Kirche gehen!" said Ruda, in his fractured German. "I'm a Cherman and I'm allowed to go church."

"Sehr gut, Mein Herr!" said Lexa. "So we're all going. What's the wedding present to be?"

⊰ ⊱

My old buddy Prema was in Australia. I learned that from his father, old Mr. Skocdopole, the one-armed legionnaire, who was still alive. But Prema wouldn't have come to the reunion even if he'd been able to. He hadn't gone to high school.

A freshly waxed and polished Hillman drove up to the hotel and Knobloch stepped out. He was wearing a leather overcoat, gloves, and a Soviet-style hat. A couple in duffle coats approached from the direction of the savings bank: the Pilouses. Knobloch stopped, ungloved his right hand, and strode forward to greet them. First he shook hands with Kveta, then with Lada, and to each of them, it seemed to me, he behaved a touch more heartily than was the custom in the land. Or maybe that was just my impression. They stood too far away for me to hear whether they had used the friendly, non-ideological "Hi!" or some more politically correct greeting, like "Honour to work!"

Ivan Vejrazka was probably not coming either. I'd run into him in Carlsbad, where I'd foolishly gone to see a woman I was chasing, but I forgot all about her the instant I set eyes on Ivan's bride-to-be. She had golden hair and was naturally flirtatious, and I was still young enough to be susceptible, so her invisible lasso settled around my neck, just as Lizetka's had done years before, and Irena's before that— Irena, who had woven her lasso from the braids she'd worn back in Uzhgorod and which she'd cut off soon after arriving in Kostelec.

So Ivan's girl held me in her lasso, but only briefly, not for many long years, as Irena or Marie had done. But she could talk beautifully. With her lasso firmly around my neck, I walked happily into the National Committee building to act as witness to their wedding. Next morning, I woke up in my hotel room with a hangover. At the reception desk they told me the newlyweds had already left. I didn't yet know they had gone to Africa, because they hadn't told me, even though it was no secret, since they had gone there legally, on business. From Africa they moved on to the United States, but that was later, and on their own, without official permission. But at least they sent me a postcard from Casablanca.

⚔ ⚔

We didn't have to take up a collection for the wedding present; we gave her a coffee mill, a one-off prototype from the Atlas Company, owned by the industrialist father of Honza Herman from grade IV A, who gave it to us gratis. Mr. Herman, an electrician by training, was said to have invented it himself, and quite possibly he had, because he had financed his rise to the status of factory owner with the proceeds from several patents like this one. The mill had a rotating steel blade that whirred around at a diabolical speed and effortlessly reduced the coffee beans to a fine powder, the kind that comes, after great effort, from a Turkish coffee mill. Mr. Herman hadn't had it patented yet; he was waiting until the Germans lost the war. He was a patriot and had no intention of letting the Germans get their hands on his invention.

Bara was delighted. "They won't get anything that original from anyone else!"

"Of course," said Lexa, "the disadvantage of the gift, my dear Miss Innemanova, lies in the fact that, apart from Mr. Herman, who no doubt squirrelled some away for his experiments, no one has any coffee."

Bara frowned. "But you can use it to grind beechnut coffee too!"

Still, the gift would be useful once the Germans had blown it. After swearing us to secrecy, Honza confessed that, apart from two prototypes, his father had already manufactured several hundred of these coffee mills but was waiting until the Reich collapsed before putting them on the world market.

The only problem was whether Miss Brunnenschatten herself would survive the war—or rather, Ravensbrück.

APART FROM HER STUDENTS, there were very few guests at the wedding. Just Mr. Cvancara, the postman and father, the groom being his only son. Miss Brunnenschatten was from Liberec, in the Sudetenland, and her relatives, if she had any, would by this time be full citizens of the German Reich. None of them came to the wedding, which tended to confirm the rumour going around that Miss Brunnenschatten was an orphan, born out of wedlock.

But she looked great. She was wearing a white gown, and her ample bosom supported a golden cross of larger than average size. None of us had ever seen her wear it before. The rest of the teaching staff came too, even the straitlaced principal, Mr. Zach, who'd once forbidden her to come to school in that white blouse because of that very bosom. Because not a single relative had shown up, Mr. Zach himself walked the bride down the aisle to the altar where the Venerable Father Meloun was waiting, his moon face aglow with otherworldly kindness and very worldly delight.

Several of the girls wept, and so did the Latin teacher, Miss Kuralova, who was leaning on Mr. Bivoj, again confirming the rumour that they would soon be standing at the altar themselves: the much feared teacher of a dead language and the mathematical scourge of the school. But that would happen, as it did, in the Czechoslovak Church, and they would be married by its brand-new minister, the Reverend Novak.

When I congratulated Miss Brunnenschatten and shook her hand, I could see her blue eyes glistening with tears, and though I tried to hold mine back, I too shed tears and she squeezed my hand and smiled at me.

At home, I sat down to write a composition on the theme Der Herbst—Autumn—which she had assigned to us the day before the wedding, but instead of delivering the obligatory description of leaves turning red on the trees and the countryside shrouded in morning mist, I began to wax poetic:

Bald kommen Winterstürme mit dem weissen Schneen
Und langsam wird zum Kot der alte liebe Pfad.

In meinem Herze kalte Winde wehen.
Es ist der Herbst. Er kommt in uns're Stadt.

The winter winds will soon be here, with white snow
Slowly blanketing the mud on the old, familiar path.
And in my heart a cold wind blows.
It's autumn, and it's coming once again.

⇥⇤

I stopped gazing out at the square, at the baroque facade tacked on to the church's ancient Gothic structure, now gilded by the Indian summer sun. I turned back to the golden-purple sheen of the hotel carpets, just as I had back then, during the war, except that now the carpets were faded and worn. I took a jacket from the closet, slipped it on, and went downstairs, descending the marble staircase that had already been worn down thirty years ago, though then I had ascended the stairs and entered the room where the bass saxophonist lay on the bed, and Lothar Kinze had seduced me into taking his place in the orchestra, using that huge saxophone as bait. *"Klingkt es nicht schön?"* he had asked. "Doesn't it sound beautiful?" And I, enthralled, replied, *"Wie eine Glocke. Sehr traurig."** "Like a bell. Very sad."

Down the marble staircase. There was no elevator in the hotel, but the place was—or used to be—beautiful. Pale pastel shades, art nouveau decor: I liked to think there was no building in the world as purely *fin de siècle* as the Beranek, not even in Paris. Or was that just fanciful thinking? Not much of its former splendour was left.

From the reception desk, which sat on a raised area just in front of the last turn in the staircase, a man in a hotel uniform shouted "Comrade!" at me. The Communist form of address clashed with his bourgeois-era uniform. At the sound of his icy tone I froze on the steps, but the voice went on, "There's a comrade waiting for you in the café."

And so I completed my descent into a world I had long since departed, a world still beautiful, but faded, a world of greenish gold, where swirls of dust danced in shafts of sunlight. At the foot of the stairs, to the left, the swinging doors that led into the café were so solid that their bevelled glass had remained intact all these years. The café was empty but full of ghosts. Irena had once sat here at a small, round marble table, and I had approached her and said, "Hello, blithe spirit!" She had frowned at me, then her eyes lit up because she saw her boyfriend and my archrival, Zdenek Pivonka, over my shoulder.* I went back to join the band, and Lexa commented, "My heartfelt condolences, sir."

They were only ghosts. From a dimly lit part of the café came the sound of clicking balls: the "comrade" in question was passing the time in a solitary game of billiards. He must have heard me enter, because he turned and a white smile appeared in his reddish brown face. "Hi," said Franta.

The ghosts vanished. Franta Jelen was real. He too was in uniform, a handsome stationmaster's uniform, minus the red cap, which he had set aside on one of the marble-topped tables.

⊨ ⊨

One day Lexa practically laid the school inspector, Heinz Dietrich Werner, flat on his back. An edict had been issued requiring that two students stand guard at the entrance to every high school. They were to allow no one in who couldn't show some ID, even if that individual was personally known to the guards or wore a swastika in his lapel, because, in the *words of the inspector, it could be "eine List des Feindes, der nie schlaft"—a trick of the enemy, who never sleeps. The edict, drawn up by some Protectorate bureaucrat,* had been beefed up by Inspector Werner with a rule, not explicit in the document itself, that physical means must be used to bar entry to any person refusing to show his ID. Thus, when Werner himself decided to put his rule to the test, a fight with him became inevitable.*

When Werner first burst into the guard booth, the skittish guards were so alarmed that they allowed themselves to be felled by a single blow, delivered by an arm trained in the Turnverein. Werner's easy entry put him in such a foul mood that he blew his stack before reaching the first classroom. There followed a chain reaction of detonations in an unusually large number of classrooms, at the end of which he brought in the Gestapo, not to arrest the hapless student guards who had let him in unopposed, but to take away Mr. Schwarz, a German teacher close to retirement, whose shaky pronunciation had enraged the inspector even more than the feeble resistance of the guards. Mr. Schwarz died in Dachau, while several other unlucky people from other high schools in Werner's jurisdiction later lost their lives in Buchenwald, in Majdanek, in Treblinka. After the war, Werner was sentenced to hang. Legend has it that the noose was not strong enough for his thick, bovine neck and the hangman had to strangle him with his bare hands. It probably is just a legend.*

And so, when Lexa's turn as school guard came up, he'd been forewarned by Werner's disastrous first visit. He refused to let Werner in without ID and, applying a variety of jujitsu holds he had picked up from a book at home, almost laid the monster on his back. Almost, but not quite. Had Lexa actually flattened the inspector, the consequences would have been impossible to foresee. Lexa might have been given the Protectorate Cross of Merit for doing his duty, or the inspector might have closed down the school and had all the teachers sent away to that place wherein all who enter must abandon hope. Lexa didn't want that on his conscience, so he suddenly exhaled and let the inspector get him in a full nelson that almost broke his neck.

Against all expectations, this mandatory altercation put the inspector in an exceptionally good mood, so he didn't burst through the first classroom door, where grade 1 B was having mathematics and Mr. Bivoj had already sweated away a couple of kilos out of sheer terror. Instead he strode briskly to the second floor, where Mrs. Cvancarova was teaching our class German ideology from that slim volume.

BENEATH THE NAME CVANCAROVA, *Miss Brunnenschatten had concealed a given name that was straight out of Wagner's* Ring Cycle, *though she never told us what it was. In those days, students did not address their teachers by their first names, so she had no reason to reveal it to us.*

But I couldn't help wondering. I asked Ruda Sepp if he knew. "I heard it's the same as your sister's," I said.

"Lorka? I dunno," said Ruda. His sister's full name was Hannelore, but Ruda was ashamed of the German sound of it and called her Lorka.

"So it's not Lorka?"

"I really couldn't say."

I left it at that. Later, as the last person to finish an assignment for Mr. Bivoj (for which I ended up getting a big fat goose egg anyway), I dropped off all the exercise books for him in his office, and when I set them down on a desk in front of his armchair, where he was sitting on an inflatable cushion (he had hemorrhoids), I saw a timetable on his desk in which the name "B. Brunnenschattenova" appeared several times.

"Her first name begins with B," I announced to Ruda.

"Bohumila?" said Ruda.

"That's way too Czech! She's such a German! She's from the Sudetenland!"

"Maybe she's become more Czech. What do I know?" said Ruda. "Are you nuts about her or something?"

I felt myself blushing.

Later, the secret of her name was unearthed by feminine curiosity. Stazka burst into the classroom and shouted as if she were out in the woods: "Girls, you'll never guess what Brunnenschatten's first name is."

"Kaltenbrunne,'" growled Ruda, although Stazka hadn't been talking to him.

All the girls shook their heads, eyes popping with curiosity.

"Brunhilde!" shouted Stazka, as if she were announcing that the Kostelec handball team had scored a victory.

The whole class burst out laughing, except me. Brunhilde Brunnenschatten. Straight out of The Ring of the Nibelung.

WHEN WERNER ENTERED, *Mrs. Cvancarova greeted him with a limp Aryan salute. We stood up and executed a variety of Heil Hitlers. Inspector Werner clicked his heels together and snapped off an exemplary salute, which we expected him to follow with a loud "Weiter machen!"—the command to take our seats. To our surprise, however, Werner uttered the command in a voice that sounded almost human and set off up the steps to the last row of desks, where Stazka Anastazova sat quivering and Gerta Woticka seemed about to faint. It was shortly after the Protectorate had been declared, and the children of Israel had not yet been forced to wear the yellow star or been expelled from school.*

The inspector sat down abruptly, right beside Gerta. He looked at her and his instincts must have told him there was something not quite right about this student. Gerta had the good looks of a fashion model all right, but a model who had posed for the anti-Semitic caricatures that even the local Kostelec News *was now compelled to publish. Werner glowered at her for a while, but then he brightened up and began listening to Mrs. Cvancarova's explanation of German ideology. She coughed after every second word; clearly, her mouth was as dry as the Sahara.*

"Der Führer und Reichskanzler des Grossdeutchen Reiches," she read in a melodious voice that was trembling like an aspen leaf. She went on in a true Sudeten German accent: "The Leader and Chancellor of the Great German Reich was born in Braunau. He struggled ..."

"In Braunau am INN!" Werner interrupted her affably. He knew, despite her ugly new Czech surname, that underneath it she had a beautiful name, straight out of Wagner. "Otherwise," he continued in German, his tone still pleasant, "Your students might think he was a Czech corporal. Das wäre ein Irrtum! *That would be a mistake!* EIN GROSSER"—*he chuckled*—"Irrtum, Frau Professor!" *And he began laughing with a devilish cackle that might have come from the throat of Beelzebub himself.*

It was an historic moment. Inspector Werner could turn gloomy and frown, he could yell and shout, but in living memory he had never been known to laugh.

There was silence in the classroom while the inspector's sergeant-major's cackle continued. Mrs. Cvancarova, as she now was, stood stiffly at attention just below the dais, then she leaned back and supported herself against the desk. Her slender legs were trembling. The bizarre sound went on for an unbelievably long time, though perhaps it was an illusion, given the historic nature of the event.

When he finally stopped laughing, we all relaxed. "Also," *said the monster,* "Das haben wir den Führer. Jetzt könnte uns jemand uber Herrn Reichsmarschall Hermann Goering was berichten." *He swept a panoramic gaze over the class, looking for someone who could say something about Reichsmarschall Hermann Goering. Then he noticed Franta Jelen's incipient blond head; his hair was, in fact, chestnut brown and it was short and dishevelled, so only a few blond traces were visible, but that was enough, perhaps, to draw the inspector's attention.* "Sie!" *he said, pointing at Franta. His voice was still quite genial, and Franta didn't see him because he was sitting in the front row with his back to the inspector. Mrs. Cvancarova cleared her throat and said, hoarsely,* "Jelen, fangen Sie an!" *Franta struggled to his feet.*

The inspector couldn't have picked a more desirable victim. Franta had always received failing grades in German. Still, with the certainty of the poorly informed, he blurted out: "Der Fewer wurde geboren."

That was all he said: The leader was born. He had clearly not understood the inspector's question. Werner didn't know quite what to make of this. After a long silence, still with no trace of anger in his voice, Werner said, "Über den Führer haben wir schon gehört. *We've already heard about the Leader. Who can say something about the Reichsmarschall?" Another panoramic gaze around the room, another deep silence. Although several of the girls had studied up on it, no one dared to volunteer an answer: it would have been tempting the devil. The inspector looked around again until his eyes were drawn to the ashen face of Gerta Woticka, and there they rested. As if hypnotized by a* snake—the one from Paradise—Gerta stood up and, in stuttering but flawless German, began to speak about Goering's distinguished record as a pilot in the Great War. "Herr Reichmarschall Hermann Goering hätte sich im ersten Weltkriege als Jagdtflugzeugführer ausserordenlich auszeichnet. Er ..." But as she droned on and on, the face of the inspector, rather than expressing satisfaction at her answer, grew darker and gloomier until suddenly he interrupted her, his voice now barely audible—another historic first, since he had never lowered his voice before.

"Bist du eine Jüdin?" he hissed. "Are you a Jew?"

Gerta swayed slightly and then replied in a tiny voice, "Ja, bitte ..."

Werner seemed to swell up to his full breadth. He shot a finger toward the door and roared like a beast: "Heraus!"

Gerta Woticka fainted.

"Weg mit ihr!" Werner growled, pointing at Stazka and at Bara Innemanova, who was sitting in the row in front of her. The girls picked up the inert Gerta and carried her awkwardly into the hall. There was a drinking fountain nearby, and there, they tried to bring her around. Inspector Werner marched down the steps to the front of the room and, in a strangely grave voice, said to the teacher, "Kommen Sie mit! Come with me!"

And then he marched out of the deep silence of the classroom. All you could hear was the clumping of his metalshod boots and the light tapping of Mrs. Cvancarova's pumps as they walked down the hall.

⊰ ⊱

"No, I didn't join the Party. You know me better than that," Franta said, after we sat down at one of the round marble tables.

"And they didn't make you pay for it?"

"Busted me down a rank or two, but it didn't matter a damn."

"The railway didn't sack you?"

"You can see for yourself, can't you? I'm a dispatcher—at Radechova."

Each branch of his family, extending back to the preceding century, was full of working stiffs, and now, because of the new historical situation, his proletarian pedigree carried with it new obligations as well. So Franta had become an amendment officer with the artillery in Kobylec.* That God-forsaken hole of our not-so-distant youth was where I'd met him for the first time since our high-school graduation, the occasion we were now gathering to celebrate two decades later. He didn't properly graduate from high school until after the war, and then it was only thanks to the liberation and because the subject that had given him the most trouble—German—had been struck from the curriculum.

Early on in the war, I used to write his German homework assignments for him. Franta had no idea what I'd written, and didn't ask, but simply passed it straight on to Miss Brunnenschatten. In the idiotic exuberance of youth, I played a practical joke on him that caused Miss Brunnenschatten to set out along the railway tracks to the little house whose inhabitants I had described, in an assignment called *Meine Familie*, in the following way: "*Mein Vater ist ein Alkoholiker, Meine Mutti eine Hure.*"

I was young and stupid. Franta didn't understand what I'd written, and Miss Brunnenschatten, in white knee socks and wearing a dirndl over her white blouse, clambered up the crushed stone of the railway embankment to discover that his *Mutti*, far from being a whore, was in fact a popular midwife and his father a non-smoker and a teetotaller. In the entire tiny house, where, like in an old Chaplin film, six people of various genders and ages squeezed into two beds, there was only a single bottle of alcohol, a bottle of Meinl's rum, a fixture in every Czech household, a tonic for the flu and for colds, carefully stashed away for that purpose and dispensed by the spoonful so that it lasted throughout the war, in this case, right up until the Communist coup in February 1948, when the railwayman got drunk for the first time in his life, polishing off the historic bottle at a single sitting.

Franta came back from the teacher's office, and I awaited him in trepidation, but he wasn't even mad at me. All he said was, "So what did you write about my family, you idiot? When Brunnenschatten showed up, my mom thought she was in trouble and needed her help. Too bad it was a misunderstanding. Might have given me a leg up in the finals." Then he added, prophetically, "The way things are now, I'm going down in flames in the Imperial Language for sure!"

Even so, a leg up from Mrs. Brunnenschatten wouldn't have done him any good. The monster, Werner, showed up at the finals unannounced, and as a result of Franta's poor showing in German, almost sent him to Auschwitz.

I did know Franta better. Of course he hadn't joined the Party.

꙳ ꙳

The dubious legality of the marriage between Dasa Sommernitzova and Tonda Kratochvil by the Venerable Father Meloun eventually came to light, but to our great relief, the rewritten registry—on which Rosta Pittermann and I had worked all night just after their wedding—remained a secret. Father Meloun's attempts to predate their marriage had been so transparent that the entire registry had to be rewritten to cover up the forgery, but not even our efforts could stand up to close scrutiny. Fortunately, no one had informed on us. The denunciation applied only to the officiator and to Dasa and Tonda, and the talk was that the informer had been Tonda's former girlfriend, Antonia Simkova, whom Tonda had dated for seven years before Dasa caught his eye. The rumours stuck, and for the rest of the war people shunned Antonia, even the boys, although she certainly would have been worth the sinning, were it not that even a sin like that would have been seen as sexual collaboration. And so, in desperation, Antonia began—in the terminology of the time—to run with German soldiers. And when the Reich collapsed in May of 1945, they treated her like a collaborator and shaved her head. Fortunately for her, the Gestapo archives soon revealed that the Venerable Father had been betrayed by the inconspicuous Mr. Alois Malina, who had also written articles for the Aryan Struggle *under the pseudonym Franz Sauer. By the time Antonia's hair had grown back in, she was almost thirty, but the fact that she had run with the Germans stuck to her, so she never married, and after the Communist coup in 1948, she became house warden—the eyes and ears of the Party—in a nationalized apartment building that had once belonged to Mr. Moutelik, where she took her bitterness out on the tenants.*

MR. MALINA, *a.k.a. Franz Sauer, was an anti-Semite, one of those unbelievable human creatures possessed by a hatred that is motiveless and therefore inaccessible to normal human reasoning. The only possible natural explanation for his act of betrayal was that he had also been fond of Dasa and she hadn't reciprocated, so his anti-Semitism might actually have been an expression of jealousy. But were that the case, we'd have known; someone would have seen them* together somewhere, or Dasa would have confided in her friends, and ultimately it would have become an ordinary public secret. But nothing of the sort ever came to light. On the other hand, Mr. Malina never railed against the Jews the way some of the Kostelec Jew-bashers used to do in the pub where he was a regular. He even greeted the wealthier Jews on the street. His doctor was Dr. Strass,* and after Hitler's Munich decree, Malina did not join The Banner, a quasi-fascist organization to which most of the Kostelec Jew-bashers belonged, together with a few politically naive people who were disappointed with Neville Chamberlain for waving his piece of paper from the airplane steps and carrying on about peace in our time.

Mr. Malina was simply a mystery. An enigma. Except that when Dasa Sommernitzova suddenly became Mrs. Dasa Kratochvilova, it must have got him thinking, since he couldn't believe he'd failed to notice the reading of the banns. After the war, Mr. Malina's secret actions were discovered in the Gestapo archives in Hradec. He'd gone to high mass every single Sunday, and attended morning mass on weekdays, paying devout attention to the Venerable Father Meloun's sermons and all the parish announcements, including the banns. And so a new denunciation was passed on to the Gestapo HQ in Hradec and a Gestapo officer showed up at the parish vicarage. Unlike the first one, this officer did not suffer from a head wound, nor did he have a weakness for the communion wine Father Meloun offered him.* On the contrary, the man didn't touch a drop of it and, from the fresh appearance of the entries in the pristine registry books, he immediately deduced what was going on. When he came to the entry recording the marriage of Dasa Sommernitzova and Tonda Kratochvil, now dated before the day the Nazi government had outlawed unions between

Jews and Aryans, he declared the Venerable Father under arrest and took him off to Hradec.

It didn't take much imagination to guess how they dealt with him there. It all came out after the war, not only that Alois Malina, not Antonia Simkova, had turned the conspirators in, but also that the Venerable Father Meloun told the Gestapo that he had rewritten the registry himself. Thus, he became our guardian angel, holding a protective hand over Rosta and me and saving us from a similar fate. The Venerable Father, along with Dasa and Tonda Kratochvil, were the Gestapo's first victims in Kostelec. They shipped the newlyweds off to Auschwitz, where they died a year later. Father Meloun ended up in Buchenwald and survived. In his place, the bishop quickly appointed a newly minted priest, Father Brejcha, as chaplain, but Brejcha was not made of the stuff of martyrs.

⚐ ⚑

"So far, Nina's here, Anka Pitasova, and Berta. Knobloch came in his own car. It's a Western model," I said, "but he's not driving a Rolls-Royce. Not yet, anyway."

"Has Vlasak shown up yet?"

"Haven't seen him."

"He's not coming," said Franta, with certainty.

IN THE END, Franta was proven wrong, but not until the very end, when the party was winding down.

By this time, we'd gathered in the private dining room for dinner. There were ten of us. The gifts brought by Pilous and Knobloch (and later by Bara, who had not yet arrived) were more or less what we'd expected. A total of seven bottles of vodka, not to mention the wine that came with the meal.

Jebavy refused to touch the Russian drink, so Pilous poured a double for himself and Kveta, and both of them began drinking like fish. Then Pilous poured everyone drinks, including Nina, who in the past had never touched alcohol. She surprised me—her moonlike face full of sorrow, the origin of which I didn't know, but sensed anyway. Then Pilous poured drinks for Anka and Berta. "Don't be so miserly, man!" Berta chided, and he got a triple. Knobloch, one of the gift-givers, covered his glass with his hand, revealing a mammoth ring that he never used to wear twenty years ago, back in school. But he removed his hand when Pilous insisted. Pilous knew Knobloch wasn't a teetotaller, and tradition demanded that he drink, or at least propose a toast. Pilous and Kveta both shared Franta's working-class genealogy, except that they now carried Party cards and drank like fish. They'd probably picked up the habit at Party meetings.

⚎ ⚎

I learned that Berta Moutelik and Gerta Woticka were in love just as we were starting our fifth year of high school. One night, I was sitting in a secluded spot in the woods with three small benches around a table where the pensioners would play cards as long as there was enough light. I was there in the moonlight, recovering from a sudden passion for Irena, who that summer had moved to Kostelec with her father and a younger sister. It was already past eleven, the woods were dark, and the pensioners had long since gone home. Suddenly, someone began pushing through the underbrush, and when he emerged, I recognized Berta Moutelik. Gerta was right behind him. When they saw me sitting there in this romantic light at this romantic hour, in a place where they hadn't expected to see a living soul, Gerta shrieked and ran off, while Berta stood his ground uncertainly, then said, "Wait here!" and ran off after Gerta.

I poked my way through the bushes and saw them running along the path through the woods toward town. Because Gerta was of non-Aryan origin, she was not allowed outdoors after eight p.m. At the time, she was living in a cottage left behind by the welder Lopatka, the father of seven small children who had moved into a villa belonging to Mr. Stein, which the local Germans and would-be Germans classified as social housing because they didn't think it fancy enough for their own purposes. They then moved three Jewish families into Lopatka's tiny house. The Wotickys were one of them.

I sat on the slope above the road, and this nocturnal event drove Irena out of my head, so that for a while I felt okay. I was fond of Berta. We'd been friends since childhood, when he had let me drive around the square in his little push-peddle car, which could also be run on gasoline. Rosta, Lexa, and I used to go over to his place to play Monopoly, a game we first came across at Onkel Otto's German-speaking camp,* where our parents sent us to improve our German, though we also took lessons from Mr. Katz, the cantor in the Kostelec synagogue.* The main improvement, though, was to our skills in the buying and selling of real estate. Berta had a room of his own, which none of the rest of us had, and it contained a beautiful school desk made of polished wood, and an accordion that the bandmaster, Mr. Mrstina, was teaching him to play.

IN FIFTH FORM, Berta gave up the accordion for track and field, for which he acquired such a passion that he even joined the Kostelec Sports Club team. He'd already tried his *hand at stationary cycle-racing, a discipline that didn't really catch on until the war. They raced in pairs, and behind each participant was a set of dials showing the virtual time and distance each had covered. Berta signed up and in the first round drew Cabicar from Myto, who was the Protectorate champion in that bizarre sport. Both Berta and Cabicar mounted their bikes while their assistants held them upright, and then they started peddling. We followed their progress on the dials. After the first five kilometres, Berta began to sweat profusely, and by the time he'd gone fifteen, Cabicar had already finished the race, which is to say he'd dismounted and was watching his opponent turning the two drums on which his velocipede was sitting more and more slowly. The bike began to wobble. By this time, Berta was red in the face, and the crowd started to encourage him. Berta didn't disappoint them. He finished his fifty kilometres, stopped pedalling, then crashed to the wooden floor with his bike, raking his left leg from thigh to ankle. But at least he'd stuck it out till the end, which was to have a certain significance in his future career in track and field. When stationary bike-riding no longer satisfied him, Berta tried the shot put, the high jump, and the pole vault; he tried sprinting, the discus, the hammer; he tried the hop, step, and jump. But he was never quite good enough in any of these events to qualify.*

Then he attempted the five-thousand-metre race and finally made the team. What qualified him was not any record-breaking prowess on his part, but his ability to endure to the end. Only Berta and the champion, Alois Bic, were interested in the exhausting event. The rules stated that each club had to enter two athletes in every race, and both of them had to complete the course. Time wasn't important; all you had to do to score a point was make it to the finish line, and Berta never failed to make it to the finish line. He was always last, but each time he ran, he surpassed his previous personal record, and in several cases, the extra point he brought in actually secured victory for the Kostelec Sports Club.

Those desolate Protectorate Sundays—before they put us all to work in the Messerschmitt factory as part of the* Totaleinsatz *program—were filled with girls' handball in the morning and track and field meets in the afternoon, with clubs from Porici, from Hermanice, and from Myto, where Fikejz, the Protectorate pentathlon champion, who also ran the five thousand metres, was a member. The five thousand metres was the last event of every meet, and in Kostelec no one bothered to work very hard for it except Berta and Alois Bic, who always came in second behind Fikejz. And so the track and field stadium, its wooden bleachers filled to the last row (since they'd banned dancing in the Protectorate, there was nothing else to do) gradually started emptying out while Fikejz was coming down the home stretch to the finish line. Bic was about half a lap behind him; one lap behind him was the second Myto runner; and three laps behind him, limping and puffing, came Berta. The stands were soon empty, leaving just me and a few club officials who had to stay to the end. Berta managed the ninth lap, then the tenth. The freshly showered Fikejz came out of the dressing room and sat beside me. "How many laps has he done?" he asked.*

"He's just started the eleventh," I replied.

"He's improving," said Fikejz, and then he shouted, "Keep it going! Only two more laps! You're almost there!" Several of the officials joined in, but they knew how dogged Berta was and how impervious to any form of encouragement. Five minutes went by, and a freshly showered Bic

joined us. Another five minutes went by, and the second Myto guy appeared. In another ten minutes or so, Berta finally reached the finish line. Bic and the two Myto runners got up and left. The stadium was now completely empty except for me. Berta came out of the showers, sat down beside me, pulled out a little notebook, and wrote down his time. "A personal best," he said with satisfaction. "Forty-one seven!" The notebook was full of such personal bests. Four six in the shot put.

I SAT ON THAT HILLSIDE and remembered Berta and how he got the track and field bug at Onkel Otto's when we had that domestic Olympiad, and I remembered my buddies Paul Pollack and Alex Karpeles. After Munich, they sent me a postcard, still full of student irony, from the English-language high school they attended in Prague. They wrote that their English teachers had escaped to England and said that for a while it seemed we'd all become citizens of the Third Reich. That was what these young Zionists wrote. Sitting on that slope in the fragrant woods, I realized I had no idea what had become of them, where they were, or even if they were still alive. But then I met Alex after the war, wearing a British uniform, just before he left to go back home, that is, to London. Paul Pollack? A question mark. Probably not even a question mark.

I WAS THINKING OF IRENA when Berta's silhouette reappeared on the path. He scrambled up the slope and sat down beside me.

"You're going on dates at night now?"

"What are you, stupid or something? Can I go out with Gerta in broad daylight?"

He couldn't. He could go out at night, of course, and

Gerta couldn't. But she was a woman, so she took risks, and not just the kind of risks that every young woman took at that time, a time of sub-standard condoms.

A YEAR WENT BY *and on the same slope, under the same full moon, across which a cloud was now slowly drifting, Berta told me how, out of pure desperation, the kind that someone without his problems couldn't even begin to imagine, he and Gerta had gone to the vicarage for advice. He knew there were no more straws to clutch at, just the tiny sliver of a possibility so remote it was practically indiscernible. Smaller than a fleck on the face of the moon. He'd gone to see the new chaplain, Father Brejcha; this was after Father Meloun had been arrested, along with the illicitly married couple, and Rosta and I were still terrified they might come after us too. We had no illusions that his clerical collar would protect him from the kind of interrogations that could turn a living saint into a dead saint. Berta went to the vicarage with his terrible dilemma, his unsquared circle. Father Brejcha heard him out, his face the colour of death. "You have to realize that what you're proposing is no longer possible, really," he said. "If it were anywhere else, but not here in Kostelec. You must know what happened to Father Meloun, and you, Mr. Moutelik, you haven't even reached the age of majority, and neither has your intended. They'll be keeping a very sharp eye out for this kind of thing now. It would be . . ." The freshly minted chaplain suddenly felt sick and ran from the room, leaving Berta and Gerta sitting in Father Meloun's former study, which Chaplain Brejcha had more or less tidied up; there weren't as many books stacked on the table and on the chairs, no more mountains of them on the couch or on the floor. The chaplain came back with a bottle of communion wine and three small glasses, and in the end the wine created the illusion that*

everything would turn out well; even though the parish reg-
ister could no longer be falsified, God would surely never
allow anything bad to happen.

AGAIN WE WERE ON *that same hillside. It was day this time,*
and we were skipping school, and behind us in the bushes
the pensioners were slamming their cards down on the table.
Berta was holding back tears as he told me how Gerta had
looked out the tiny window in the railway car. "She was cry-
ing and, man, I was weeping too," he said, "and so would
you if..." A train whistle hooted in the distance, a different
train, but all the same—Irena was not Jewish, and she didn't
have to leave town in a cattle car jammed with people bound
for Terezin, which was said to be a ghetto, but the Jews knew,
or suspected, or rather were in a state of uncertain certainty
about, what it really was.

And Irena walked by below us, arm in arm with Zdenek.
And such is our world. Berta.

⊰ ⊱

The glasses, one after the other, clunked down on the table,
and then there was silence. Before that, a few formal greetings had been uttered, and I paid careful attention to what
they were. I didn't hear a single "Honour to work," the stan-
dard comradely greeting the Party insisted on. All I heard
was "Your health!" the clinking of glasses, and then silence.

At a previous party, back when we were still in school,
where a tiddly Bara had once asked me why I was ignoring
her friend, there had never been a silence like this, not at the
beginning and certainly not at the end. Pilous tried to break
it with a meaningless comment: "I hear the A class haven't
had their reunion yet."

"No one's organizing it," said Anka.

"But they've got Nosek.* He was always one to organize things."

And with that, the conversation was off to a limping start. I turned to Nina. "Why so sad, Nina?" I asked.

"You don't know?" she said. We lowered our voices; it seemed to me that Kveta Pilousova, across the table, was straining to hear what we were saying. "You're not interested in your old classmates anymore, are you, Danny?" Nina said. "You're famous."

"You know how it is, Nina."

"I don't know how it is. But yes, I am sad, because I'm a widow with four children to look after."

⊣ ⊢

A miserable afternoon among the rocks, not like those times with Irena, who went there to climb, but because we were holed up in the cottage belonging to Bara's parents. On the upper bunk, slow movements became faster and faster, and then I knew what I was hearing and something in me froze. What? Was I measuring Nina's moonlike cheeks through the filter of Hollywood standards out of adolescent insouciance? Out of boneheadedness? Because I was a goody two-shoes whose oral muscles worked very well in conversation with Marie and Irena, but who was otherwise uptight and useless, always missing his opportunity? All of the above? Terror puellae. Up above us, the movements became faster and more urgent. In the lower bunk, Nina and I were playing cards and, too late, I regretted having come. What had I been thinking? Vlasak, in the upper bunk, howled, and a moment later Bara gave a muffled cry, and tears flowed down Nina's cheeks; a steaming jungle inside the cottage.

The day after that lost weekend, I rode my bike to Her-manice. Why? What was I thinking? Nina didn't measure up to my Hollywood ideal. She was no Judy Garland, but after that tropical outing I felt I was in love—almost. And then came the cold shower: "Nina's not home."

She'd promised to wait. "When's she coming back, Mrs. ... ?"

"I have no idea, young man ..."

I didn't tell her who I was, and I ran away like the little boy I really was, still wet behind the ears.

I waited in the café on the square, from where I could see her house. It was almost dark when she appeared. I ran out of the café and pounded across the square, managing to catch her just before she went inside. "Why didn't you wait for me, Nina?" Her cheeks were tearless, betraying no emotion, carved in stone. Was she offended? Wounded? Disdainful?

"Just because," she said and turned and disappeared into the passageway.

I rode home in the moonlight about as sluggishly as Berta had managed to cycle on those two drums.

Then time drew a veil over those things.

❧ ❧

Very quietly, Nina told me how the Communists had locked up her husband, the Reverend Novak, because he had refused to condemn the so-called Vatican conspirators from the pulpit, although he was a clergyman in a church that was thought of as being more likely to collaborate with the devil himself than with the papists. But there are exceptions to every-thing, and whether they prove the rule is something I dare not judge. I do know that Nina's husband was one such exception. So the Communists included him, incongruously, as a participant in one of the minor Vatican conspiracies they were cooking up, and to the usual charges of having provided unspecified intelligence to unspecified agents of the Vatican, they added the sin of opposing the execution of Milada Horakova,* an opinion he had uttered not in private, but from the pulpit, so that the informer assigned to entrap him had an easy job of it. In his homily, the Reverend Novak had informed his congregation that Dr. Horakova would be hung by the neck until she was dead for a political mis-demeanour—he did not say "crime," and the informer's report had emphasized that—and then he added that throughout the ages, Christianity had always treated such acts (thus elevating "political misdemeanour" to a moral "act," and that was also in the report) as deserving of mercy and atonement.

Perhaps the reverend had imagined that the head of state, Klement Gottwald, was a Christian at heart because he had inaugurated his presidency with a celebratory mass in St. Vitus's Cathedral;* from the pulpit, the reverend had referred to this event "out of context" (in the informer's words), but he couldn't have been that dumb. The court chose to inter-pret his reference to an historical fact as an "inadmissible criticism of our comrade president," and so, in addition, they accused Reverend Novak of listening to foreign broadcasts for the purpose of spreading seditious information, of com-plaining about the food supply (overheard by the informer at a bakery) and of a number of other misdemeanours—or perhaps they were crimes—to which they even added a sin he had allegedly committed during the war: the provocative christening of a German child.

"And you know the story behind that," Nina said.

I knew.

≒ ≒

I knew, and I even knew how it began. Dr. Schmidt had said, "My dear lady, get pregnant. Mr. Soucek is an expert. Get pregnant. It's the only thing." Miss Brunnenschatten—I still used that Wagnerian name even though it was no longer hers—laughed nervously. I wondered how Soucek's expertise could help Miss Brunnenschatten. Cvancara said, as if he were apologizing, "We wanted to wait until after the war to start a family. You understand, Doctor. Then it would no longer be a problem ..."

"I understand, of course," said Dr. Schmidt. He turned to Mrs. Brunnenschatten. "Did Werner really give you an ultimatum?"

She nodded.

"I have no idea how their laws work," said Dr. Schmidt, "but are you certain, ma'am, that he really has that kind of power?"

Now Soucek got into the conversation. We called him Detective Babocka because we knew our Apollinaire. Soucek embodied an Apollinairian bon mot: he was a man who knew everything there was to know about things no one needed to know anything about. Until recently, that is. Now Babocka's knowledge was obviously of some use and, it appeared, was of particular use to Miss Brunnenschatten.

We were sitting around the kitchen table—Dr. Schmidt, my father, Babocka, the Cvancaras and I—and guided by hints from the know-it-all, we were attempting to play bridge. The game was Dr. Schmidt's idea. He was an anglophile and desperate to master a game he associated with English aristocracy. I wasn't doing very well, and Dad was completely at sea. We were playing in the blacked-out kitchen, under a lamp that had been pulled low over the table, like in American movies. But now something alien had entered the atmosphere. Soucek said, "Have no doubt about it, Doctor. By marrying a Czech, Miss Brunnenschatten—from their point of view, of course—has committed so-called Rassenschande. *It's true that we Czechs are also considered Aryans, but I suspect that will last only as long as the war does. In any case, we are Aryans of an inferior type. That could be put to rights if the gentleman here," he nodded toward Cvancara, "would adopt German nationality, as was offered to him."**

"I don't get this," Cvancara interrupted him. "My wife has committed a racial misdemeanour, but my own racial status will be upgraded if I betray my nationality?"

"We're not living in a democracy anymore," said Babocka, "and your racial status won't get upgraded. It just means that your wife's case won't be so blatant. And you," he added, "will get drafted into the army."

Cvancara and his wife looked at each other. We were all silent. Babocka broke in: "The best solution—from their point of view, I should emphasize—would be for you to get divorced."

My teacher and her husband energetically shook their heads.

"Your wife would probably be safe, but you, sir—if you did not accept their offer ..."

"You mean if I refused to betray my nationality," Cvancara said with disgust. "And by the way, they offered it to me solely because of Brunnie here. After the divorce, they probably wouldn't accept me and I'd probably get drafted all right—straight into a concentration camp."

"You may well be right," said Babocka thoughtfully. "Which brings me back to my original suggestion."

The couple looked at one another and then at Dr. Schmidt.

"It's the best thing," Dr. Schmidt said. "You're at an ideal age, ma'am, and I know the state of your health. It's also ideal."

We all stood up, and the couple said their farewells. Then Babocka made a stupid remark: "Here's hoping your efforts are successful!"

Dr. Schmidt shot him a nasty look. Babocka realized what he'd just said and blushed. Dr. Schmidt turned to the couple. "From a biological point of view, I haven't the slightest doubt things will work out. And if anyone should ask you, ma'am," he said in a confidential tone, "you're already in the second month."

Miss Brunnenschatten nodded, but then she suddenly caught herself: "But what happens next?"

"Next?" asked Dr. Schmidt.

"They'll take the child away from me and send me to— to the same place Werner's threatening to send me now."

Dr. Schmidt laughed uncertainly. "By that time the circumstances will be quite different. In the fall, the Germans will have other things to worry about. In the worst case ..." he looked at Cvancara and added quickly, "but by then you'll be breastfeeding and that can be declared essential to the health of the child for at least two years. And by that time ..."

"I hope you're right," sighed Miss Brunnenschatten, to let him off the hook. "I sincerely hope you're right."

※　※

"What happened to you, Ferda?" I asked Knobloch. "You dropped out of sight after graduation."

The question was pointless. The fact that he owned a Hillman—at a time when the roads were cluttered with carefully maintained pre-war Aero sports cars, gutless wonders that slowed traffic down to a safe speed so that Hillmans could easily, and dangerously, pass them—said it all. But I wanted to hear it from Knobloch.

"It was you who dropped out of sight, you notorious bugger!" He was referring to the scandal around the operetta that, out of ignorance, I referred to as a musical.* "I ..."

Into the wine room came a whiff of *L'esprit de Moscou*,* followed by Bara Innemanova, twice the woman that I remembered. "Evening, all!" She put two bottles on the heavily laden table and, starting on the other side, pressed everyone's hand and mumbled a greeting she probably wanted no one else to hear. Nina sat there like a sphinx, staring at nothing.

Pilous handed Bara a glass before she got round to our side of the table. "To your health ..." He was about to say "Comrades," but he caught himself in time. "Ladies and gentlemen," he intoned. "Bottoms up!"

⊰ ⊱

After the Cvancaras left, Dr. Schmidt laughed and turned to me. "Do you know how Mr. Soucek came up with that idea?" he said.

"Having a kid was Bab ... Soucek's idea?"

It turned out that this particular scientific solution had first occurred to Detective Babocka a year before, in Vienna, where he'd been sent to work on a construction site. He'd gone to see a German movie called The Golden City, *because for reasons unknown it had been banned in the Protectorate. After he saw it, Babocka understood why. In the movie, a Czech man seduces a German virgin, and the censors must have decided that the story might stir up unrest among the citizens of the Protectorate. Given the German experience* in Bohemia and Moravia so far, any unrest was extremely unlikely, but the war situation had worsened to the point that officials weren't about to take any chances.

In the movie, neither the Czech seducer nor the wronged German virgin escapes retribution. She commits suicide by drowning herself, although she is carrying in her womb a child that, while it may have been half-German, is still Aryan, after all. The part was played by a Swedish actress, Kristina Söderbaum, a one-hundred-percent blond Nordic type who had also been blessed by marriage to the director of The Jew Süss.* The Germans had a nickname for her: they called her Reichswasserleiche—the Imperial Water-corpse— because she ends up drowning herself in several other films directed by her husband.

When Babocka learned about the young couple's problem from Dr. Schmidt, who hung out with Cvancara, he remembered The Golden City and got to thinking about the case. He came to the conclusion that German officials would not send a pure-German woman who was carrying a half-German, but clearly Aryan, child in her womb to a concentration camp and thus to her death. And if the father would simply wise up, the child could be completely German. Besides, the father would have nine months to reconsider, and if he did, the rescued child could ultimately be as German as a fence post.

THAT NIGHT, I couldn't sleep. I thought about my pretty German teacher, of whom I was so fond, even though she tormented me by constantly correcting my pronunciation of the German "e," which poor Mr. Katz had failed to teach me properly. The torment, however, had forged a kind of bond between us, and I was terrified of what might happen to her. I knew that the inspector, Heinz Dietrich Werner, *actually did have that kind of power. He had demonstrated it several times already, although he had not yet used it against German teachers who had committed* Rassenschande, *only against Czech teachers whom he merely disliked. He had that kind of power.*

⚔ ⚔

Bara. I remembered her when she was half her current girth. She was even further from the Hollywood ideal than Nina. Her cheeks were like pancakes. Right after the war, her old boyfriend, Vlasak, had gone to work for the Ministry of the Interior. The secret police.

I looked around. Some invisible chief of protocol had seated us precisely according to the criteria of the historical situation: "us" on one side of the table, "them" on the other. Erwin Pick sat on our side as a kind of guest of honour. His Party card had earned him no favours, instead costing him six years at an address that it was better not to ask about. Lexa had served two years with him at the same address, and now he was lounging next to me on a well-upholstered chair, puffing on a Virginian, and when Bara's perfume preceded her through the door, Lexa had turned to Knobloch and said, "Your Excellency, what kind of eau de cologne do you employ after shaving? Is it an import from Paris?"

Knobloch did not reply, but from the way the muscles moved in his cheeks, you could tell he was gritting his teeth. But the school inspector—Bara—had already arrived, twice the woman she once was, uttering her colloquial "Evening all!" Now it was the turn of our side of the table to stand up and mumble our awkward greetings—whatever they were— in response to Comrade Innemanova's warm and ample embrace. Whereupon Pilous again yelled out his drinker's invocation, getting it right this time, "Ladies and gentlemen!" he said, raising his glass.

I looked over at Nina. Her delicate cheeks had turned pink.

Berta, Franta Jelen, Anka Pitasova, Nina, Lexa, me, and Erwin Pick as our guest of honour on one side.

Bara, Pilous, Kveta, Knobloch, Jebavy on the other.

So far we outnumbered them by two. Jebavy, it seemed to me, was sitting on the wrong side.

"Ahoy!" I said to the aromatic school inspector, but I did not embrace her. She hesitated, and when she got close to me, she said, "Ahoy!" under her breath, and her blue eyes, submerged in the consequences of a life unknown to me, the life of a school inspector, now rested on Nina.

Nina sat as straight as a yardstick. She didn't say "Ahoy!" She didn't say anything.

"Excuse me, Your Excellency!" Lexa called to Knobloch. "How could I have been so wrong?" and to Bara, "*Eau de Moscow*, if I'm not mistaken?"

Bara was rescued by a voice from the door. "Greetings, my friends! My train was greatly delayed, and I offer my sincere apologies to you all," said Mirko Kulich, pompously, like the specialist teacher of the Czech language that he was. He placed himself on the correct side of the table, beside Jebavy, who had sat there by mistake.

"Is Stazka coming?" asked Inspector Bara. A safe question. We all knew that Stazka wasn't coming. So did the inspector.

"Stazka's in the sanatorium in Dobris," said Pilous needlessly.

"My word! Is she still there?" said Kulich. "Indeed, it was my distinct impression that the poor woman had already been completely cured."

※ ※

It was a dull rainy day, and Jebavy asked, "Why is her candle broken?"

"It's an ancient custom in the Roman Catholic Church," Kulich instructed him. "After all, she and Stejskal were engaged, weren't they? So she's laying her fiancé to rest."

We were walking in the funeral procession for Stejskal through the chilling drizzle, Stazka in a cheap, flimsy black mourning dress that clung to her in the damp, the rest of us bundled into winter coats. In the affectation of youth, Stazka may have wanted to die too, and she nearly succeeded. She caught tuberculosis, not from the cold, but from her fiancé. And she survived. Back in primary school she had thrown her lasso around my neck, but I didn't really understand what she was doing to me. I was an only child, with a sheltered upbringing, barely ten years old. By the time Irena did the same thing to me three years later, I had an inkling of what was going on. It was as though God had turned on a huge lantern in heaven. Light flooded the world. Irena walked with her skis over her shoulders. I turned around to look at her as she passed, her long braids bouncing against her back. It was evening, winter. The lantern went on shining brightly.

※ ※

"Gentlemen, why isn't Vejrazka gracing us with his presence?" inquired Lexa. Of course he already knew: he wasn't that uninformed. Those on the opposite side of the table fell silent. There was an approved phrase they might have used to account for Vejrazka's absence, but for some time now, it cropped up only in the newspapers, not in polite conversation. I interrupted the silence, setting both sides up, not so they could smash the ball back at us, but to get something like a human conversation going. No other kind was possible. That much I knew.

"I was his best man last year in Karlove Vary," I said.

"Who did he marry?" asked Anka.

I shrugged my shoulders. I had no appetite for delving too deeply into the Vejrazkas' convoluted history. I had known about their escapade long before anyone else, but I didn't go around broadcasting it. On a postcard from Africa, from Casablanca, where the newlyweds had gone on a business trip, they had added a brief note just below their signatures: "From here—across the Pond!" Casablanca is a port city. There was only one Pond. At that time, Czechs were certainly not making any business trips to the other side.

Franta spoke up. "It was someone from Vary. I was a conductor on the Prague Express at the time, and I met them when they were going to visit Vejrazka's parents in Porici."

"But who was she? Surely he introduced you to her?"

"All he said was, 'Meet my little Dotty,'" and she gave him a slap on the elbow."

And so the conversation staggered promisingly into life, a more human conversation than I had hoped for, but Lexa, whose irony had been steeled by two years in a correctional institution, was not interested in seeing anything human emerge from this evening. He turned to Kulich and said, "Deml is running a little late too. Or," and he adopted a theatrical tone, "could it be that he's avoiding us?"

Silence. They didn't want to respond in set phrases. Kulich was not about to provide information that was probably news to no one.

※ ※

Not long after Werner's disastrous visit to our classroom, the principal, Mr. Zach, showed up when we were expecting a lesson in German ideology and announced, in a voice that was softer than normal, that Mrs. Cvancarova had been transferred to the Ernst Udet Public School, whose students, with the exception of the local German, Kvetuse Pelozza-Lukitch, had all been evacuated from Hamburg and Berlin, and for whom they had set up a residence in—and here the principal paused for a moment, but then finished what he was going to say—in the former Masaryk Municipal School.

The Masaryk School had been relocated to the business academy in Parkany, where they had introduced an afternoon shift for students of accounting. We were going to be taught German by a new teacher, the principal said, from Prague, Mr. Puchwein.*

The new teacher was standing beside the principal, and several of the girls noticed right away that he looked like Robert Taylor.

When the principal left the room, Puchwein began his instruction in German ideology with a statement about Dr. Goebbels, whose name he pronounced "Gables."

During recess, a discussion got under way among the girls about whether Robert Taylor was married. But I couldn't get this sudden change out of my head. We talked about it in the boys' washroom, and long before Ruda Sepp confirmed that it was true, we had figured out that Werner was behind it. Ruda had come to say goodbye to us because his father had been elevated to the position of Treuhänder, *a supervisor, or trustee, appointed by the Nazis to look after businesses confiscated from Jews, among them the largest Kostelec dry goods store, which belonged to Mr. Strass. Given his father's new position, it was out of the question for Ruda to continue attending a Czech high school, so the* Treuhänder *sent him to the brand-new Horst Wessel school, in Braunau—the one that was thirty kilometres down the road, not the one where Hitler had been born. For the duration of the war, the Horst Wessel school ran an accelerated program, and because Ruda was sixteen he would finish his high-school diploma in less than a year and then go off to war to fight for the Leader and his country. For Der Fewer, as we called him in Kostelec.*

Ruda wasn't happy about this turn of events, and he revealed some secrets, which may have been official German secrets, that he'd uncovered at a big dinner party organized by his father for the school inspector, Mr. Werner. "I have transferred Frau Professor Brunnenschatten to a German public school," the monster had said over his Wiener schnitzel. "It's a preliminary warning because she insists on remaining married to Mr. Cvancara. If Frau Professor Brunnenschatten does not file for divorce, or as long as Mr. Cvancara refuses to take German citizenship . . ." The monster paused and then set about instructing the Treuhänder *and his son: "A grandmother of Herr Cvancara, on his father's side, was half-German. His mother is one-quarter German, which makes him more than a quarter German, and therefore he has enough German blood in his veins to . . ." Werner, who at that point had in his own veins at least four glasses of French cognac, imported for the Kostelec German community from Paris, shrugged his shoulders and fell silent again. Ruda, who had been going to Father Meloun for private religious instruction, told us later that he was almost expecting Werner to call for a bowl of water to wash* his hands. But instead, he went on, "In that case, it would be quite impossible for a woman who is racially and nationally so compromised, who is so completely unfamiliar with the new German ideology, to go on spreading confusion among the German children in school, let alone in one that proudly bears the name of Ernst Udet."*

Given the percentage of German blood in Cvancara's veins, whatever it was, it didn't seem to me that Miss Brunnenschaten was terribly compromised, but it was certainly true that she had made a hash of teaching us German ideology.

WE DECIDED TO GO AS A CLASS to bid her farewell. No one was excluded. We took up a collection for a giant bouquet, which Bara and Vlasak were to present to her. The only one who didn't show up was Stejskal, who by that time was already in the sanatorium, but Stazka came, though she looked as if she'd rather have been there with him. Kveta and Pilous brought a bottle of homemade slivovitz from Kveta's uncle's farm in Moravia, and Anka and Nina baked something resembling Christmas cookies.

But it was a sad occasion, not like the time we'd given our teacher the coffee mill as a wedding present.

Miss Brunnenschatten sat in an armchair under a portrait of Emperor Josef the Second—hung there by Cvancara's mother, who was one-quarter German but spoke Czech—and cried the whole afternoon.

No one felt like saying much. Lexa made jokes about Josef the Second, famous from Czech literary classics as the brightest of Empress Maria Theresia's fifteen—or was it seventeen?—children. But his jokes fell flat. The teacher wept and her husband was gloomy and quiet. Then, quite formally, he asked to speak. We fell silent, and Cvancara *announced what I already knew, and knew as well that it was not yet true: that they were expecting a baby in about seven months.*

So we drank a toast with the Moravian slivovitz, except for our teacher, who, out of consideration for the not yet existent baby, drank tea. And I began thinking that this child, who was meant to save her from Ravensbrück, would be, in fact, an almost perfect German. I ran the numbers: one great-grandmother, who was half German; one grand-mother, a quarter; the father perhaps only one-eighth; how-ever, the mother was as German as it gets—ergo, the child had, or rather would have, in his or her blood ...

I realized how hard to master this racial science was, but by my calculations the child would be at least three-quarters German. If I'd done the math properly, that is. So when she really was pregnant, the German officials wouldn't let Werner send her to Ravensbrück, unless of course he really was a very big shot ...

At that age I was not used to slivovitz, and I'd already made a fool of myself once before, overindulging with the one-armed legionnaire Mr. Skocdopole,* and so a queer thought occurred to me. Perhaps Cvancara wasn't the patriot he was making himself out to be. Perhaps he didn't want to take on German citizenship because, as a quarter—or perhaps one-eighth—German, they would draft him as they had Ruda, even though Ruda was tainted by a serious fault in Nazi eyes: Jew-loving (if, that is, it was true that Ruda's grandfather had been a gravedigger in the Jewish cemetery).

I took another drink ...

How I got home, I don't know.

Next morning, with a hangover, I prayed that my teacher would conceive, and I wondered how many months would go by before the war was over.

⊣ ⊢

Silence. They didn't want to respond in set phrases. Nina spoke up, her voice tremulous.

"Deml betrayed his country," she said, with exaggerated irony.

It was a Communist label once applied liberally to those who committed the crime of leaving the country without authorization, now slightly dated, and I could scarcely believe I was hearing it from Nina's lips. Before I could respond, three waiters marched into the room carrying the national dish—pork, cabbage, and dumplings—first serving those on the other side of the table, who started to eat, eagerly clacking their knives and forks and heaping exaggerated praise on the cook. Then the waiters came around the table and served us.

It was as though someone had told them which side of the table to wait on first. Mentally, I shook my head in disbelief, though of course it must have been unintentional. I too began eating the pork, while observing my former classmates—the comrades—across the steaming bowls of dumplings. Bara was staring intently at Nina, and just as intently, Nina was looking down at her plate. All at once, Bara, a piece of meat on her fork, casually remarked, "Deml is in Switzerland. Apparently he got some kind of menial job with Nestlé."

"Deml betrayed his country," Nina repeated, still looking at her plate. She spoke quietly, but there was no mistaking what she had said.

Perhaps anticipating a showdown or at least an unpleasant scene, Bara gave a weak little shudder and continued looking intently at Nina. In her eyes was uncertainty, amazement, and something else. Everyone fell silent, their cutlery poised.

Was that something else hatred? No, it wasn't that. They'd been too close. They had sat together in the last row from the first to the eighth grade. I had a sudden recollection of that bunk bed in the Innemans' cottage, each of the two friends with a different guy, and I shook my head, pushing the memory back into an abyss in my mind. When Mr. Liska tried to seat them separately because they were interrupting his chemistry lessons with their giggling, they marched into the chemistry department together and, the story went, got down on their knees in front of him, begging him to relent. No one had seen them do it; it was only a rumour, but it was probably true, because they were allowed to go on sitting side by side in the last row, though they were thereafter more circumspect during chemistry classes, apparently paying attention to the lesson, but each of them almost certainly somewhere else in her thoughts.

The silence was sepulchral. Pilous tried to smooth things over. Instead of following where his human curiosity would naturally have led him—back to the interesting question of Vejrazka's ditzy wife—he said, "In Deml's case, it sort of makes sense. His family owned a children's biscuit factory in Dobruska, and it was nationalized; he had nowhere to go—so you can explain it that way if you want. In Vejrazka's case, it's perhaps understandable—"

"But not excusable," Nina interrupted emphatically. "Deml behaved like a class enemy, and he betrayed his country." She looked her former friend in the eye. "And he doesn't have a *menial* position. He's director of production in the baby formula department."

"How do you know that?" said Knobloch darkly.

"I have my sources," said Nina. "After all, I'm a class enemy too." She paused to let that sink in. "Because of my husband. That's why they locked him up in the correctional facility. That's why he contracted TB. That's why two months after they let him out he was dead."

The terminology Nina was using could scarcely be heard in public anymore, not even in the main Communist Party newspaper, *Rudé pravo*, and if such phrases did appear there, most readers would automatically skip over them. They could no longer be used in polite conversation, except perhaps at Party meetings. An absurd idea flashed through my head: I imagined that Knobloch would now send our side of the table out of the room, the way they used to do at meetings of the Union of Dramatic Artists when opinions began to diverge too greatly and it was necessary to get everyone back in line. Once the inner circle had decided on what that line was, they would call us back to the table. An absurd notion, right through to its logical conclusions. Meanwhile, our dinner was getting cold.

Then another thought flashed through my mind, one that was not absurd. Was Nina perhaps trying to follow in the footsteps of her dead husband? Vlasak wasn't here, but of those who were ... I looked around at them: Pilous and Kulich had their noses in their plates, Knobloch was frowning at Nina. Bara—were those tears in her eyes? Jebavy was looking at Nina dumbfoundedly.

No. It was unlikely that anyone here would report this conversation to the "appropriate places," another phrase that had gone out of circulation. Unless—Kulich? That master of grammatically impeccable, and therefore artificial, Czech?

But this wasn't a whodunit. The rule about the least suspicious didn't apply here. Nina's cheeks were burning; she sat as stiff as a plank. By sheer force of will, I pulled myself out of this unreal reality and came back to a subject that interested even the women on the other side of the table. As though it were the greatest joke in the world, I said, "Someone told me that Vejrazka is in California, working as a gofer for a construction engineer on the San Francisco–Los Angeles freeway. Apparently, his wife's nickname, Dotty, has caught on among the Czechs who live there. But I've met her, and I would say she's far more crafty than dotty."

Nina stubbornly, anachronistically, said, "Vejrazka's another traitor."

"Knock it off, Nina," Berta muttered. "You're spoiling the mood."

"You're a class enemy too," said Nina, calmly. "And you're suffering the consequences."

"Now listen here, Novakova," Knobloch broke in, in a loud voice. "Are we celebrating the twentieth anniversary of our matriculation, or are we at a political meeting?"

"In the words of Lenin, my friend," said Lexa, "politics is everywhere. Even in mathematics. That's why a non-political soul like myself never managed to matriculate in math."

LENIN MAY HAVE SAID THAT, and if he didn't, then someone else did and attributed it to him. The body of work Lenin left behind isn't big enough to contain all the so-called quotes of Lenin. Lexa's citation from the highest authority turned my mind to the politics in which his matriculation exams had become entangled. Bivoj had given him a goose egg, but he'd entered the mark only in his private records. On the report cards, he granted a general pardon and would have let Lexa pass had Werner not suddenly appeared out of the blue, well informed as always, aware that the Gestapo had recently executed Lexa's father. Thus did Lexa become the son of an enemy of the Reich, and his final mark in math reflected this, confirming Lenin's observation, if in fact Lenin had ever uttered it.

Knobloch said nothing, and we went back to our meal. My thoughts swept me back into the past.

⊰ ⊱

Ten years after the war, halfway through the dark 1950s, I came back to Kostelec to put flowers on my mother's grave and then, with another bouquet, I set out on yet another pilgrimage to Nadia. It was autumn, and I climbed up along the road, past the orphanage where Mother had died and then up a path through the fields to a restaurant called Na Vyhlidce—so called because it afforded a great view—and I paused to look around. By now I was higher than the castle that dominated the town, and below me I surveyed the beautiful valley of my swell season, the town that held the secrets of many young girls, the woods that surrounded it. It was a view, as Father Meloun used to say, that lifted one's thoughts toward God. But by this time I knew that all this beauty concealed a cruel and never-ending struggle, a struggle for everything imaginable, including life itself. The Venerable Father had emerged from that battle more or less intact. Nadia had not, and I was making a pilgrimage to honour her memory. My thoughts were raised toward God, but I wondered what kind of God he actually was.

I walked up the steep path through the woods, the timeless fragrance reminding me that what I had lived through long ago had actually happened and was not a fantasy spun out of memory. I walked up to a point just below the bare peak of Cerna Hora, that black mountain where I had once carried the slender Nadia, barely making it to the top.[*] *I scrambled up to the summit and walked toward the village. Nadia's house was on the outskirts. Her husband lived there now with his second wife, with whom he had several* *children, for that's how it must be. Nadia would not have minded.*

A man wearing a coat and a cap walked out of the village with a crowd of children tagging along behind him, little boys and girls about seven or eight years old. They were making their way toward Jirasek's chalet, where there had once been a pub, although shortly afterwards they closed it down and tried to build a Young Pioneers camp, complete with the never-to-be-used pitch for gorodky *(a comical Russian substitute for lawn bowling) and a much-used Olympic-size swimming pool. But the scheme collapsed and the upkeep of an Olympic pool on the summit of Cerna Hora proved too expensive. So they abandoned the whole idea, leaving neither pub nor pool. Sometime later, the pub was reopened, and the chalet became once more what it had been.*

I recognized the man in the cap.

"Jebavy! What are you doing here?"

"What are you *doing here?" said Jebavy.*

"Rekindling memories," I said. "I haven't been here for ten years."

I looked at the gaggle of village kids, who had also stopped and were staring at me. "I thought you were teaching at Hradek."

"I was," said Jebavy. "I finished up there about eight years ago."

Hradek was a district town in the mountains with a nice new school that had been built during the war.

"Where are you now?"

"Here. In a two-roomer."

"So, what did you do wrong?" I asked. Given the historical situation, there was no other way to phrase the question.

Jebavy looked around at his students and issued a command in his teacher's voice. "Form two lines. We're going up to the plateau in front of Jirasek's chalet." The pupils lined up as they were told and waited patiently for their teacher to lead them off.

"Hey," Jebavy said. "This is my last lesson of the day. I'll finish up, send them home, and we'll go for a beer."

"Certainly. I've got time."

"You go on ahead. I'll catch up with you."

"Good," I said. "I've got something else to do here."

"Here? On Cerna Hora?" asked Jebavy.

"A private thing."

Jebavy glanced at my bouquet. He must have wondered about it. I might have been going on a serious date. Given my literary notoriety, which he must certainly have heard of, that would have been the most likely explanation.

"So, I'll see you in about half an hour," he said, turning to face the double line of pupils. He gave an order and the lines moved off and disappeared on the other side of Jirasek's chalet. I walked to the little cottage. I'd seen the inside of it only once, while Nadia was still living there. I knocked on the door. A dog emerged from a kennel and began barking ferociously at me. I'd expected something like this, and I placated him with a sandwich I'd brought from Prague. I knocked again, but no one answered. I grasped the latch. Locked. There was no one home. So I laid the bouquet by the door, with the ribbon on top to make it easy to read: IN MEMORY OF NADIA—DANNY. I recited the Lord's Prayer and a Hail Mary. The dog finished the sandwich and began growling at me. So I crossed myself and set off slowly toward Jirasek's chalet.

Jebavy was still teaching. I stood around the corner so he couldn't see me. I found a sunny spot that had a magnificent view over the autumn countryside. The surrounding hilltops were like scenery flats in a theatre, one behind the other, *extending away to the horizon and the white peak of Snezka. Jebavy was busy testing his pupils' knowledge of the local geography, my familial landscape. They knew most of the answers. I went into the restaurant. It was empty, and I sat down at a table at the lookout window, which they much later started calling the panoramic window.*

The same view of an unreal world, wrapped in the real and unlovely world of the historical situation. I saw the little heads of Antonin Jebavy's pupils, the blond, beribboned hair of the girls, and even a couple of old-fashioned braids, but I couldn't hear anything they were saying. I looked at the countryside and saw in it events that were long since past. I lifted my eyes to the sky and wanted a God to be there, but a different God, a kinder God. I closed my eyes and saw Nadia. My thoughts were without rhyme or reason. Marie, in her ski outfit, with a friend from Prague, giggling over some young girls' secrets. It was in winter, long ago, far too long ago ...

⊰ ⊱

While I was lost in the past, a discussion had developed at the table. I started paying attention.

"Today," Knobloch was saying, "they don't deal with things quite so ... harshly."

"That's a fact," Pilous nodded.

"But, of course, they're still traitors," said Nina stubbornly. "Deml, Berta, and Lexa—"

"They've already done their time," Pilous interrupted her. Then he caught Berta's eye and said, "And, Berta—well, that was a mistake, actually."

"And it still is, comrade," said Lexa.

"Come on, guys," said Berta. "Just drop it!"

"And what about my husband, Pilous?" Nina retorted. "Was he a traitor, or a mistake?"

"Your husband, Nina, did his time too. And if ..." Pilous suddenly stopped. What would Reverend Novak be doing now if he'd survived? The same as many other such reverends, pastors, brethren, venerable fathers, and eminences were doing: they were ditch-diggers, night watchmen, labourers on the construction sites of socialism. The Reverend Novak's employment prospects would have been rather limited, and entirely menial.

Nina's thin voice, still incredibly girlish, was saturated with despair, hatred. Hatred? No, not hatred. Regret, perhaps. She said, "And if he hadn't died, then what? He's not a traitor anymore. He's dead. But was he a mistake?"

She looked around the table. Those on the other side seemed to have suddenly caught colds and were sniffing into their handkerchiefs. After a moment, Kulich said harshly, "Your husband dragged politics into the church, Nina."

The moonlike cheeks darkened. "But is he still a traitor, now that he's dead? Now that he's not only served his time but died as a result?" She stared into Kulich's evasive eyes and suddenly shouted, "Or was he a frigging mistake?"

Anger or regret or whatever it was shook her slender figure. It seemed unbelievable that she'd given birth to four children. I felt a shudder of horror. Was anyone here actually on the job, a designated informer? Vlasak hadn't come, at least not yet.

Lexa interrupted my moment of fear. "An interesting problem, ladies and gentlemen!" he cried. "How shall we put it in the terminology of today's socialism, which, in this country at least, has finally been achieved?"

"Careful," said Kulich darkly. "You're in dangerous territory."

Could he be the one on duty?

"I'm not in dangerous territory, sir," Lexa replied. Nothing was ever sacred to him. Or was everything sacred? "I only wish to be completely in the picture, if you're familiar with that popular turn of phrase."

Jebavy looked up from his beer and spoke. "You know, that would interest me too. I mean, purely from a terminological and logical point of view."

I was surprised at how erudite this teacher from a two-room schoolhouse sounded. And he went on: "For instance, Deml, according to the established terminology, is our class enemy because of who he is, and a traitor because he left the country. But betraying the enemy is an oxymoron."

Jebavy could speak with a certain sophistication. Perhaps he could even give himself licence to say what he said. His working-class pedigree was unassailable. He was a graduate of our humble school. Both his parents had walked to work, a three-kilometre trek from Lipi to the Mautner's knitting mill down in town. His grandparents used to have a small field in Lipi that was not enough to sustain them, so they took on various odd jobs, some of them in Kostelec, which meant they had to walk those three kilometres up a steep hillside to get back home. I didn't know much more about Jebavy's family, but they were certainly not from the upper crust. (His priest would have known more, but he was in prison.) Jebavy's class background was no doubt unblemished, so perhaps he could get away with talk that paid no heed to the historical situation. I couldn't.

Then I heard Berta, the peacemaker: "Why don't we get together and talk about this some other time," Berta said, raising his glass of vodka. "*Nunc est bibendum!*" It's time for a drink!" It was one of the many fragments of Latin that Miss Kuralova had taught us. She was dead now, having survived the sudden death (from overweight) of her husband, Bivoj, by a mere three months. *Nunc pede libero pulsanda tellus*...and Berta started singing in his high tenor:

Gaudeamus igitur
Iuvenes dum sumus
Post iucundam
Iuventutem
Post molestam
Senectutem
Nos habebit humus

Under Berta's bold voice, Kulich hissed angrily at Jebavy, "As a Communist, you ought to be familiar with Party tactics."

"As a matter of fact, I am," said Jebavy.

⊨ ⊨

As we drank beer by that beautiful window with the magnificent view of a countryside sullied by the historical situation, Jebavy told me all about it. He didn't use the stilted, hypercorrect language that Kulich did, but rather spoke a living vernacular, a compromise language from which he had expunged the vulgar words while leaving intact, like drops of mountain rain, fragments of the idiom of the countryside of our birth, though we'd each grown up in a different part of it. Naturally, he was a member of the Party, but by this time it seemed unnatural to him. "You know how it is," he explained. "I don't have the balls to quit, unfortunately."

Right after his second round of state exams at the teacher's college, they'd sent him to his native town of

Hradek, to a new five-room school built during the war, and by then he was already feeling somewhat out of place, given what was going on in the country and given what those whom he now addressed (because he had to) as "comrades" were up to. His first task in the new school—in response, of course, to orders from above, which he had not received in writing but which were clear nevertheless—was to fire the former principal. Until this point, the principal had also served as choir master and organist in the small local church, though it was only once a month, since the sole remaining chaplain in the large diocese wasn't able to serve mass there any more often than that. Instead of turning the old principal (who was two years from retirement anyway) over to the work office, to be assigned to some appropriate— that is to say manual—job, Jebavy, contrary to orders, merely shifted him laterally, from the sunny principal's office where Jebavy now sat alone, haunted by his conscience (the principal had once taught him, back when the school was a mere three-room affair), to the no-less-sunny staff room, where his former employees continued to address him as Principal. Jebavy did not try to stop them.

He looked out at the magnificent countryside where he had lived since birth. The historical situations that had unfolded in his life had prevented him from seeing other landscapes equally as beautiful, or more so, often a great deal more so. He looked at the gilt peeling off the cupolas of the ducal palace far below us, where, when we were still young, there lived, or ruled, or whatever it was, a little old princely gentleman with his little old butler, both of whom were sent away after the liberation to nearby Chudoba, about ten kilometres away but on the other side of the Czech-Polish border, where in a dank basement apartment, the two old men had soon passed away.

"I managed to iron things out in Prague," Jebavy said. He finished his beer and turned for another one, which he received at once because we were sitting alone in the pan-elled tap room and the barman was keeping his eye on us, probably because he had nothing better to do. "They had me on the carpet, but I appealed to their social conscience, if you can call it that. I said that the principal had only two years before his pension kicked in, and by now he was a bundle of skin and bone and couldn't have handled physical labour. Take my word for it, it wasn't easy." He took a drink of his beer and then looked out the window, as if gathering strength from the landscape. "This was right after the Feb-ruary coup, and some of the colleagues were damned tough customers, partly because they had a reason to be. I expect you know what I mean when I say they had a reason to be."

I nodded.

"So I managed to sweet-talk them into going along with it, but like I said, it wasn't easy. The thing is, the principal was a dyed-in-the-wool Masaryk man, which didn't make things any easier. Well, I squeaked that one through, but then the end of the school year came and I recommended sending a student of mine, Vostrel, on to high school." He took another drink. "And this time, my friend, I fell flat on my face."

And he told me the story. Vostrel was the son of a Kulak, a pernicious term for a private farmer, but appropriate, given the historical situation. The father qualified for this deadly classification on the basis of a decision made by the chair-man of the Party in Hradek. He owned almost a hectare less than the land required to make him officially a Kulak, but the chairman took into account his political opinions, which, Jebavy said, would have been as clear as a kick in the shins even to the village idiot. The problem—for Jebavy—was that

Vostrel Jr. was a brilliant student. Jebavy's predecessor had recommended that the lad be sent to a school for the exceptionally gifted, but even a year before the February coup, school boards were already quietly taking class origins into account, though not yet required by law to do so. Vostrel remained at the school in Hradek, Jebavy inherited him, and at the end of the school year, he had to decide on Vostrel's fate. "He could have started right in teaching instead of me," he told me. "He could have gone straight on to teach high school!" He took a drink and looked me in the eyes. "And so I recommended him for high school, even though I knew giving the children of Kulaks a secondary school education was against the new guidelines. I figured that for a talented kid like that they would, exceptionally, make an exception. Well, my friend," he sighed and took another drink, "they said, 'Only after he shows his worth through hard work in the mines,' the usual blather, and I got rapped over the knuckles for not being vigilant enough, and they sent me off to Vyhlidka to smarten me up. Ideological training, reeducation, whatever. Well, that was some punishment. You know Vyhlidka, right? You used to play there during the war."

"I know it," I said. "You had it pretty good there, didn't you?"

He'd been there at a time when the à la carte menus in teaching institutions like Vyhlidka, which later entirely vanished, were on a par with those in the international hotels.

"It was nice there," said Jebavy. "There was dancing every evening, and some of those lady teachers, man, they were worth the sinning, even though there were also these trade union types as well..."

"I know, but what about those who were worth the sinning?"

Jebavy laughed in a way that could only be described as knowing and said, "I married one of them, and she's stuck by me to this day, even though she's teaching in Hradek and they've sent me here. I go home to see her on Sundays. But that Vostrel, man! Just listen!"

It was not long after the victory of the Party in '48. There were still gaping holes in the Iron Curtain. Vostrel the Kulak took his wife and his brilliant son, and with the help of his brother-in-law, who had a little farm in the Sumava mountains down near the West German border, they disappeared over the hills.

"Today he's a professor of nuclear physics at Yale," said Jebavy with some satisfaction. "I mean, the son is—I don't need to tell you that—but the old man made out okay too. He has a business selling grain. When I came back from my 'schooling,' the inspector hauled me in and I got rapped over the knuckles again. 'Comrade, do you have any idea who it was you recommended for high school?' he said. 'Too bad you didn't follow my advice,' I said. 'Who knows what kind of damage this kid might do to us now he's abroad.' The inspector turned red, and then he said, 'Well, on the one hand, you might be right, comrade. On the other hand, the comrades should have been keeping a sharper eye on that border.' So I said I entirely agreed with him, and he looked at me like he was making sure I wasn't taking him for a fool. But he couldn't very well say anything, so he made up for it the next time."

⊰ ⊱

Berta took me by the sleeve.

"How about a little fresh air? Anka's about to toss her cookies."

Knobloch, Kulich, and Nina, in a cloud of smoke, were up to their ears arguing about a theory that could hardly be applied to anything anymore, but was still officially in force. Bara was silent, her eyes fixed on the floor, and she was slowly getting drunk. I looked at Anka and saw what Berta meant; she was a little pale, but smoking with the rest of them, so I nodded at Franta and Lexa and we all got up from the table.

Bara called after us, "Where are you going?"

"Where even the emperor himself had to go on his own steam, your ladyship," said Lexa. "Unfortunately, ladies are not admitted."

Bara looked at us and then at Anka, reproachfully, it seemed to me, and said nothing. We could hear Nina's thin, high voice emerging from the cloud of smoke: "So will someone please amend this terminology for me!" It occurred to me that we shouldn't be leaving her at the mercy of her former classmates, but the others had already left the room and I walked out as well, with a heavy conscience.

※　※

It was three weeks after Mother's death. I had no other reason for going to Kostelec, except that I felt sorry for my father. He was all alone in a flat where he and Mother and I had moved when he'd been promoted to manager. The building that had just been completed. We'd been to see the flat when it wasn't quite finished, and the kitchen floor had been freshly covered with some sort of reddish cement called xylolite. The superintendent, who was showing us around, said we couldn't go into the kitchen yet because the floor was still soft, so I got down on my knees in the doorway and with my finger—a tiny finger because I was still a little boy—touched the dark red material. It really was soft, and my finger sank into it. My mother yelled at me, but everyone else, including the superintendent, laughed. They stood me up and my mother gave me a symbolic slap on the bottom and dragged me into the next room, our future living room, where the parquet flooring was already laid down. I managed one last glance behind me, and I saw that my finger had left a tiny impression in the red cement.

So I went to Kostelec to please my father, though I had never thought much about his welfare while Mother was still alive. The air inside the train was freezing, despite the steam locomotive. I felt sad, but then the countryside, as always, began to change, and past Skalice that magic landscape opened out—the country of my childhood? No, nothing that subjective. The land suddenly began to undulate, hills appeared, then mountains, and the train went into its long, slow, inclined curve around the town, and I could see Cerna Hora, and I made up my mind to go on a pilgrimage to Nadia, to honour her memory. Then I remembered I was there to see my father. The train pulled into the Kostelec station and screeched to a halt.

I walked home, along Kamenice Street, past the Hotel Italia, to our five-storey apartment building, constructed in no particular style. It was just a building, with two shops at street level and flats for seven families, since the owner's brother occupied the entire third floor himself. I walked up the stairs to the fourth floor—there was no elevator—and remembering why I was there, I thought about my mother, who had been alive only three weeks before. I rang the bell and my father opened the door. He embraced me and my tears blurred the world but, oddly, my father's eyes seemed dry. We sat at a table in the living room. My father had bought a cake and he poured coffee from an insulated flask and smiled at me and then suddenly said, "Danny—what would you say if I got married again?"

I looked vainly for some metaphor to describe my feelings, but I could only think of my mother's heavy breathing and how some time had gone by before I realized it was her death rattle.

"Well, what can I say?" I said, and when I added nothing more my father told me that Mrs. Hercikova had come to see him and let it drop that she had just the woman for him, someone he'd known for a while, and Father, after all, was a war invalid and needed looking after, and the woman in question was a nurse, the head nurse, in fact, at the nursing college in Prague. My father went on about what the matchmaker had told him but I no longer paid any attention. She was clearly a smooth talker, that was all I knew.

The next day I went into the woods and, despite the frigid air, sat down on the bench where I'd once seen Berta and Gerta—she was dead now too—but that was long ago, and Nadia had been dead for a long time as well, and my father had known her for a long time, this woman who was now the woman for him, and an ungovernable wave of memory swept me away.

WHEN I GOT BACK TO PRAGUE, I went to visit Uncle Fara at my father's urging. The last time we'd been to see him was in 1940, but only my aunt was at home; my uncle had taken his two daughters to see Krivoklat Castle in West Bohemia. Uncle Fara had been an inspector of art instruction in Uzhgorod, and when the Hungarians annexed the sub-Carpathian region in 1938, he moved to Prague. Whenever his name came up in conversation, I was always reminded of Irena, because her father, the alderman, had also come to Kostelec from Uzhgorod with his two daughters. It was mainly because of this

association that I took the streetcar to Pankrac, where a mod-
ern apartment building with a green portal stood on The Sev-
enth of November Street, and I took the elevator to the fourth
floor, rang the bell, and promptly put everything else out of
my mind—my mother, Irena, Nadia, Lizetka, Marie, every-
one and everything—because I was young and foolish and
my cousin Danica, whom I'd always called Dinah because
that name evoked memories of jazz, *had struck my heart*
with that legendary arrow. She was only two years older than
me, with a cheerful disposition and large eyes, and she was
very sexy, though no one used that term in those days. The ex-
pression we used was "a looker," and that she was.

Not long afterward—it was May, that legendary month
of love celebrated in Czech romantic poetry, a time of ren-
dezvous with young women, love-making, apple blossoms—
I was out walking with Dinah on Petrin Hill in Prague when
it started to pour. We ran to the nearest "mushroom." (At
irregular intervals along the pathway, there were round
benches with thatched roofs over them that looked like
mushroom caps, erected to shelter lovers from the rain.) On
the other side of the post supporting the roof, a man and a
woman were wrapped in a passionate embrace, their backs
to us. By now, the rain was coming down heavily. I looked
around at the couple and realized that I knew who they
were. The woman, who was about forty, was the one my father
intended to marry; the man, though, was partially obscured
by the thick post between us. I craned my neck for a better
look and, to my shock, realized that it was my father. I don't
know what I did next. I think I yanked Dinah back into the
rain. We got soaking wet, of course, but she took it in good
humour, and perhaps she was even happy to have her dress
cling to her body, because that year May was as warm as
July. I don't know anymore.

⊰ ⊱

As we walked down the hotel stairs into the relatively fresh air, all of this was running through my head: this class, this band of friends; Stejskal's funeral (he was the first of our class to travel to that land that has no name), Stazka dressed in black, Jebavy asking about the broken candle she was holding; the monstrous Inspector Werner, nightmare of our student years, and how this group of friends, as one, held their breath and stared at Professor Propilek when he insulted the monster's German (*Ich spreche Goethes Deutsch, nicht Schweindeutsch, Herr Inspector!*)* and miraculously survived this tossing of the gauntlet, for what else could it have been but a miracle when a monster more dangerous than a naked high-tension wire accepted, or ignored, or simply did not hear, what this tiny tubercular teacher had said; this class attending the wedding of our—of my—beloved, though German, German teacher, and how we all feared for her when Werner, the savage dinosaur, threatened her. This band of friends, this class.

What had happened?

IN SEARCH OF SMOKE-FREE AIR, to make Anka feel better, we took her deep into the bowels of the hotel, where they still ran a little dive bar, a remnant—of what? Of something lost? As long as you were willing to walk through the underground corridors into the kitchen, you could summon a waiter. Franta vanished in that direction, and we sat down at the bar.

"Why do they say that you're a mistake?" Anka asked Berta. In this underground room, her colour had returned, and she lit up immediately. American cigarettes. Marlboros. God knows where she'd got them.

"They mistook me for someone else," said Berta. "I should have been demobbed long ago, but they confused me with another Moutelik, who was also with the Black Barons, because his old man had stabbed the Party chairman in a brawl somewhere up in Hejsovice and they hanged him for it. In the meantime, my father was decorated as a model worker, and I pointed that out to them, but it took them two years, and even then it didn't go through the Party process, or whatever it was. The fact of the matter is, I'm serving past my time. Originally I was with the Black Barons based on a valid law, but now I'm there because of a valid mistake."

"Isn't that old man of yours also a mistake?" asked Franta, who had just come back with the barman in tow. "But a different kind of mistake?" The barman pulled a bottle of cognac out from under the bar, gathered some bulbous glasses from the racks, gave them a cursory wipe, then poured us drinks. "I mean, because they let him stay on as manager in your department store?" Franta added.

"What d'you mean 'manager'? He's the so-called senior clerk on the first floor. On the second floor, where the toys are, old Klimes is still in charge, the one who was working for us in the old store, if you recall."

"I don't," said Franta.

"Right across from the savings bank. It was a small, dark little hole in the wall. They had to keep the lights on during the day. Then my old man went and borrowed a lot of money and bought a department store, and Pelozza-Lukitch has my dad's old office on the third floor and now he's the boss."

"Are you talking about Branko Pelozza? That quisling?" said Franta, surprised.

Berta shrugged his shoulders. "They couldn't prove it."

"But everyone knew it," said Franta. "He was a *Treuhänder* at Krauses."

"He was absolved of his guilt through the agency of clemency," said Lexa. "The Party, my friends, has the capacity to forgive even the greatest of sinners."

For a while no one said anything, and the cognac began to warm my stomach. It was a pleasant sensation. Lexa turned his snifter around in his hand, and the evil liquid cast a golden glow on Anka's sad face. Lexa ...

꒳ ꒳

He was single again because his wife had died barely two years after he'd gotten out of prison. He'd married Marenka while he was in the internment camp, though not directly. Without writing to Lexa about it, she had made an official request to marry him, even though he had more than a year left in his sentence. The clerk asked her if the reason was pregnancy. Marenka blushed and said, "No, Lexa's been in the concen- ... in the correctional institution for a year and a half," and the clerk flashed her a twisted smile and told her that not long ago, in the camp where Lexa was interned, a civilian miner—who was still a miner, the clerk said, but no longer a civilian—smuggled fresh sperm from one of the prisoners outside the gates in an insulated bottle. A lady was waiting for him there—the clerk laughed—and she took it straight to the midwife and while it was still warm ... and he chuckled, and Marenka blushed and couldn't think of anything to say. A moment later, the official stamped her request loudly, Marenka rushed over to the town hall and they married her to Lexa in absentia.

Lexa knew nothing about any of this because Marenka wanted to surprise him. When a guard told him he should write home for a black suit, he was terrified, because he'd already escaped death by the skin of his teeth once before.

They had originally sentenced him to the gallows for allegedly giving overnight shelter to an American agent. It was a trumped-up charge, but the criminal police—unusually, in this case—managed to track down the real person responsible for harbouring the agent, and when they came to arrest the man, he pulled a gun, shot at the police, then ran away. When they finally arrested and hanged the right man, Lexa's sentence was commuted to three years, since they weren't about to let anyone who'd already been sentenced go scot-free.

Lexa became obsessed with the idea that the black suit was for laying him out in a coffin, although the practice was to execute prisoners in their work clothes and either bury them in a common grave or send their bodies to medical schools for dissection. He was completely baffled, he said later. After all, they'd reduced his sentence to three years; why would they execute him now? But man proposes, he said to me years later, and the Party disposes. Blessed be the name of the Party.

When the suit arrived, Lexa put it on and then, as pale as candle wax, stumbled after the guard, who led him to an unknown destination, which turned out to be the warden's office. Lexa's head was reeling as he stood at attention before the warden. The guard steadied him and whispered, "Hang on, buddy! There's worse things than gettin' hitched." In his confusion, Lexa wondered when they had started using the euphemism "getting hitched" for hanging. And then he heard the warden's voice addressing him in a tone that promised no good:

"Prisoner Lexa!"

"P-p-present," said the prisoner.

"The Comrade Minister of Justice," the warden went on—and Lexa felt the ground sway as if he were already on the

gallows—"has seen fit to comply with the request of your fiancée to join with you in wedlock. Do you wish to marry her?"

"Ye-yes," said Lexa, slowly awakening from his nightmare. He looked around to see where Marenka was. Could they actually have let her in here? But all he saw was the guard standing beside him, and he heard the warden say, "Prisoner Lexa, you have now entered into the state of matrimony." Then the warden gave Lexa a silly grin and said, "You may now kiss the bride!"

The guard turned to Lexa, made a face, then turned to the warden and said, "Is that an order, Comrade Warden?"

"Dismissed!" roared the warden, and Lexa no longer felt dizzy, but was floating on the euphoric clouds of this mistake, or joke, or whatever it was. He floated all the way back to the barracks, where he announced to the men who were just coming back from their shift, "Gentlemen, they've just handed me a life sentence!"

"No shit! What happened?" asked a prisoner by the name of Baloun.

"I'm a bigamist. So far they haven't discovered this, but it's merely a matter of time before the truth is out."

"What the fuck are you talking about, asshole?"

"I never told Marenka I was married already, although I wasn't living with my wife when we met, and when they arrested me I was too ashamed to tell her, and so, comrade prisoners, she married me in the Prague Town Hall without my knowledge!"

᠁ ᠁

I smiled at the memory, because that was just Lexa being Lexa. He wasn't a bigamist, just a clown. He always wanted to have the last laugh. I remembered a time even further in the past, New Year's Eve, 1944, midnight blues on the ski jump on Cerna Hora in the freezing cold, in the dark, playing to a semicircle of faithful zoot-suiters gathered below us. With every inhalation, the frigid air invaded our lungs, and Lexa blew a sour note on the clarinet because his fingers were stiff from the cold in spite of his woollen gloves with the ends of the fingers cut off.* We were playing "West End Blues," the melody soaring over the valley and flowing down the snow-covered slopes with the wind and the snowflakes, and it sounded so strangely new, so beautifully absurd up there on Black Mountain, in the German occupation on that thirty-first of December, nineteen hundred and forty-four.

And then the year nineteen hundred and sixty-three pulled me back from memories of that wonderful night, back to our band of friends, to the words of Franta Jelen.

"Pelozza-Lukitch? They let him join the Party?" said Franta.

Berta got his hackles up. "That's a dumb question! I told you he was the boss in our store, didn't I?"

That silenced us. I thought about the third floor, where Berta had a darkroom where he'd developed his notorious snapshots of the uprising in Kostelec against the Germans. The shiny little peddle cars sat there, though the best one, which had an auxiliary gas engine, was on display in the shop window.

After a while, Franta spoke again. "All the same, your old man is some kind of a mistake, or whatever you want to call it. Look at Kubelka—I mean the goldsmith, not the watchmaker. They tossed him in prison, and his shop didn't even have two floors, like yours. And get a load of the name! The City of *London* department store! I'm telling you, your old man must have been some kind of pretty damned exceptional mistake!"

I looked at the bottle the barman had set on the counter

because, quite rightly, he expected it to be used again. It was Martell.

"All of those things are the mysteries of the faith," I said. "Let's drink to it. May no one ever explain them."

⚑ ⚑

It was the spring of 1945, and it occurred to me to go to the vicarage to ask if there was any news of Father Meloun, who had been in Buchenwald for the last four years. Almost no one was showing up for work at the Messerschmitt factory by that time, and to harbour any doubt that the war was almost over, or to believe that the Leader's miracle weapons could turn the tide, was a sign of pathological denial. The British pilots had quickly learned how to intercept the v-1 buzz bombs and bring them down by using the wingtips of their Spitfires to flip them over and send them crashing to the ground. The v-2 rockets were harder to deal with, but by now Patton and Montgomery had occupied almost all of the launching pads, so that that hope was also extinguished. The psychopaths harboured one last hope: the v-3, which was supposed to be flown to New York by a female suicide pilot who was madly in love with the Führer.*

Everyone in Kostelec who'd supported the war had given up hope, including Mr. Sepp, who would hobble across the square to the Beranek café every day on crutches. His AA gun in Berlin had been hit by a bomb, and he'd escaped with nothing worse than a broken leg, so he'd come back to Kostelec to recuperate. Some recuperation! Sometimes you could already hear cannon fire from Kladsko, across the border.

As Rosta and I had once done, I walked up the wooden stairs to the second floor of the vicarage, where Father Meloun had had the parish register all ready for us to copy. My knock was answered by Chaplain Brejcha's voice, and when I entered, he was sitting at a desk that was barer than when Father Meloun had occupied it. No more stacks of books, only a black crucifix with a tiny yellow Christ on it, carved from ivory to conform to the strictest precepts of tradition, which dictated that the body of Our Lord must be fashioned from a different material than the cross. Father Meloun had had a crucifix too, but it was always completely buried under piles of breviaries, so that all you could see of the Christ was the head with its crown of thorns. That crucifix was brown and made of porcelain, and so was the Christ, except that in this case the porcelain was coloured, the head a deadly shade of pale with tiny droplets of red, representing blood, a compromise with the strict dictates of tradition.

"What brings you to see us, Mr. Smiricky?" said Father Brejcha in a flat, expressionless voice. He had lost a lot of weight, and his collar was so loose it made his neck look like the stem of a poppy.

"I wanted to ask if you had any news of Father Meloun."

The chaplain lowered his head and was silent for a moment, and I couldn't help noticing that his lips were moving. My mention of the Venerable Father had obviously triggered some kind of little prayer. Then he looked up, stared at me with bloodshot eyes, and shook his head.

"Well ..." I wanted to say something, but I couldn't think of what, and then he spoke with the desperate voice of someone being stretched on the rack. "I blame myself for the fact that he was arrested by the Gestapo." He crossed himself.

"But, Father—you weren't even here yet when they came to get him."

"No, no. God was testing me. Because he's omniscient, he knew that I would fail terribly, Mr. Smiricky. Twice—twice,

Mr. Smiricky—I've refused to do what the Venerable Father did, what you and your friend helped him to do. And it's not just that, it's—well, you must remember, I refused to wash away the hereditary sin of an innocent child. The babe couldn't help who its mother was, and its mother, after all, couldn't help being German. And she and her husband couldn't possibly be blamed for the kind of regime we live under."

The chaplain reached under his gown and pulled out a handkerchief. Tears ran down his cheeks. I still couldn't think of anything to say.

"And it was my responsibility as an anointed priest— my responsibility, Mr. Smiricky—to risk life itself to help my neighbour. And I was afraid. Christ our Lord also knew fear, and yet he carried his cross to Golgotha and allowed himself to be nailed to it. I was in no danger of so ghastly a death, and yet, out of fear, I did none of the things I should have done."

He turned away to dab at his tears.

"Well—but I ..." I still didn't know what to say or how to make him feel better. I only remembered my own fear, the fear that poor Nadia had helped me overcome. Chaplain Brejcha had no Nadia, nor could he have had. Poor chaplain.

Then he confided in me that every hour, even at night, using his rosary, he prayed ten paternosters for Father Meloun, and told me that if the Venerable Father did not return from Buchenwald, he, Brejcha, would join the Brothers of Mercy and go to Africa to work in a leper colony.

Though I felt sorry for him, though I suspected—no, I knew—that in his situation I would probably have done the same, and though I could see that he was as much a coward as I was, I still couldn't help feeling sceptical about his innocent notion of atoning for his guilt in this romantic way.

Outside the rectory window, the town square shone in the brilliant sunlight, and the dark shadow of the church fell on the cobblestones.

As things turned out—though I couldn't have known it at the time—Brejcha's fate would not be romantic in the least.

After the war, Father Brejcha did not enter the Benedictine order, because Father Meloun survived Buchenwald. But he still ached to make amends for his self-confessed wartime failures, and this he accomplished through acts of penance, by fasting and by praying day and night. His daily routine was so strict and so fanatical that he soon began to resemble a concentration camp survivor himself. In the end, Father Brejcha did manage to make amends for his shortcomings. He helped an agent provocateur *escape across the border, but instead of making it out of the country himself and living out his days in Germany, he was arrested and sent to a Communist concentration camp, Rovnost, where he died soon afterward in solitary confinement.*

⚑ ⚐

"Other such mysteries of their faith …" mused Lexa. "Jebavy once attempted to reveal them to me, but we had consumed an excessive amount of intoxicants and never got around to it. Why is Jebavy, with his impeccable working-class credentials, a lowly teacher in a two-room schoolhouse on Cerna Hora?"

"That's no mystery," Anka said, frowning. "He defended Horakova."

"Seriously?" I asked. I had thought the reason for his degradation had been the trouble he got into over his old principal and his brilliant student. "If that's true," I asked, "shouldn't he have ended up in the mines, not teaching school?"

"As usual, he bamboozled the comrades," said Anka, gaz-ing into the bottom of her glass. We all quickly emptied our glasses, and the barman refilled them. Anka may have been as brilliant as Jebavy's old student, though she never got to be a professor at Yale. She was the first in our class to get her Ph.D.—in the natural sciences—and she was immediately offered a position in the academy with Professor Heyrovsky. She got a bonus for discovering some methodologies I didn't understand; otherwise, I knew nothing more about her. But she had never married, and all of us were now approach-ing forty.

"Jebavy agreed that Horakova had committed an anti-state act," Anka continued. "But when everyone was required to unanimously demand the death penalty for her, he pulled a list out of his pocket with the names of all the women who had been executed in this country since the revolution of 1848. I don't know where he came up with it."

"I have no doubt he made it up," said Lexa. "A teacher from Hradek could scarcely be expected to have such pro-found historical knowledge."

Anka shrugged her shoulders. "In any case, the list re-vealed that all the women hanged had been murderers, mainly poisoners, and Jebavy said the last thing we wanted was for Horakova to be the first woman executed in our country for a political misdemeanour. 'The enemy,' Jebavy said with a straight face, 'would have a field day with that.'"*

I WALKED WITH THE BARMAN down the long and winding corridor to the kitchen and thought about Nina's husband, who had paid with his life for essentially the same crime. Jebavy had merely been shunted into a lower-salaried posi-tion. How many people, I wondered, had paid the price in one way or another for an act like Horakova's?

A new bottle of cognac cost a thousand crowns, the better part of a teacher's monthly salary. I returned with the barman behind me, carrying stuff that was better than what they were drinking upstairs, and I heard Berta say, "Jebavy's list wouldn't have been of any use to Horakova anyway. In those days, they didn't give a damn what the West thought."

"Apparently, they had a meeting about Jebavy at the highest level," said Anka. "But given his class—I'm not talking just about his working-class origins here, but about an actual pedigree that goes back to the Middle Ages—his punishment ended up being a two-room schoolhouse in Cerna Hora."

"Originally," said Lexa, "he was supposed to hang by the neck along with Horakova. But, indeed, that family tree stretching back to the dark ages got his punishment reduced. Originally, though, he was meant to have got the rope."

"In those days, how else could it have been?" I said, and the thought made me very sad.

⊰ ⊱

Anka and I had met only once in all those years—a few months before our reunion—in Prague, on Narodni Street, a place where people were always bumping into each other. Her beautiful black hair was streaked with premature grey. I invited her to the Café Slavia for coffee, and we were soon sitting over glasses of red wine.

"What's it like being famous?" she asked.

"You should know. Seven international patents, or was it more? I'll bet you spend more time at conferences abroad than you do in your lab with Heyrovsky."

Anka nodded and, inappropriately, I recalled her knickers, laundered so often they were grey; it was so long ago, it scarcely seemed real anymore. I took a drink to banish the thought.

"I've been to Moscow five times so far, Warsaw twice," Anka said. "Twice in Sofia, three times in East Berlin, and four times in Budapest." She fell silent and then added, "Not long ago I was in America for the first time, at a conference at the Massachusetts Institute of Technology."

That had been the year before. 1962. "The times are slowly changing," I said. "Slowly, but they are changing."

Anka looked out the window, beyond which nothing ever changed. People still fed the gulls on the riverbank, and couples drifted across the murky waters of the Vltava in wooden rowboats.

"Mother's still alive," she said. "I don't know for how much longer."

Though I didn't know her mother, I reassured her with a smile: "A country woman like her? She must have some pretty good genes."

"You think so?" she replied. "The doctors say she only has half a year to live. And Janek is already gone, the year before last. He wasn't even thirty-eight."

Who Janek was, I didn't know. Her brother? I couldn't remember if she had a brother. A lover? So I asked her a tactical question: "Where did he die?"

"In Cambridge, Massachusetts." Anka looked me in the eye and smiled. "I got two official invitations to go there. Our authorities turned them both down. At that point, Janek was still alive. This year, when the third invitation came, they let me go."

It was simple enough to understand. Janek was dead, her mother alive. Very simple indeed. I didn't attempt to make Anka feel better about her mother by mentioning how often doctors are wrong or how quickly the times change, and might still change. It didn't really matter.

⊰ ⊱

All at once Erwin Pick appeared at the entrance to the bar. He was practically carrying Nina, who was sobbing heavily in his arms. He set her down on a bar stool, where she perched precariously, while the barman, without being asked, put a glass of cognac in front of her. It occurred to me that if someone didn't help her sit up straight, she would pass out and fall off her perch. But she managed to right herself, wiped her nose, and said, "Damn it, I will have a drink." She lifted the glass and drained it. The barman poured her another.

"What happened?" I said quietly to Erwin.

"Kulich told her that her husband had been sentenced strictly in accordance with the laws as they applied *at the time*,* and he emphasized that, and so she punched him in the nose."

I remembered Brunnenschatten. I always remembered my beloved German teacher in connection with Reverend Novak, the clergyman of the Hussite congregation of the Czechoslovak church, or as it was called then, the Czecho-Moravian church.

"Upstairs they're still hard at it, solving the problems of the faith," said Erwin. "I've already solved them for myself, and Nina's a non-believer."

Nina squinted at the full glass, but the cognac got the better of her before she could take another sip. She burst into tears and collapsed with her arms around Anka's neck. I looked at Franta, nodded, and stood up, and we walked out of the bar.

⊰ ⊱

Miss Brunnenschatten's baby was born in the eleventh month, but no one was paying attention anymore. There were no German clergymen in Kostelec, except perhaps in the Horst Wessel barracks, and my teacher did not want to go there, though her child was almost pure German. A kind of religiosity awakened in her, or maybe she'd always been devout, so she started attending the church of St. Lawrence, and some of us began going there with her, to the displeasure of Father Meloun, who reminded us that there was a consecrated assembly hall right in the school building.

When the baby was finally born, the rookie chaplain, Father Brejcha, was as terrified as he had been when Berta and Gerta came to him—Gerta, who by this time was very likely dead. Given the circumstances, Father Brejcha would certainly have known that, had it not been for the baby, my teacher would long ago have been sent to Ravensbrück for marrying a Czech, and in his terrified state, the very thought of christening a child whose mother ought to have been, and now probably would be, sent to Ravensbrück preyed on his mind: he was afraid and he made excuses. My teacher brought him the child, wrapped in a little duvet. Cvancara argued with Brejcha, but he could not dispel the cloud of fear hanging over the priest. Father Brejcha was haunted by the red posters the Nazis put up every day with a list of current executions. He was a timid man by nature, and the historical situation had made his cowardice complete. Despite his recent ordination, he lost the sense that he was a priest, of what it meant to be a priest.

Cvancara was getting nowhere with him, and at last he stood up, as did his wife. The baby started crying, and Cvancara, to vent his frustration, snatched the metal crucifix and flung it at a relatively valuable baroque painting by the Italian master Donatello depicting the sufferings of St. Stephen, puncturing the canvas. With the sobbing child in tow, they walked across town to the evangelical congregation, but there too they encountered fear, this time probably justifiable. Reverend Hejda's son had been in Buchenwald for six months already, and it was said that Hejda was being closely watched. And this, said the reverend—because in Kostelec, by now, everyone knew the Cvancaras' secret—is a somewhat problematic child.

This time, Cvancara didn't make a scene, and they went next door to the Chelcicky Unity of Brethren Church. That congregation had a reputation for acts of charity—at least, I had always imagined their members as mild-mannered people who had somehow come to terms with their fate, and who were also courageous in matters of their faith, which included a strong component of generosity toward one's neighbours. They probably really were like that. But the cloud of fear had cast its long shadow even over the unpainted window frames of their tiny place of worship, and the arguments they made were couched in a form of insincerity. The bearded pastor trembled and expressed surprise that they were coming to him with a bawling child when both the parents were Roman Catholic. Cvancara came clean with him, though he omitted to mention the heretical gesture that had damaged the more or less valuable baroque painting. The pastor smiled; he was still nervous, but managed to be uncommonly persuasive. He promised to speak to Father Brejcha and explain things to him in a way that he would understand, though it was clear that Father Brejcha understood everything only too well and that Cvancara had spoken plainly to him. He said that, despite differences in matters of faith, he and Father Brejcha were good friends, and so on. And then the pastor, bowing and scraping, ushered his visitors out the door.

So they found themselves on the street. With the still unchristened, almost-German child, they made their way back through the town to where they lived in community housing. At this point, God suddenly intervened, taking upon himself the unlikely shape of the Reverend Novak, the pastor of a church that changed its name according to the political situation in the country, but who himself behaved like a man whose faith was unshakeable and who would not be intimidated, although the black cloud engendered by those daily posters hung over him as well. The Reverend Novak listened to their problem, nodded, turned around, and invited the couple, with their child, who by now was something of a hot potato, to follow him into the nearby church, an unlovely construction cheaply erected by a master mason when the denomination was founded in haste in 1918. There, in the light of the setting sun—for that was how long the pilgrimage, begun before noon, had lasted—Reverend Novak asked, "And what will the child be named, Mother?" The father replied in her place, somewhat awkwardly, "Brunhilde. After her mother." The mother quickly intervened: "No, Fath-...I mean Reverend... her name is Ruth."*

The reverend looked at the mother, then at the father, and the father looked at the mother and said, "But, Brunnie ...I thought we'd already—"

"I've changed my mind," said my teacher firmly. "Ruth is a beautiful biblical name, and I like it."

"But it won't go down well with—"

"Exactly," said my teacher. "Darling, this is a Czech baby, after all."

"Well..." The father was thinking hard, and wanted to say something, but he swallowed it. "All right, it's a Czech baby. At least—well, I can't do the math, but—if you ... if you say so, darling." He turned to the clergyman. "Ruth," he

said, in a tone indicating that, despite his apprehensions, he was giving in.

And so Reverend Novak christened the child from the metal baptismal font with the blood red chalice on the side that faced the congregation. A mere seven years later, that act was added to the list of his other political sins, but it wasn't the Nazis standing over him in judgement this time, it was the Communists. By the time he christened the baby, the Nazis were no longer paying much attention to this sin—if a sin it was—nor did Inspector Werner give much thought anymore to my German teacher, since he was no doubt preoccupied with how it would feel to have a noose around his neck.

⚞ ⚟

Upstairs in the dining room, it was foggy. At first I thought there was something wrong with my eyesight, but it was only the fog of a political meeting, a fog of nicotine and sweat, and out of the fog came voices speaking in a language that was not of this world.

"... the official line ... such slander ... the Party ... setting serious objectives ... resolutions ..."

"What year is this, Franta?" I said rather loudly, but the voices from the fog safely drowned out my words.

"You know, I could have sworn it was 1963, man," Franta shouted into my ear. "Now I'm not so sure."

The voices continued arguing about angels on the head of a pin.*

That gang. That class.

⚞ ⚟

Putych, Haryk, and I were walking along Narodni Street sometime in the mid-sixties. Putych was all decked out, as usual; all that was missing was his walking cane with the secret compartment for whisky. He was wearing a velour hat made to measure for his big, watermelon noggin, and a custom-made sports jacket that had set him back eighteen hundred crowns, plus another two hundred straight into the pocket of the master tailor, Mr. Havlin. Down the street toward us came a rock and roll band on a flatbed truck decorated with posters in English saying "Rock 'n' Roll Forever!" The singer was wailing into a microphone, her English pronunciation a wonderful imitation of what she had heard, though what she was singing made no sense, clearly not even to her.*

"There's no way they can stop that now," I said.

We stood watching as the racket receded.

"I hear that in Prague alone there are at least several hundred rock bands like that. There's no way they can stop it."

"You don't think so?" said Putych.

"Well, do you?"

"All Comrade Kral has to do is wag his finger," and *Putych pointed to the singer on the flatbed,* "and then where will they be?"*

"In the shithouse," said Haryk.

They both shared my profound belief that everything would turn out the way it had to.

⚐ ⚑

Suddenly Vlasak emerged from the fog. As the smoke around him parted and every one of us saw him, we stood up.

"Good evening," said Vlasak breezily. "Sorry I'm late. My chauffeur had a spot of trouble."

Franta looked at me, I nodded, we got up, and in a moment we had walked through the fog and descended into the depths of the hotel, where the air was fresh.

DOWNSTAIRS, we said our farewells and I kissed Anka and Nina goodbye. Anka left on foot to walk back to her native village in the mountains. Nina's train left at five minutes after midnight.

A familiar scent floated down the stairway into the bar, followed by the one wearing it, different now from when I knew her before. She looked around. By this time, the air in the bar was pretty smoky, mainly from Erwin Pick's pipe, though Anka, too, had been smoking. Bara went up to Nina.

"I have a car here, Nina."

Nina looked off into space and said nothing.

"I'll give you a lift home to Hermanice. It's out of the way, but it's worth it. What do you think?"

Nina said nothing.

"We haven't actually talked since ..." Bara hesitated. "I can't even remember how long it's been. Come with me, Nina." And then she added uncertainly, "Wouldn't you like that?"

"No thanks," said Nina. "My train leaves in fifteen minutes."

CLASS
REUNION
1993

Twilight. Honey and blood. Indifferent to the historical situation of nation and town, it spoke to me, aged sixty-nine.

I had first stood here long ago, a whole eternity ago, in a room papered in purple and gold. The bass saxophonist lay on the brass bed, a half-dead old codger, while I held his saxophone in my hands, his asthmatic breathing behind me.

I had stood in this place another time, when we met here to celebrate, if that's the word for it, the twentieth anniversary of our high-school graduation. Celebration or not, the room was still aglow, as it had been then, like a greenish-yellow lantern, as the warm autumn sun cast its golden rays through the trees outside.

As now. But now the wallpaper was new, though the pattern was the same as then, purple and gold. God knows where they found it. The entire hotel was like new, with a colourful *fin de siècle* rendition of the Kostelec coat of arms on the main doors, to match the building's original style, popular so many, many years ago. They'd removed the scaffolding that had hidden the facade for seven years before the fall of the old regime; they'd put new tubs in the bathrooms, probably custom-made, since they too were styled in the *fin de siècle* fashion, squared off, with taps in the shape of mermaids.

The room glowed like a green and gold lantern.

I drew aside the curtain, which was also new, and concealed behind the golden fabric, I looked down on the square. A thin man in a clerical gown was walking out of the church.

THE VENERABLE FATHER MELOUN had been dead a long time, having passed away in the care of the Franciscan sisters, whom the Communist regime had allowed to continue working as nurses, because lay nurses refused to look after hopelessly immobile cripples and aging priests, though in the latter case, their refusal was buttressed by an ideological imperative. The Venerable Father, then, had died in a home for aged clerics called The Cross. In fact, he really had no right to be there at all, since he was barely sixty years old, but he'd come back from his four years in Buchenwald twenty or thirty years older than when he went in. For eight more years he served mass, after a fashion, at the church on the square, though he could scarcely hold up the chalice, would forget the Latin responsoria or get them mixed up with the altar boys' lines, and he moved about with a cane, often depending on an altar boy for extra support. That was how he was the last time I saw him, thirty years ago, and I never saw him again. I didn't speak to him that time; I merely saw him from the window—the same one I was looking out now—hobbling along, leaning for support on an aging ministrant. They took him in at The Cross soon after that, thanks to some personal connections. Long, long ago he had gone to the same elementary school as Bishop Zeleny. Zeleny had gone on to study at the seminary with the archbishop, who, years later, was evicted from the archbishop's palace by the Communists. Bishop Zeleny, now a night watchman, albeit in a classy locale—the Loretta—put in a good word for Father Meloun with the archbishop, who was under house arrest. The quasi-prisoner then gave an order to the administrator of the archdiocese (who had kept his position at the pleasure of the secular authorities), and the administrator came through. When faced with a choice between the two great fears—God and the Party—he yielded to the more remote and transcendental one and granted permission for the Venerable Father Meloun to die in dignity at The Cross.

When I was still an altar boy—in a world that was no longer real, just a cocktail of memories and fantasy, with fragments of historical reality floating about in it—the Venerable Father used to tell me, in a reedy voice with a hint of longing in it (though how that voice could roar when he was teaching religion and someone disrupted the class!), that once he'd retired from his teaching job at the high school, he would move to Prague, where they always needed priests, and there he would explore all the Prague churches—all of them!—one by one. It was the dream of a poor priest. He died of cancer at The Cross, half a year after they admitted him. Whether he ever managed to make that tour of the holy places in the city of a hundred spires (I could see him hobbling about on his cane, supported by Sister Udelina, who needed supporting herself) I don't know. I couldn't get him out of my mind.

AN OLD MAN EMERGED from behind the church, pushing a wheelchair with an elderly, overweight woman sitting in it. I didn't recognize them, but I knew who they were: Pilous, with his wife—Kveta Hruskova, as she used to be. I had learned about their tribulations from Berta, with whom I had begun to exchange letters right after November 1989.

Berta was also planning to come to this reunion of relics and leftovers. After extracting my promise not to tell a soul, he revealed to me, over the transatlantic phone line, that he was bringing a surprise to the party.

✠ ✠

"Who, for crying out loud?" I said. "I thought we'd agreed that husbands, wives, children, grandchildren, and great-grandchildren aren't invited—except for couples who were already going out together in high school, and both of them had to be in our class."

"This is no family member," said Berta, his voice sounding far away in the hum of the ocean that separated us. I had a horrible, though improbable, thought.

"Don't tell me you're planning on bringing Vlasak?"

"Don't insult me!" Berta said. "You lose your marbles in Canada, or what?"

I assured him I hadn't, at least not to that extent. Then another possibility occurred to me, one that was not horrible at all. "Miss Brunnenschatten? She must be at least ninety, if she's not already dead."

"No, she's still alive. She lives with her daughter in Prague and, yeah, she's about ninety. Of course we invited her, but she said she was too old. Apparently, she can't walk and that."

With her daughter. That would be the baby who started complicating things the moment she was born. Not for her mother, but for the pastor who christened her. But the complications didn't start until the second regime took over. A mere five years had gone by between the christening and the complications.

I thought of Ilse.

"Not Ilse?" I said.

"Which Ilse?"

"Seligerova."

Ilse was living in Austria, although Berta might have

tracked her down there. I knew she'd survived the war. I vividly remembered running into her in a German pub in Toronto called the Oompahpah. "Die Welt ist ein toller Platz," she'd said to me. "The world is a crazy place."

"She's been missing since the war," Berta said. "You remember what a good little German Mädchen *she was? Maybe she hooked up with the army, or joined the concentration camp ss." He paused for a moment. "Or maybe she was killed in an air raid. No one knows what became of her."*

So now I had a little surprise for him, but I decided to save it for the party.

"So who is it, then?"

Berta was silent as the clock ticked and the dollars drained away into the ocean, but it was a brief pause, and then he said, "Know what? You'll get your surprise at the party, with all the rest."

He hung up. I thought it over. Deml and Vejrazka were no longer with us. Both of them had died in exile; I knew that. Berta had excluded Vlasak. Knobloch? Was he still alive? But he wouldn't be much of a surprise. Who, then? Ruda Sepp? I had spoken with him in the Beranek café a couple of months before the end of the war, and he'd been in uniform. But had he survived the war? God knows. If he had, and it was him Berta was talking about, I would pretend to be surprised, like the rest.

⚞ ⚟

I walked slowly down the marble staircase, the steps as worn down as they had been thirty years before, the only thing the new owners hadn't replaced. They hadn't installed an elevator either, but the hotel was beautiful in its pale pastel, *fin de siècle* colours. From the reception desk, still set on its raised area just next to the staircase, two pretty young women in uniforms greeted me, and one of them said, "Two people from your group are waiting for you downstairs, Master."

I thanked her and smiled, not because she'd addressed me as "Master," but because she was pretty and as young as those Kostelec girls had been fifty years ago. Irena. Marie. And there were others, many others, some from farther away. Krista from Myto. Karla-Marie and Marie-Karla.* And others.

I was only ever addressed as "Master" here in the old country. It is a silly, old-fashioned local custom, reserved for aging artists.

I walked down the last few steps, past the doors to the café, which had new polished glass panelling, the Kostelec coat of arms etched into them, then I turned and went down a narrow flight of stairs to the cellar where the air was fresh. To the dive bar. Thirty years ago, I'd come the same way with Franta Jelen.

⚓ ⚓

"Come on, you ain't twelve years old anymore, man," Franta had said to me. It was 1968, five years after our first reunion. "You don't really believe that! Miscegenation? Brunnenschatten was a real piece back then, and she was supposed to have committed miscegenation with Cvancara?" Franta chuckled. "You can bet Werner would've loved to miscegenate with her, but he needed Cvancara out of the picture. And race had nothing to do with it—at the very most, it was a church thing, because Brunnenschatten was a married woman."*

I thought about it. No, I wasn't twelve years old anymore, but my understanding of events in my hometown hadn't changed since they first happened. Though twenty-five years had gone by, I saw them now exactly as I had seen them then. I was an only child, and well brought up—meaning I was completely ignorant of the ways of the world and didn't immediately suspect the worst of people. I was the kind of person who assumed that others never did or thought things he would never do or think himself.

We were sitting over beer in the railway restaurant at Denis Station, and the Prague Spring was going on outside.* Not the annual May music festival. Not that Prague Spring. The other one, the one that turned out badly, the brief rule of a benign and naive Party boss, Alexander Dubcek, that ended with a mighty bang when the tanks arrived. The season of danger.

"Is that true? Who told you? What makes you so sure?"

"Ha!" said Franta. "You're not going to believe me, but it's definitely true."

He polished off his beer and waved to the waiter for another. He was good at dramatic pauses, and this was a long one. The waiter finally came over with a rosetta of beer mugs in each hand, pausing briefly to set one down in front of Franta. Franta drained about a third of it in one go.

"So, who did you get it from?" I asked.

"From my daughter, Olinka," Franta said, and then he told the story of how his daughter, when she was in her first year of medical school in Prague, became friends with Ruth Cvancarova because they had a biology seminar together. They would go with a bunch of medical students, all of them young women, to the Green Frog bar after lectures to drink Becherovka and shoot the breeze about everything under the sun, but mainly about the goings-on in their small world, or in the slightly larger world of their parents.

❧ ❧

A lone couple was sitting in the bar: Kveta, the woman in the wheelchair, which her husband had pushed up to a table, and Pilous. I couldn't remember what his first name was. We'd always just called him Pilous.

Their greeting was tentative. I kissed Kveta on the cheek, pressed Pilous's hand. We drank a toast to the encounter with wine from bottles already set out on the table for our half-century reunion. I felt what almost seemed like a chill; the conversation started off aimlessly, awkwardly. "So, what's new with you folks?" I said.

"What's new with you?" Pilous countered. "You're the world traveller." He had something in his voice, an echo of something bad. Was it some kind of deep disappointment? I looked at his feeble, elderly wife. Was he disillusioned with life? With history? It wasn't the voice I remembered from our past reunion, when they'd had that discussion on the problems of the faith, in which I had taken no part because it wasn't my faith.

And yet, could it have been? Once, long ago, Benno, who had played trumpet in our band, had caused me to waver.* We were sharing an apartment at the time, and he was what, in the jargon of the time, people called a "merged Social Democrat," meaning a de facto Communist, since his old party, the Social Democrats, had been swallowed up by the Communist Party. Then there was the Marxist atmosphere at university, and the innocent, Stalin-loving Ivana Hrozna— Ivana the Terrible, the girls at the Social School called her— the good-natured indoctrinator of future high-school teachers at the mountain retreat in Vyhlidka. These were the ghosts that haunted me. But then there was also Zdena

Prochazkova and her unwavering, though very private, view of the faith's main saint, Vladimir Illyich Lenin, his body now stuffed, embalmed, and on display in a glass case for the adoration of pilgrims and the amusement of American tourists. And there were also lecturers and professors who referred to the faith as a "coalminer's faith," and then there was the news in the main Party organ, *Rudé Právo* (available for sanitary purposes in the toilets of the mountain retreat), about the trial of the Boy Scout leaders who, although all of them had yet to reach the age of majority, were handed out sentences totalling several centuries, in institutions with the Orwellian attributive "re-educational." And other things, and events, and people, so many of them.

I decided to get straight to the point. "So," I said to Pilous, "are you still a Party member? And you?" I added, turning to Kveta.

They both shook their heads. Pilous said, "Matter of fact, no, we're not. As the saying goes, we saw through them. Took us a while, that's true—a long while, actually. But in the end, the scales fell from our eyes."

＊　＊

He was a factory owner's son—though at the time his father was no longer a factory owner, but a man with the unusual job description of "production master" in a factory that had once belonged to him. The father had built it up from an electrical shop on the town square into a small manufacturing plant on the banks of the Ledhuje, by which time it had a name: Atlas. The son, Honza Herman—the one who had managed to get the unusual coffee grinder for Miss Brunnenschatten—told me all about it. We were sitting in the Film Club in Prague, where I'd invited him for dinner. I knew Honza would jump at the chance, because there was always a film star or two hanging around the club—actresses, I mean; actors didn't interest him—so I didn't have to ask him twice. Over cocktails, he told me the history, or the story, perhaps embellished over time.

In the days immediately following that evil day in February 1948 when the Communists took power,* the Party cell in the Atlas factory deliberated, while the owner—Honza's father—sat twiddling his thumbs in his office, waiting for the verdict, though he knew what the verdict would be and was prepared for it, his desk cleared, the drawers emptied. He sat there, drinking coffee, while the Party cell deliberated.

In that time of zero tolerance, however, Atlas was something unique, a monument to the power of individualism. The chairman of the cell called for a vote on a motion to toss out the owner, and a forest of hands went up. But the chairman failed to notice, in this forest of hands, that one comrade had not raised his. Pro forma, he asked, "Anyone against?"—though he spoke the words in a triumphant tone of voice that said, in effect, "Of course there's no one"—and the previously unnoticed comrade raised his hand.

"And you know who it was, Danny?" Honza said. "It was that classmate of yours, Lada Pilous. So according to the rules of order, the chairman was obliged to call for discussion, and again, no one asked to speak—except Pilous."

My classmate's contribution to the discussion was, in effect, a political character reference for the factory owner. He said that Honza's father was of pure working-class origins, and though it flew in the face of all the obligatory notions about what factory owners were, it was still true. He told them how Honza's father had worked in the underground resistance movement against the Germans, to the extent that after the war, Mayor Prudivy presented him with a

*medal for valour in front of the Kostelec town hall. He said
Mr. Herman had become a factory owner not because he
exploited his workers, but because he was smart and had
taken out several patents—*

"For the coffee mill," I interrupted.

"*There was that, too. After the war, the mill was a
money-maker, but Dad came up with several other patents
as well, and with the money they brought in, he expanded
the original Atlas from a little workshop with thirty employees to a factory with two hundred craftsmen.*"

*Honza took a sip of his White Lady, another attraction
of the time, because apart from the Film Club, you could
only get a White Lady in the biggest international hotels,
places it wasn't really advisable for ordinary citizens to
enter. This was still the early 1960s, and you could feel the
thaw only here and there.*

"*It was a stroke of luck that this happened right after
the February coup, when people, at least workers and the
occasional Party member, weren't yet afraid to speak their
minds. And Dad was truly popular. He never fired anyone;
he went about the factory in coveralls and spent more time
out on the factory floor than in his office—he had an assistant to look after the paperwork. So when the chairman of
the Party cell asked for another show of hands, it was just as
unanimous as the first time, except now they had one more
vote—from Pilous—in favour of merely confiscating the
factory, that is, nationalizing it, yes, but also making Dad
production master, or whatever it was.*"

⚞ ⚟

I remembered that evening in the Film Club now, as Pilous,
with that strange hollowness in his voice, told me that the

scales had fallen from his eyes. I knew his class origins were the same as the factory owner's, but though he had a degree in engineering, which the factory owner did not have, he wasn't as smart, and never came up with any patents of his own. But he was a slogger, a plodder, a workaholic, like many others who ended up as he did, with that hollow echo in their voice. At our last reunion, thirty years ago, he had sat on the other side of the table, along with the celebrants of the Bolshevik black mass, and he had stood up to greet Vlasak.

Vlasak? He was probably what Zdena Prochazkova had called the mummified head of state in the glass sarcophagus. "The Devil!" she had said,* in that lilac-bowered town, in thrall to an evil mafia and its hit man, Ponykl, in that beautiful year—1949—of the miracle in the rocks near the church of the Virgin Mary under Mare's Head.* For me, it was the final year of young love, shrouded in what felt like permanent night, though given the many bright lights of my youth, I did not really feel its weight. In that age of dangerous darkness, those words uttered by the no longer youthful phys-ed teacher resonated so strangely that I was alarmed, not by the words themselves, but because of the ears that may have been lurking in the darkness around the lilac bushes. The Devil!

But I said nothing of this to Lada Pilous, whose first name had come back to me when I recalled that conversation with Honza. What I did say was: "I'm glad to hear that. You did the right thing." Then Anka arrived to liberate me from the conversation.

She appeared in the doorway, and I was startled. She was walking on two canes and looked like an old woman. Like Kveta Pilousova.

Right after her, Stazka swept into the bar. She'd long since recovered from her tuberculosis.

⚔ ⚔

The strange ways of the world, or of destiny, or of just simple coincidence: my good friend Lester's daughter, Jana, also attended medical school with Ruth Cvancarova. Jana was born in the fifth month of the year the war ended. She was also a regular at the Green Frog, but she claimed she only drank beer, until it came out that she chased it with rum, and her father gave her a slap for it one evening when she came home tipsy. Lester's daughter asked Ruth the same question I'd asked Franta. Not that Jana was well versed in matters of recent history; of all historical periods, the young are most ignorant of the one their mothers and fathers have lived through; they find Tutankhamen far more interesting than Gottwald or Dubcek, who seem to them like characters in a forgettable shadow play. So she wasn't that well-informed, except that the evening before that encounter at the Green Frog, the conversation around Lester's dinner table had turned to the seven baptismal certificates required, in an even earlier shadow play, to demonstrate one's origins— not class origins, but Aryan origins. You had to show that there were no Jews in your family tree, Lester explained.*

"Are you saying there were Jews in our family tree?" asked Jana.

"There were and there weren't," Lester said. "It's just that your great-grandmother—my grandmother—her maiden name was Silbernagelova. Uncle Vaclav, who was a priest in Kladno, managed to get those seven baptismal certificates for us, and that's where he came across the name Silbernagelova. This worried him, so he studied the Nuremberg Laws very carefully—probably the only one in the whole Protectorate who ever did." Jana, of course, asked what the Nuremberg Laws were, and was told. "And there he found a clause that saved us," her father went on. "Not from the concentration camps—we wouldn't have had enough Jewish blood in our veins to warrant that—but certainly from some unpleasantness, perhaps digging ditches, who knows? The clause said: If the race of the grandparents cannot be established with any certainty, and if the record shows that the person is registered as belonging to the Christian faith, then such person shall be deemed to be of Aryan origin. Granny Silbernagelova died giving birth to her first child. She was eighteen, and any witnesses who could attest to her non-Aryan origins were either in the other world or they resorted to lies, claiming faulty memory, advanced age, whatever—or maybe it was just that no one was willing to rat her out. And so, Jana, you have an officially Aryan great-grandmother, and I have a grandmother who was born Silbernagelova, and voila! We are all pure-blooded Aryans!"

And so, instructed in the Nuremberg Laws and, in the course of another conversation in the Green Frog, about other sore points of life in the Protectorate of Bohemia and Moravia, Jana asked Ruth Cvancarova essentially the same question I had asked Franta Jelen in the restaurant at the Denis train station: "How come your mother was able to marry a Czech during the war, Ruth?"

At that point, Ruth was well under the influence of the disgusting but popular yellow bitters known as Becherovka, and she replied, "Some guy called Werner smoothed things out for her with the German authorities. Dad was probably one-eighth German, or maybe a third, because of his grandmother, and that helped. But it would never have happened without Werner. He was some kind of Gestapo agent or something like that—an influential guy—so they were able to get married. Except..." Ruth fell silent, thought for a moment, *then tossed back the Becherovka and held up her empty glass to the bartender. She was thinking intently about something.*

Jana was impatient. "Except what?"

"Oh, nothing. It's just that ... well, Mom had an argument or something with this Werner guy, and he suddenly changed his tune and started threatening to send Mom to Ravensbrück because she had a Czech husband—my father, that is."

"Send her where?" asked Jana.

"Ravensbrück. It was a concentration camp for women," Ruth said. "And one of Dad's buddies—a Czech, naturally— advised her to get pregnant, because then they wouldn't send her to the camps because that would endanger the life of the unborn child, who in their books was practically a pure German. There was a high mortality rate. In Ravensbrück, I mean."

"And you were the impregnantee, right?" Jana said.

"What?" said Olinka, Franta's daughter. "Isn't that a neologism? And a morphologically doubtful one, at that."

Ruth laughed and said, "You guessed it. The impregnantee was me. It was something like shotgun weddings back in the olden days, when a man had to marry a woman he got pregnant. No one talked about why he had to marry her, because everyone knew."

"I'd say that this was just a little bit different," said Olinka.

"A little bit really different," said Jana. "Your parents were moved to conceive not by passion, but by historical circumstance."

"Or the way historical prejudices forced people to get married in the olden days. In the end, it's all the same thing," Olinka added.

Jana thought for a moment. "I'm not so sure," she said finally. And then she expressed herself as a member of her own generation, so different from the generations of her ancient non-contemporaries. "Look, you said your mother had an argument with this Werner fellow and then he started threatening to send her to this—this woman's concentration camp. So my question is: What did they argue about?"

Ruth said nothing, but quickly downed another dose of the yellow bitters, which went right to her head. The med students looked at each other and grinned in a way that the girls from Kostelec would probably never have done—or perhaps they would have, and I'm a victim of petrified memory.

"So what actually happened?" Olinka insisted, and Ruth told them.

I don't know if Marie or Irena would have revealed something like that about their own mothers, even though the sexual aspect of the argument with Werner was not my old teacher's doing. The well-groomed daughters of my day never talked about things like that.

But perhaps, again, I'm a victim of the fact that my knowledge and notions of the other sex somehow remained frozen in the historical circumstances of those distant years.

⊰ ⊱

I embraced Stazka and we kissed, the first time we had ever done so. Our lives had parted ways when we were eighteen, and I hadn't seen her in all those years.

In fact, our lives had parted ways even before that, though not physically. Stazka still sat in the last row in Second, Third, and Fourth Form, right up until Eighth, but at the end of our second year I fell in love with Judy Garland, which suited me just fine at the time because, after a serious case of pneumonia, I became what they used to call a sickly child. When I went back to school that winter, I had to wear a white hood my mother had knitted for me, and on top of that, the eye doctor, Dr. Krousky, prescribed glasses for me. I didn't have to take phys-ed classes; I had a doctor's note exempting me. Before the discovery of penicillin, international medical science—represented in Kostelec by Dr. Strass, who used to go all the way to London to attend medical symposia—recommended such exemptions as part of the cure for serious bouts of pneumonia. All these measures actually made me worse, though I wasn't sure why; when I read Freud's *Introduction to Psychoanalysis* in Fifth Form, I understood it a lot better.

Every evening, I went through a bedtime ritual in front of a photograph of the girl from Hollywood. I would arrange my fountain pen, my pocket diary, and a ring with a large Venetian cameo my mother had given me in precisely the same way on my night table. I was able to give this behaviour a name only in Seventh Form, when I had moved on to reading Freud's famous student, Alfred Adler, who taught me about inferiority complexes, as he called them. By this time, my illness had lifted, and I had started to become a bit of a show-off in front of the girls in my class.

I looked at Stazka. She wasn't an old woman at all. Her face was wrinkled, her grey hair combed back in an uncertain style, but her clothes still clung to her and she was as slim as she'd been back when, in her frugal mourning clothes, she had carried that broken candle in her fiancé's funeral procession. I had long ago slipped out of her lasso, but I had always been fond of her, though I hadn't realized it at the time. I was indifferent to the other girls in my class—apart from Anka—and I hadn't known that either. It wasn't until years later, in

Canada, that land of memories, that I realized I was still fond of Stazka. Nina was another chapter altogether.

Now I smiled at Stazka, and she smiled at the small gathering and said how happy she was that we'd got together again, remarking that even I had come, an emigrant.

"An exile," I corrected her. "I didn't leave to better myself; I went for the freedom."

As true as that was, it sounded like a newspaper cliché.

Stazka and I sat down away from the others. Among the bottles of wine on the table was a lone bottle of whisky, and I asked her which she preferred, wine or Scotch.

"What?"

"This stuff," I said, pointing to the bottle. "The drink of anglophiles."

"You know, I've never tried it before."

"So, now's the time."

I poured her a shot of whisky, neat, and she tossed it back—you could tell she was used to drinking slivovitz—and made a face. "Brrrr!" she said. "Now that's a good drink!"

I poured her another shot, and one for myself, and suggested that, since it was such a good drink, it was better to sip it slowly. So we sipped away, and then I said to her, "Did you know I used to be in love with you, Stazka?"

"I know. In First Form."

"So how come you never . . . ?"

"You were so gauche. But you snapped out of it one day when I came to school with a hole in my skirt—in Second Form."

"I remember that. The hole was on your bottom."

"My ass," Stazka said. "I'll bet you never heard any of the other girls say that word then, did you? Then you gave it to your actresses to say in just about every line of dialogue you ever wrote."

She was right. Not in every line, but I was the first one, after all those blood-soaked years of utter politeness, to bring that word to the stage. Because the first girl I'd ever heard say it was a pretty girl, alive and mercurial. Then she caught TB from her lover.

⚔ ⚔

The mailman brought the wedding announcement straight into the classroom. The address on the envelope was "Grade VIII B, State Grammar School, Kostelec." Later, we discovered that it had been delivered to every teacher who taught us a matriculation subject. There were only two weeks left before the exams, and the mysterious announcement caused a sensation.

"Erazim Pokryty? What kind of jerkwater name is that?" said Franta.

We looked at each other, but no one knew.

"Maybe she made it up," said Berta.

"The name of the jerk," asked Lexa, "or the wedding?"

"But why?" asked Knobloch.

"It's not even half a year since Stejskal ..." said Bara.

"Love, oh love, oh fickle love," I paraphrased, in English, to the old tune.

"Don't be such a show-off," said Nina. "What's 'fikel' mean, anyway?"

Mr. Bivoj came into the room and stood by the blackboard holding a piece of paper: the wedding announcement. Bivoj was frowning when he said, "Does anyone know what this is supposed to mean?"

Silence.

"Or who Erazim Pokryty is?"

Silence.

Bivoj looked around the class. "Or where Anastazova is?"

Silence. Then Anka put her hand up. "Please, sir, Stazka's probably ill. Yesterday she told me she probably wouldn't be coming to school today."

"And do you have any idea, Pitasova," said Bivoj in his sternest voice, "who this Erazim Pokryty is?"

"Please, sir, no, I don't."

"With whom on the …" he looked at the announcement, "twentieth of June …" and he paused again and took a closer look, then looked around. "With whom, on the very day of your—and her—matriculation exams, your classmate intends to get married?"

It was a question directed at all of us. Bivoj looked darkly around the room at the silent class. No one said a word, then Lexa put up his hand. "Sir?"

Bivoj grumbled something and nodded.

"Sir," Lexa said, "she's afraid she'll get a failing grade from you, sir."

Bivoj did a double take, then strode with heavy steps to the chair on the raised platform at the front of the classroom and sat down abruptly. The chair creaked under his weight as he asked, in a scandalized tone of voice, "And that's the reason Anastazova is getting married? To a man whom, it would seem, none of you in this class have ever heard of?"

No one said anything, though some heads shook, and then Lexa said in a stage whisper, which, because the class was silent, Bivoj could hear: "That's the kind of foolishness only a woman is capable of."

Bivoj lost his temper and sent Lexa to the board, and shortly thereafter we watched him write the usual "F" in his notebook with a calligraphic flourish. We knew it was an

"F" because he did it so often we could read the movement
of his stubby fingers and the sharpened pencil.

≒ ≓

Berta came into the bar, alone. I got up and went over to him,
and we shook hands.

"So, where's your surprise?"

"Oh, God!" Berta said. "It's . . ." Then he stopped and
made a universally understood gesture: he ran the edge of
his hand horizontally across his neck.

"Seriously?" But in fact it didn't surprise me. "Ruda
Sepp?"

"Matter of fact, yes. He cut his own bloody throat. His
wife wrote me—she knew we'd been corresponding."

And I remembered a snowy afternoon in the fifth year
of the war.

≒ ≓

I stumbled out of the Messerschmitt factory after thirteen
and a half hours on the job. We'd been working long hours
for about six months to increase our output. I had no way of
knowing if the long shifts were making any difference to the
war effort; probably not, because along with our patriotic
tendency to slack off, there was now the added factor of
boredom from all those extra hours on the production line.
We'd recently begun assembling a component for some-
thing, though no one knew yet what it was. It looked like a
huge round laundry tub with no bottom. Then Rosta lent
me a new copy of Signal, *a magazine we both devoured*
because they always ran pictures from the battlefront,
drawn by war artists. Rosta had collected Signal *since the*

*beginning of the Protectorate. He had a painter's eye and
was able to show me, based on tiny, almost imperceptible
details, how realism (which, a few years later, and in a different historical situation, was called "socialist realism")
had, over the course of the war, begun subtly morphing into
something very close to naturalism.*

*At the time, we had not yet seen the pictures these battle-
front artists had been making privately. Long after the war
was over, we saw examples of their unofficial work in a
fancy art catalogue sent by Benno's uncle, who had managed to escape to America before having to come up with
those unattainable seven birth certificates. The catalogue
contained reproductions of material seized from the Germans that had ended up in the war archives of the American army. The pictures showed men whose bodies were
ripped apart, bullet-ridden, frozen like icicles; soldiers of an
army that, with unbelievable ferocity, had fought a doomed
rear guard action in the Russian winter. The war artists
hadn't submitted these drawings to* Signal, *but had hidden
them in their rucksacks, and God knows how many of them
were killed, not by the war, but because of those very drawings. They were killed by a political system that saw in such
drawings not merely a defamation of the army, but high
treason.*

From the illustrations in Rosta's copy of Signal, *I sur-
mised that we were making intake nacelles for the pilotless
jet-powered bomb, the v-1.*

I DECIDED TO TAKE A LOOK *in at the Beranek, hoping there
would be someone there besides Ruda's father, Mr. Sepp, in
his* Flugabwehr *uniform. The last time I was there, he had
been regaling a group of Kostelec Germans about his super-
human exploits in anti-aircraft marksmanship as the Flying*

Fortresses bombed Berlin. He was speaking so loudly I could hear him in the corner, where I had sat by myself with a cup of beechnut coffee, hoping someone would show up. His German had improved, and he looked more like a Kraut than before, perhaps because of the uniform. He'd recently had another son, despite being about sixty, with a wife at least fifteen years his junior. The word was that they'd had the child in response to a directive from the Führer that was intended to transform German couples into producers of cannon-fodder, though it would have to have been fodder for some future war, since these potential soldiers would scarcely have made it into this one. The little boy was given a beautiful German, or rather Nazi, name—Horst—and the municipal commissar, Mr. Horst Hermann Kühl, was the godfather. Kühl's original name was said to have been simply Hermann, but when he joined the Nazi Party, he tacked the name of its patron saint onto his own.

The Kostelec Germans, who were hanging on Mr. Sepp's every word, were an odd bunch. Two of them—Anton Jahoda and Josef Skrezeny—were actually Czech, and a third, an Italo-Serbian mongrel named Branko Pelozza-Lukitch, had declared himself a member of the German community long ago, before it was advantageous to do so.

I walked quickly along Kamenice Street. It was snowing, and a penetrating wind made it seem colder. Suddenly, on the corner by the apartment building where Irena used to live, and where old Mr. Lewith, God rest his soul, had a small shop that sold liquor, a German soldier stepped out into the pale blue glow of the blacked-out street lamp. We managed to avoid a collision, but in that fraction of a second when our eyes met, we recognized each other and stopped.

"Ahoy, Danny!" The German sergeant spoke Czech with pure local intonation.

"*Holy cow! Ruda!*" *I said. I was taken aback, and couldn't think of anything else to say. "Let's go somewhere, okay?"*

"*Where?*" *said Ruda.*

"*I was just on my way to the Beranek,*" *I said.*

"*The Beranek? You want to go there with a German grunt? Are you out of your mind?*"

I had been feeling a rising disgust for the current disposition of the citizens of Kostelec, a disposition I had shared, of course, and I was stabbed by a memory of how I had once snubbed Ruda, pretending I hadn't seen him. Now I saw him clearly. Ruda. Ruda Sepp, who had disappeared in Fourth Form. His father had sent him off to a German grammar school, and he had vanished without a trace, at least for me, for us—for us, I thought, he was lost forever. But then I ran into him once when I was walking Nadia home from the factory—we hadn't started doing those fourteen-hour shifts yet—on the low road to Montace. He was wearing a mountain commando's uniform and had a Riviera-like tan. He stopped and flashed a broad, white smile, and because of Nadia, because of her highland patriotism, I walked on as though I hadn't seen him, though I automatically made up an excuse, telling myself I hadn't recognized him because his face was ruddy from the Luis Trenker–style wind. I must have flushed red myself, because I felt a hot wave pass over me. But I didn't look back.*

I never saw him again, until now, when he appeared in the pale glow of the street lamp, in the swirling snow and wind that made it feel almost like Russia. Or at least how I imagined Russia to be, like the pictures in the art catalogue, though it would be years before I saw them.

"*I mean it—the Beranek, Ruda,*" *I said. "It's not your fault they drafted you, since you're German." And then, less brashly, I added, "Anyway, you could swing a cat in there now.*"

⊰ ⊱

"Ruda needed an oxygen tank to breathe," Berta said, tears running down his cheeks. He wiped them off. "And, matter of fact, Danny, I …" He broke down weeping.

My eyes filled up as well. I remembered him as he was—God, half a century ago—and so I wouldn't start weeping like an old whore, I coughed and then said, "Poor Ruda."

I thought about him for a moment, but I was really thinking about how I could blanket that tragic tale with a similar memory, but one not as bad.

"Berta, do you remember asking me once about Ilse Seligerova? That echt-German girl from the old gang?"

Berta wiped his eyes with a cotton handkerchief. Paper tissues had obviously not yet made it as far as the village of Neznasov, where he now lived. "You mean the Gestapo gal?"

"You're being too hard on her, Berta. I met her once in a German pub in Toronto."

Berta fixed his bloodshot eyes on me. "Seligerova? She lives in Canada now?"

"No, she was there visiting her son. And she's not Seligerova anymore, and she was never in the Gestapo. She was just a real *Deutsches Mädl*. She's long since outgrown all that."

⊰ ⊱

Cvancara died with a weapon in his hands in the uprising against the Germans in May 1945. Three years later, when the mildly hopeful times morphed once more into a new era without hope, his widow, my old German teacher, took advantage of the opportunities that the new Federal Republic

*of Germany—or maybe it was still called the Western Zone,
I can't remember—offered to ethnic Germans and moved
there with her little girl, Ruth. Ruth was about five at the
time and spoke German as well as Czech. At first, I was surprised to learn that the mother spoke German to her daughter, given how little good she'd experienced at the hands of
her compatriots. Her decision had obviously been pragmatic.
Despite the post-war aversion to German (when I applied
to study English, along with about eight hundred other
pent-up students eager to start university, there were five
people enrolled in first-year German), the language was—
let's face it—far more widely used in the world than my
mother tongue, and it was also, literally, the mother tongue
of the little girl with the hybrid name, one Biblical and one
from the heyday of Czech cabaret: Ruth Cvancarova.*

*But my former teacher's experience in Germany was
hardly encouraging. She lived with distant relatives in Düs-
seldorf, and though she was among kith and kin, as the saying goes, these people were not really her own kind at all.
Their collective memory was of a world of daily and nightly
air raids, of an atmosphere that began with a distaste for
war, and then, as the victories began to pile up, was gradually supplanted, against their will, by a kind of jingoism,
soon to be displaced by the horrors of carpet-bombing and
finally by perpetual fear, no longer of bombs, but of the potential, and often actual, terror perpetrated by a Gestapo
that knew its days were numbered. The horrors my old
teacher had had to face sprang from the same origins, but
she had lived through them against the backdrop of the tiny,
tranquil northeastern Bohemian town of Kostelec. None of
her relatives had experienced anything like that during the
war, and so, in Germany, she felt like a foreigner. Most of
her colleagues at the high school where they gave her a job*

were female, since the male teachers were usually missing. Either they were alive somewhere in Siberia, or they had frozen to death or fallen at Stalingrad. All she had in common with her colleagues was their most recent experience of individual, private fear. It was not an agreeable source of fellow feeling.

After the reversals of Chairman Khrushchev, whose denunciation of Stalin in 1956 naturally led to similar, if not quite as spectacular, backflips in the Soviet satellite countries (at the time, even such petty acrobatics seemed hopeful to me), my teacher decided to come back to Czechoslovakia. And return she did, to a country that was unlike, and at the same time very like, the Germany that no longer existed, the one once ruled over by the man who was not from Braunau in Bohemia, but from Braunau am Inn, as her sinister compatriot Herr Werner had once pointed out. But she returned to Prague, not to Kostelec. Why, I did not know. But she had come back when the similarities between Nazi Germany and Communist Czechoslovakia had become less pointed, and she discovered that she didn't really have a lot of adjusting to do. At first.

Ruth made a smooth transition to Czech in a school run by a comrade who, to the initial horror of her mother, bore a strong physical resemblance to her old nemesis Werner. The resemblance, though, was purely superficial, because the principal was a woman, and she had a kind heart. The tears that welled up in her eyes at the mere mention of Stalin's name were genuine, and she did battle with her less kindhearted and often quite evil superiors over the fate of every pupil who was threatened with expulsion because the father had been arrested, or had falsified his class origins.

Ruth did exceptionally well in school; she had her mother's keen mind. Even her command of German, which was still not used by many people in polite society, came in handy.

There was another Ruth in the same class. She was about two years younger than Ruth Cvancarova, but she'd been born at a time when the school regulations allowed her to enter the same grade. This Ruth's Old Testament name seemed more suited to her than it did to the fair-haired Cvancarova, for she was the outcome of the long and desperate efforts of two forty-five-year-old Auschwitz survivors to bring her into the world, hoping against hope. Both parents were Prague Jews, and had it not been for the Nuremberg Laws, the mother would have been considered German. This Ruth, whose last name was Stribrna (originally Silbernagelova, just like Lester's grandmother), learned Czech quickly from the other children at her school, not from her mother. She was dark-haired, and—as the cliché goes—had gazelle-like eyes.

Both Ruths soon discovered that German was an ideal secret language, since no one in class, not even the teacher, understood it, and even if some of the other teachers did, it wasn't something they would have flaunted. In any case, the two girls spoke it only when they were around their fellow students, for whom German might as well have been Latin, which was no longer taught. And so both Ruths would chatter away in a language that was practically taboo in the country. They spoke it even when they were walking home together alone and didn't really need a secret language. And when Ruth Silbernagelova came to Ruth Cvancarova's for a visit, which she often did, they spoke the secret language with Mrs. Cvancarova, because it was, after all, her mother tongue.

But years later when I came to visit—unannounced, as was the custom in that place and time—it would never have

occurred to me to speak the language I had once, long ago,
almost mastered, thanks to the efforts of Mr. Katz, who died
in Terezin, and Miss Brunnenschatten, who fortunately did
not die in Ravensbrück, although, had it not been for Mr.
Soucek—Detective Babocka—she might well have.

⊰ ⊱

"You look good," I said to Nina when she walked into the
room. "You look swell. How do you do it? You haven't
exactly had an easy time of it."

"How do *you* do it?" said Nina, grinning. Her face was
still like a little moon, like the Venerable Father Meloun's,
but it seemed to me that the lines in her face that I remembered so vividly from that first reunion, thirty years before,
had softened. "It can't have been very easy for you, either,"
she said, "living abroad."

"It's not exactly 'abroad,'" I said. "I have a new homeland." And I flashed her a Clark Gable smile, but she'd long
since forgotten him, if she'd ever known he existed. "Will
you have a drink with me, a little something that's pretty
much the national drink in my new country?"

We sat down at the bar. Unlike the last time, it was actually open, but the barman in the white vest had nothing to
do, since no one in our little group had ordered cocktails. For
the most part, they didn't drink anymore, or at least not a
lot. They were old folks now. We were all old folks.

Nina pretended to think it over, but of course she'd already
made up her mind. "What the heck—I will have one," she
said, just as she had at the last reunion, thirty years ago,
though her situation was different then, and much worse.

Tentatively, I asked the barman for two Manhattans. He
didn't express the slightest surprise at my request; he merely

nodded and, with an experienced hand, mixed Canadian whisky and vermouth with a dash of bitters in a shaker.

"To tell you the truth, this isn't really the national drink of my new homeland," I said. "Martinis are more the national drink of my spiritual homeland to the south. But I like them. And so will you."

I was right, and because she wasn't used to martinis, the liquor let her tongue off its leash. There was no need to worry about keeping the conversation going: she launched into a monologue that no conversation could have equalled. It quickly became very personal, and all I had to do was listen. It was as though she needed to confide in someone from another world—as I was—and, at the same time, someone from her past who, after all these years, she could still see in the light of how ridiculous he'd seemed to her then, a spoiled, sickly only child and, in fact, a goody two-shoes, as she reminded me.

"Ah, but then, you weren't really in love with me, and that lets you off the hook," she said. And then, completely unselfconsciously, she told me how, in Eighth Form, she'd fallen head over heels for the new minister of the Czechoslovak Church, with the commonest of all Czech last names, Novak. It was as if she had never told anyone about her rather limited experience of sex, and a lot of other things as well, until now. She told me they had produced four children in rapid succession, one a year, although he wasn't Catholic and therefore wasn't forbidden from using contraceptives. They deliberately gave them all patriotic Czech names: Vojtech, Vlasticka, Libuska, and Sarka, a boy and three girls. And then the babies stopped coming, because their quite ordinary, but genuine, marital happiness suddenly came to an end. When Reverend Novak began mentioning Milada Horakova— the first woman ever executed in Bohemia for her political convictions—in his sermons, castigating the court for its verdict, he had, in the eyes of the regime, committed the crime of promoting religious thinking. So it was off with him—not to Auschwitz, Majdanek, Treblinka,* but to Bytiz, Svornost, Jachymov, new final destinations in the new historical situation.

And they had four little children.

"How did you manage, Nina? How did you make ends meet?"

"How does a minister's wife make do, Danny? His congregation—you're Catholic, so it would probably never occur to you—they were real Christians."

⊰ ⊱

When I first met Ruda in uniform, on the low road to Montace, as tanned as if he'd been at the seaside, and when, because of Nadia, I pretended not to see him, it occurred to me that our non-encounter might have been a highly significant coincidence. Not long before that, I had had a run-in with Ruda's sister, Hannelore. She was sitting in for the ailing Werkschutz, Bajer, *as guard at the factory gate, as I was leaving the factory that day. She stopped me—in the annoying, self-important voice of a member of the* Bund Deutscher Mädl, *where she was still a* Scharführerin *(or maybe it was another rank; I wasn't really up on how they did things in the League of Young German Women)—and ordered me to open up my briefcase. I did so quite willingly, because I wasn't in the habit, as others were, of smuggling stuff out of the factory. I wasn't a do-it-yourself type, and in any case, I wouldn't have known what to do with a piece of duralumin, though some hobbyists would make letter openers from it, or they'd etch drawings, sometimes risqué, into the soft metal. Then I realized—but it was too late, because Hannelore's attention was drawn to a notebook I wrote poems in. If she had read them and merely failed to understand them, it would have been awkward but not dangerous. But I'd written them in a secret alphabet, not one I'd invented myself, but one that Mr. Mervart had taught me: the Cyrillic script.*

Mr. Mervart, a photographer by trade, had been liberated from a Soviet prison in Smolensk by the German army, and when they questioned him, it came out that he was a Czech with Czechoslovak citizenship, which made him a citizen of the Protectorate of Bohemia and Moravia. When they heard his story, they shipped him back to his native town, which happened to be Kostelec. But no one knew who he was anymore, since Mr. Mervart had left Kostelec in November 1918, when the Great War was over, and had gone to Russia to photograph the famous battlefields of the war for an enterprising Prague publisher. For a while he was shadowed by the Cheka, an early predecessor of the KGB, and then they arrested him as a spy and locked him up. In prison, he ran into a streak of luck: there was no prison photographer, so Mr. Mervart ended up taking mug shots of freshly arrested detainees. Because their number kept growing, particularly when Stalin became head man, Mr. Mervart, by some miracle, or perhaps by an oversight, managed to go on practising his craft until the German victory in the first Battle of Smolensk in 1941, which turned out to be a real boon, for him at least.

Back home in Kostelec, the long-forgotten Mr. Mervart made a living as a clerk in the municipal office. Occasionally, the local Nazi authorities would compel him to give lectures exposing the harsh reality of Soviet life, and he made money on the side by giving private lessons in Russian. He'd already

had a decent command of Russian when he first left Kostelec,
because he loved Russian poetry. His lectures—"Scenes
From the Soviet Paradise," as they were advertised on
posters in both Czech and German—attracted a growing
audience because he would always start by declaring that
he knew the Soviet paradise exclusively from his time in
prison, and then he would briefly describe what he'd done
there and how it had saved his life. And then, as if by sleight-
of-hand, he would to segue from what was meant to be anti-
Soviet propaganda into a talk on Russian literature. In his
overly dramatic but strangely engaging voice, he would re-
cite from Lermontov, Pushkin, Jesenin, and many others I'd
never heard of. After one of these lectures, I asked him if he'd
give me private lessons in Russian. And so, almost until the
end of the war, I would go to his place, a rented room in a
tiny cottage hidden away behind some lilac bushes on the
slope of Black Mountain just below the Kostelec Castle.

His method of teaching Russian was as unique as his
anti-Soviet propaganda. First, I had to learn the Cyrillic
alphabet, which was no problem, and then, in each lesson, he
would dictate to me three words starting with A, three with
B, three with C, three with D, three with E, and so on. Then
he would recite to me long passages from poems in which
the words in question appeared at least three times, always
indicating a word's occurrence by raising his voice, but he
would continue the recitation long afterward, until each
word had appeared ten times or more. An alarm clock on the
table would go off, and I would get up to leave, making way
for the next student, who by this time would be waiting in
the kitchen.

As a result of his teaching method, the only aspect of
the Russian language I ever learned properly was the alpha-
bet, but I didn't regret it, because in between recitations of

his favourite poets, this eccentric teacher gave me a very useful private education in what was later, in America, called "Sovietology," which dealt with matters that Mr. Mervart never mentioned in his public lectures in the Beranek or anywhere else. That interested me far more than declining nouns and conjugating verbs.

Hannelore lifted the notebook full of poems out of my bag. She knew me through her brother, of course, but when she'd leafed through several pages, she asked me, in German: "Was ist das?"

"I write poems, Hanka," I said in Czech. "But so no one else can read them, because I'm just a beginner at this, I write them in ... in a kind of shorthand."

Hannelore examined a page or two, and then declared, rather threateningly, and in Czech, "This doesn't look like shorthand to me."

"I have lousy handwriting," I said. My handwritten Cyrillic really did look like something that Mr. Borisin had tried, without success in my case, to teach us in high school.

"Lese mir was vor!" The Scharführerin had reverted to her putative mother tongue.

So, with reasonable fluency, I read her a poem:

You tint your cheeks with carmine,
Your eyes reach out, like tentacles,
And pull me in.

When I had finished, she seemed to soften a bit, insofar as the military set of her face revealed anything at all, and she coaxed me, in German, to read more:
"Noch was!"
So I read on:

I gaze into young women's eyes,
And dream, and talk of pleasant things,
Giving no thought to what I say
Nor saying aught of what I think.

I stopped, fearing that she would start to hate it. But Hannelore said, in Czech, as if she were rather moved, "I had no idea you were such a poet."

I was obviously just such a poet—the kind who loves flattery.

"I've got one here in German," I said proudly.

"Read it!" Her military voice again, but she was speaking Czech.

And so I desecrated a poem I had written out of love for Miss Brunnenschatten by reading it to this young woman, who was practically in the ss.

Bald kommen Winterstürme mit dem weissen Schneen
Und langsam wird zum Kot der alte liebe Pfad.
In meinem Herze kalte Winde wehen.
Es ist der Herbst. Er kommt in uns're Stadt.

The winter winds will soon be here, with white snow
Slowly blanketing the mud on the old, familiar path.
And in my heart a cold wind blows.
It's autumn, and it's coming once again.

As soon as I began to recite the poem, I thought: Now I've really shot myself in the foot. As indeed I had. Either Hannelore didn't like my pronunciation, perhaps because there were traces in it of the elocution lessons I received from Mr. Katz, or she had managed to overcome a moment of un-Teutonic weakness. Whichever it was, she held out her hand and said, "Gibst mirs!" And I gave her the notebook. The contents were harmless—they were all love poems— but their form was highly dubious, and, ordering me to wait, she marched away like a general to the personnel department just inside the gate.

All of a sudden, I felt nervous. I'd never heard of Hannelore actually turning anyone in to the Gestapo, although otherwise she was such a model Nazi that wherever she showed up—in the Beranek, say, or at Mr. Mervart's lectures (and she never turned him in, even though his recitations could easily have been taken for enemy propaganda)— everyone would fall silent and then start talking about football. Still, if she were to give the notebook to one of her compatriots, and that person were to recognize that the poems were not written in shorthand at all, but in the alphabet of the enemy . . .

So, as I awaited her return, little rivulets of perspiration began trickling down my back. Then I remembered that her chief in the Personalabteilung *was her compatriot Mr. Kleinander, who was not a Nazi and who was given such an important position only because he was German, and a real German at that, though his Czech was flawless. His two sons, Harald and Rheingold, had attended the high school, one year and two years ahead of us respectively, where they were about as popular as Ruda, the brother of this annoying* ss *girl, if that's what she was. Both the Kleinander boys were drafted shortly after the war began, and both of them were killed in action, though—as far as they were concerned—it was not for the Führer (they were not Nazis, after all, like the Sepps). Harald died early in the Polish campaign, so in a sense fate was kind to him in that he avoided a great deal of suffering. Rheingold came home once wearing an* Afrikakorps *uniform; then he returned to the desert, where he ended up being buried.*

So I had an encouraging thought: Since Mr. Kleinander was Hannelore's boss, I might be in the clear.

Scarcely ten minutes later, Mr. Kleinander, a tall bean-pole of a man, too old now for army service, appeared from around the corner, holding my notebook. Hannelore, her face red, followed behind him. He grinned at me and said, in Czech, "Your shorthand is very good, very legible. And these poems ..." And then he began to read them. He read them fluently, and as I was slowly recovering from my astonishment, I remembered that he had been to our place one Sunday on a visit, and from the chit-chat over coffee, I learned that both my father and Mr. Kleinander had fought on the Eastern Front, my father for Emperor and country—a service that ended in a serious wound that saved his life—and Mr. Kleinander, likewise, for Emperor, though a different one, the German one. He avoided further military service by getting captured by the Russians and remaining a prisoner until the day the Bolsheviks signed a peace treaty with his emperor. This explained the fluency of his recitation from the Cyrillic. Mr. Kleinander read aloud in a German that Mr. Propilek, in the presence of the inspector, Herr Werner, had daringly called the German of Goethe:

Und nach dem Winter folgt die Zeit der Blumen,
Die warme Sonne scheint, der Wind ist mild und sanft.
Mein Herz ist wie erneut. Der See flüstert den Namen
Und voller Sehnsucht leg' ich in dem Sand

Am Ufer. Die Zeit ist kurz und wird bald kürzer werden.
Wie heißt der Name? Wird der See verraten?
Die Zeit rennt wild. Die Hoffnung liegt in Scherben.
Der Name faßt unlesbar ... Brunhilde ... Brunnen-
    schatten ...

When winter's gone, the time of flowers comes,
The warm sun glows, the wind is soft and sweet.
My heart feels born again. The sea whispers that name
And I, full of longing, lie down upon the sand

By the water's edge. And time is short and soon will
*   shorter be.*
What was that name? Will the sea yield it up to me?
Time runs wild. Hope lies in ruins.
The name is barely legible ... Brunhilde ... Brunnen-
*   schatten ...*

Mr. Kleinander stopped reading. Hannelore stared at me with her mouth open, and then her boss spoke. "Your German leaves a lot to be desired, young man, but it would appear that you have some talent. It actually reminds me of something similar I read somewhere. Was it in Reiner Maria?" He didn't say "Rilke"—the poet was probably not a favourite in the **Bund Deutscher Mädl**, since the Nazis considered him a "decadent artist." "But of course, a young poet has to learn his craft somewhere, am I right? Still, I'd leave the poetry outside the factory, if I were you, and concentrate on work."

He turned to Hannelore and said something to her in German in a half-whisper that was meant to smooth things over. Hannelore appeared to object—her face was still red—but Mr. Kleinander probably had some kind of sway over her, some erotic power, perhaps, since he was still a rather handsome man and, moreover, in the Great War he'd been decorated, like the Führer, with the Iron Cross. Hannelore was quickly mollified. Her normal complexion returned, she smiled a toothy smile, and Mr. Kleinander handed me back

*the notebook. I took it quickly, thanked him, and disappeared
as fast as I could.*

Nadia was waiting for me just outside the gate.

I WALKED THROUGH *the woods with Nadia, thinking of
Hannelore. I heard she later came to a bad end—though, of
course, I couldn't have known it at the time. But it was a terrible end. When the Red Army was nearing Kostelec, Mr.
Sepp took his wife, his daughter, and little Horst, whom
Hannelore carried in her arms, and on the railway track
through the Branka Gap, they jumped under a train. I heard
that all that remained of them was a bloody mass of flesh,
mixed in with bits of Mr. Sepp's uniform and fragments of
the women's dresses. There was nothing recognizable left of
little Horst.*

*I may not have known that at the time, but as I thought
of Mr. Kleinander reciting my Czech poetry from the Cyrillic
in my notebook, and of Hannelore, from whose clutches my
father's* Frontkamerad *had rescued me, her brother suddenly
appeared before me in a mountain commando's uniform
and a tan that might have been acquired on the Riviera.*

⊰ ⊱

Nina took a sip of her Manhattan. "Our eldest, Vojtech—
he was five when they killed my husband—was taken in by
Mrs. Broumovska, who was married to a factory foreman at
Kudrnacs. She had three children of her own, but they were
a bit older by then, and each day when she went by our place
on her way home from dropping her kids off at kindergarten,
she'd stop in for Vojtech and take him home with her," Nina
said. And then she went on to tell me how it was the same
with Vlasticka, who was four. She was taken in every day by

Mrs. Rechnerova, also on her way back from kindergarten. Her husband was a clerk in the municipal power company. Nina left her three-year-old, Libuska, with a neighbour, Mrs. Reinisova, a pensioner and the widow of a late government advisor, and she took the two-year-old Sarka to the Simans. Mrs. Simanova was a modestly well-off widow who was getting on in years. She had no children of her own, and she modestly hid her Christian good works under a bushel of enthusiasm: each day, she would say, dawned brightly when Nina dropped her little girl off in the hallway and hurried off to work.

"What about the state nursery schools," I asked hesitantly.

Nina looked at me scornfully. "Didn't you used to live here too, Danny? Ah, but you weren't interested in children, were you?" She stared at me with forget-me-not blue eyes, and her cheeks began to remind me of the kitschy portraits of the Virgin Mary that customarily hung over connubial beds. Then she lowered her gaze to my national drink and said, "Maybe it was supposed to be part of the punishment for my husband's misdeeds, or else someone was doing it to us deliberately. Nursery school! Back then, even people who didn't have a fraction of the stigma I was carrying around had a hard time getting their kids in."

"Forgive me—it was a dumb question," I said. I was struck by her mention of the possibility of deliberate revenge. In a time of heightened, official class struggle, the execution of general Party decisions were often left to the arbitrary will of some comrade or other whom Nina may not even have been aware of.

"At first I had a pretty good job," Nina went on. "It was with Mr. Moutelik, Berta's father. They let him stay on in his former department store, the City of London."

"Do you have any idea why they didn't just toss him out? His case seems to me rather unique ..."

Nina shook her head. "I don't know. Some people found it suspicious, but I never let it bother me. Mr. Moutelik is— I mean, he was—he's been with the Lord for quite a few years now—Mr. Moutelik was a generous, good man. Catholic, church-going ..."

"That makes it all the odder."

"So be it," said Nina. "He got me out of a jam, and at that time, not everyone would have done that. It was right after the show trial against the Vatican conspirators, with the Hussite tossed in for good measure."* She took a drink. "I needed a job to put food on the table for the kids, but no one would hire me. They'd all been given some kind of advance notice requiring them to be vigilant, or on their guard, or whatever the phrase was. Mr. Moutelik was the only one to give me the time of day. He said—not to me, but to some of the comrades—that I wasn't responsible for my husband's errors. And at the time, people had begun to stop acknowledging my existence, even some of the nervous Nellies in our own congregation."

Life is one huge mystery. It's a cliché to say so, but sometimes there's no better way to formulate the truth. Life is a mystery, from the cosmic "whys" of existence among arbitrarily exploding stars that can suddenly obliterate life on an unknown planet, the life of intelligent creatures like ourselves, or unintelligent creatures like those poor dinosaurs, all the way down to a secret decision taken by the Municipal Committee of the Party regarding the more or less enviable fate of a former department store owner. All of it a mystery. Did Berta's father have powerful interceders? And why did they intercede? Was someone like Ivana Hrozna involved? But she was concerned only about the children of people like

Mr. Moutelik. And his children didn't come out of it wonderfully well. Berta ended up serving time in the Black Barons, which amounted to an open-ended sentence. Pavlik, a younger son, was also sent to the Black Barons, but he served only two years, perhaps because inherited class antagonism was deemed weaker as each new sibling came along. But Berta served for years and years. Why? Did Mr. Moutelik know something about the wartime conduct of his interceders? Later, after the war, it came out that Mr. Moutelik was involved in hiding an illegal transmitter used by the resistance during the war, and he even got a medal for it. The story that didn't come out was that one of Mr. Moutelik's future interceders had been secretly working for the Nazis, and the man who owned the illegal transmitter found out about it, but meanwhile the double agent had joined the Communist Party, who suppressed the information. Had it all been just coincidence, luck, a caprice of fate? Or had one just man, a merciful man, been found in Sodom? Or was it all simply an enigma?

Regardless, the mysterious Mr. Moutelik helped Nina get a clerk's position in his magnificent two-storey department store, the first such establishment in Kostelec. During the war, it had fallen on hard times, and then during those three miraculous but uncertain years between the demise of one system and the rise of another, it had come up in the world, and then it was gradually transformed into that strange socialist phenomenon: a store with nothing to sell, the shop clerks picking their nose from boredom and behaving rudely to female customers who were searching in vain for garter belts.

I gestured to the barman, and he started making two more Manhattans.

"Not for me," said Nina. "I'd like a Coca-Cola, please."

The barman did his job, and then put both drinks in front of us at the same time. We each took a sip. It was pleasantly quiet by the bar, not like the time thirty years ago when Franta Jelen and I had slipped in here, and then slipped right out again. And it was dimly lit, the way I loved it, like the bars in my new country. Such a bar is a good place for a man to be alone. Alone with another person.

"When Mr. Moutelik got me the job, the store was still pretty busy," Nina said. "And he always looked the other way when I had to take my kids to the doctors, or had some government office to visit." She sighed. "It goes without saying that those heavenly circumstances didn't last. They almost never do, not for long." Nina glanced at the department store owner's son, who was bending Pilous's ear in the corner, and her forget-me-not blue eyes had none of the sadness in them I had expected. There was, instead, a kind of levity that may have been Christian—happiness that she had survived everything with the help of God and His faithful followers, that her children had turned out all right, that all three of her daughters had married, "and one of them," she said, "is in Canada—some place called Thunder Bay. She married a Baptist minister she'd been going out with while they were still here. I mean, originally he was a pastor in the Chelcicky Unity of Brethren Church, but in America, the closest affiliates are the Baptists." Again, she glanced over at Berta Moutelik. "And Vojtech's an X-ray technician in the hospital in Jicin."

"I'm happy to hear that, Nina," I said.

Nina eyed my second cocktail over her glass of good intentions. I waved to the barman again. It was the kind of physical exercise I'd had a lot of practice in.

"I'll get all hopped up," Nina said hesitantly.

"There are no hops in a Manhattan. My understanding

is that it's made from drinks produced from rye and grapes."

In place of the Coca-Cola, Nina now had before her another conical glass filled with my national drink.

"Just sip it, Nina. Very slowly."

She took a sip and said, "Anyway, it didn't even last a year. Mr. Moutelik got seriously ill, and they gave him an invalid's pension and a new boss took over the store. He was hard-core, if you know what I mean. He carried out to the letter what the Party—in the person of someone called Vosahlo—ordered." She was silent for a moment. "Do I have to spell it out for you?"

"Vosahlo said the word, and you were out the door."

Nina shook her head. "They weren't as crude as that. They gave me a job in the local municipal office, as a typist."

I didn't understand that. Nina looked me in the eye. "Does that surprise you?"

I nodded.

"It's simple. The worst they could have done at the store was to throw me out; I'd have found a job as a night cleaner in Kostelec at the Mautner factory, or another job like it, something no one else would do. At the municipal office, they had other opportunities. I scarcely had time to warm the chair."

"I'm trying to guess what happened next."

"Guess away. They transferred me to the village of Nejdalov. On orders from the Party, in the person of Comrade Vosahlo. I had to commute there every day—three and a half hours, Danny. It was only an hour by train from Kostelec to the little station in Nejdalov, but it was three quarters of an hour's walk to the village, and there was no bus. Multiply that by two, and then add time onto that in winter."

Nina's eyes still had something Christian in them, though they were now slightly awash in the Manhattan.

Then my former teacher, Miss Brunnenschatten, stepped out of my memories. I didn't know why at first. Then I knew. Nina and my old teacher had shared similar tribulations. Miss Brunnenschatten's had been more life-threatening, but they were just as timeless. *Cherchez l'homme.* You camouflage human nature under some grand idea that sooner or later gets forgotten, though at the time it was useful.

"Did Vosahlo want something from you?" I asked.

She looked at me with those Christian eyes. "Meaning ... ?"

"That's exactly what I mean."

She took a sip of her Manhattan, and then gave a tiny nod. "You're right, of course," she said. "And obviously I never gave him what he wanted. So they bundled me off to Nejdalov on the pretext that they needed a typist. Of course, they didn't need one at all, but in those days they didn't throw people out of work. And so I took my place among the hidden unemployed, know what I mean? And it made my life miserable, or at least a part of my life. Just as it did Marie's."

"Which Marie?"

"Yours, of course," Nina said. "Not that you'd have made her life miserable; no, you were such a goody two-shoes that I'll bet you never even pushed her that hard, did you? And so, instead of that, you made an international scandal of her—or maybe you made her famous all over the world. Right, Dannyboy?" Nina said, using Marie's favourite way of addressing me.* She must have taken it from one of my comedies, because Marie had never called me that in the company of others.

"I hope I did," I said. "But not that famous, and in a pretty insignificant part of the world."

"In Kostelec, for sure. And it was more of a scandal, don't you think?"

I shrugged. The reminder of that long-ago card game in Bara's parents' cottage had struck me to the quick. As the truth always did. I said, "You said I was a goody two-shoes, so it couldn't have been that much of a scandal."

"And you didn't make her that famous, either," said Nina. "It's just that every once in a while, a group of Czech literature fans shows up in Kostelec, and Jarka Mokry takes them around the places you hung out. And if they happen to run into Marie, they all stare at her like she was some kind of freak of nature." She took a sip of her martini; more than half of it was left. "All the same, though, the one who made her life miserable—or part of it, anyway—was called Comrade Hribe. He was chairman of the municipal Party organization, and he made Marie's life a proper hell. I didn't know her very well from school, only that she was really good-looking. She still was when I got to know her well, which happened because we always met at four thirty in the morning at the station. Both trains came in at the same time, mine to Nejdalov and hers to Lesni Mesto, and they were usually both late, so we had time for serious conversation. And Marie told me what happened between her and this Hribe guy."

"A little Czech Werner?"

"He was a small, but specifically Czech version of that old Nazi, yes," Nina said. "What he did was report her because, despite his repeated offers, she refused to join the Party. Can you believe it? And he wasn't even after her body. As far as he was concerned, your Marie wasn't worth the sinning. She had just sinned against the Party, that was all."

"You mean he made it up?"

"No. He was right about that. She refused to join."

We were quiet for a moment while the implications of the comparison with Werner sunk in. I polished off my Manhattan, hesitated briefly, then waved my hand at the barman.

≼ ≽

As I expected, you could have swung a dead cat in the Beranek. The head waiter, Roubicek, was on duty that day. He knew Ruda from the gang he'd hung out with in high school, and he even greeted him more or less cordially. The dead cat could only have hit two baldheaded chess players in the corner, completely shut off from the world, and absorbed in their strange game. On the other side of the pillar you could hear the billiard balls clicking. One of the players rounded the pillar into the main room, on his way to the toilet. Pelozza-Lukitch. He made straight for Ruda and pumped his hand for several hectolitres worth of false camaraderie. The chess players paid no attention. Roubicek merely made a face and brought us beechnut coffee in pre-war glass teacups set in silver holders.

We sat down at a small, round marble table in the opposite corner from the chess players and stirred our coffee in silence. The memory of that encounter on the path below Montace, when I had pretended not to see Ruda, loomed between us. I had done it for selfish reasons, since acknowledging him could have ruined my standing with Nadia. Or maybe it was just the fact that snubbing Krauts was de rigueur *in the atmosphere of reverse political correctness that held sway in occupied Kostelec. Ruda was silent, and I considered explaining it to him truthfully, but it would have seemed like a lie. Was he waiting for me to broach the subject, when only a short time ago, in the dim blue light of the blacked-out street, it had been he who had greeted me?*

Roubicek sidled up to us and said, almost in a whisper, "Can I bring you some rum?"

"Rum?"

"Shhh," said Roubicek. "The boss got it from an Austrian at the Horst Wessel barracks, traded it for some homemade sausages. So keep it quiet. D'you want some?"

We both nodded, and Roubicek furtively poured a small shot of rum into our teacups in the silver holders. We each took a drink, and things between us began to thaw out.

"You were just pretending not to see me, I guess," Ruda said. He didn't have to explain what he was talking about. "Was it because of the girl?"

"Yeah, that was it, Ruda. You were mad at me, weren't you?"

"Not really." Ruda laughed bitterly. "I'm from here, not from the Reich, and so if I'm wearing this uniform, I know it ain't all that easy to say hello to me. Especially in front of a girl."

"So you're really not mad at me?"

Ruda shook his head. "I'm really not. It hurt, but it wasn't your fault. The thing is ..." But instead of finishing the thought, he just waved his hand dismissively.

The historical situation.

I took a drink of beechnut coffee spiked with rum.

SOMETIME EARLIER, I had learned, through Hannelore, that they'd transferred Ruda's division to Stalingrad. Not that she would have told me on her own. Before the war, we used to greet each other on the street, but after it started, we barely nodded to each other, if that. But Hannelore bragged about her brother to Mr. Kleinander shortly after Hitler's exceptionally fiery speech, which the Führer ended with a colossal and memorable miscalculation: "Ich werde Stalingrad errobern!"*

The speech, broadcast live, was then repeated several

times by all the German radio stations. A few days later, they called me in to the personnel department to talk about the factory band. It was a ragtag group of boys from our swing band who'd been caught by the forced labour edict, plus some polka players from Mr. Mrstina's orchestra, a couple of fiddlers whose origins I knew nothing about— though they couldn't have belonged to any band because they could barely play—and one virtuoso gypsy who had miraculously avoided being sent to Auschwitz. So it was a band of hacks, but there were some advantages, like hours off work under the pretext of rehearsing our new repertoire. Mr. Kleinander was able to hold a protective hand over the band because it had started up at a time when the Germans were winning, or at least they'd got their second wind. When they stopped winning, I was summoned to the personnel department to receive a verdict intended to seal the band's fate. And that was the end of it. The Germans never did catch their third wind. They continued to fight hard, but though they reduced the breadth of the front, it didn't help. We started manufacturing parts for the v-1s, and the factory orchestra became an anachronistic luxury.

When Hannelore brushed by me in the corridor, I noticed she'd been weeping. She had the hiccoughs—the kind people get when they've been crying hard.

Mr. Kleinander notified me of the band's demise, as I knew he would, and I asked him, "Did anything happen to Hannelore's brother, Mr. Kleinander? I mean, she was crying."

*"Ruda is right there in the pocket. At Stalingrad."**

Ruda, whom I had denied, as Peter had denied Christ.

I returned to the assembly line, and I must have been pale, because Nadia asked if there was anything the matter.

I shook my head. "No, Nadia, it's just that ..." A phrase came to mind, the fragment of a song that Nadia certainly

didn't know, and anyway, she didn't understand German:
"...Ich hatte einen Kameraden..."*

But now, over our beechnut coffee and rum, I could reach out and touch Ruda. He had made it out alive. Out of Stalingrad.

⚜

"You didn't know that?" said Berta, astonished. "You? You were such an admirer of Irena."

"I got over it while I was still living in Kostelec," I said. "But I didn't forget about her."

"So then, how come you didn't know about it?"

"I left Kostelec for good. Before I went to Canada, I was only back once, and then I only met Marie."

Berta surprised me. He had turned—at least as far as I could judge, though women might have seen him differently—into a rather handsome gent with a neat little moustache, wearing a three-piece business suit, although he was only the pub-keeper in a village near Jaromer.

I had known his wife—who had died in the meantime—only by sight, and I had always thought he'd married her out of desperation, as ex-prisoners and Black Barons often did, ex-prisoners in particular. They were terrified by the jokes the guards would crack at their expense, jokes about the impact that mining uranium would have on their future sex lives, if they were lucky enough to have one. But what terrified the ex-prisoners even more than impotence was sterility, the fear that they would not be able to have children. To my mind, it was a kind of mystical way of thinking, keeping alive the blood line, the clan, the family, or just life itself. Rumours would circulate through the camps, permutating into legend, then hardening into gospel truth. After the general amnesty in 1960, many of the ex-prisoners grabbed the first skirt they could get their hands on at a village dance—and they didn't bother with niceties like contraceptives; they used live ammunition, and the girls usually got pregnant right away. Most of the marriages didn't last, they merely produced children who were then shuttled back and forth between the divorced parents, or sent to live with relatives.

"It was all about one of the main evils of capitalism," he said, "about the root of all evil—which is money, as you certainly must know, since you've lived under capitalism for practically thirty years."

⚑ ⚑

I used to think Irena and Zdenek were truly in love, but they probably weren't. It just seemed that way to me. At that age, people appear bound together by common interests, and all the time it's just sex. And if it's only sex holding you together, you seldom die of a broken heart when that bond breaks. At least, that's what I think.

In Irena and Zdenek's case, the common bond was mountain climbing, or more precisely, sandstone rock climbing, because there were no mountains in the Protectorate— they were all in the Sudetenland, and we lost that in 1938. So people went on weekend excursions to Ostas, to Rough Rock, and stayed over in a tourist hostel where the sexes were not separated. Irena probably lost her virginity in Rough Rock, though maybe I'm wrong about that. She was a sociable person, and that hostel would not have been the most appropriate place for such a momentous event in the life of a young woman. More likely, it happened one afternoon at her place, when her sister, Alena, had gone off to a basketball tournament and the alderman was at work in his office at the town hall. Or it could have happened in one of those small hotels on the rock-climbing circuit. Zdenek, who was from Prague, was streetwise enough to know how to bribe the hotel owner, since without proper proof—either a marriage licence or an entry to that effect in the ID booklets the Germans made us carry—couples were not permitted to spend the night in the same room. Or maybe they did it the way it was usually done: they booked separate rooms. Zdenek had plenty of money, though it was only Protectorate currency, which had no value after the war and not much during it, either—the kind of currency that turns misers into free spenders. However it was, Irena admitted to me that it had happened, but she complained that it hadn't happened as early in her life as I'd suggested in a juvenile novel of mine in which she figured. (It had the innocent title Inferiority Complex.)

Zdenek's mother (his father had already passed away) owned a company in Prague that made high-end lingerie for the smart set, and my guess was that they'd get married as soon as the war was over. Indeed, there was a wedding, but it was only Zdenek who got married, obedient to his mother's wishes. He married the daughter of a liquor factory owner; during the war, it had been refitted to produce soft drinks and soda water, but as soon as the war was over, it reverted to booze. It was the perfect cliché: the rich bride invested her substantial dowry into high-end lingerie. Irena, the daughter of a municipal employee whose greatest asset was the title "Alderman," had no dowry at all.

It did not break her heart. Irena immediately began going out with Dr. Capek, an intern at the Kostelec hospital, and what bound them together in this case was a love of classical literature (one of the sources of my complex:

compared with Irena's, my knowledge of such literature was almost zero) and sex, though probably in reverse order.

But there was more to her affair with Dr. Capek than there had been with the mountain climber, for their relationship became associated with a plague of blowflies that had hit Kostelec about a month after the war.

⚔ ⚔

"I'm astonished you never heard of it, Danny," said Berta, stroking his moustache the way they used to in the movies. "I'll bet you've never heard of a girl demonstrating devotion to her beloved in such a peculiar way."

I hadn't known anything about the plague of blowflies, nor of Irena's part in it, because by that time I was living in Prague, so Berta filled me in. From somewhere, no one knew where, enormous swarms of shiny, fat flies with disgusting black legs suddenly descended on the town. They got into the food, which made them hard to kill. If you used a fly-swatter, they left behind ugly, bloody splotches, and shooing them away was fruitless, because they'd come back and land on your plate again and start sucking up the cream sauce with their disgusting proboscises. Shoo one away and three more would land and start feasting, bringing more with them, until the plates became a stomach-turning, writhing mass of shiny living matter. It was horrible. They'd never get caught on flypaper; it was as if they'd inherited an awareness in their genes and passed it down to their offspring, though I hear that's nonsense.

It was a serious problem for the town, Berta said, and no one claimed to know where this Egyptian plague had come from. Today, that seems highly improbable, because everyone knew of the massacre at the brewery.

The problem landed squarely in Dr. Capek's lap, for in addition to being an intern at the hospital, he was also the municipal medical health officer, a position he had assumed after the sudden death of the previous officer. As he racked his brains out loud, Irena listened.

"Anyone who can figure out where these little devils come from will earn a personal citation from the mayor," he said.

"And from you, too, sweetheart?" Irena added seductively.

"Of course," said Dr. Capek. He was distracted by the blowfly epidemic, and his answer sounded somewhat offhand.

She said goodbye to Dr. Capek, who had to go to an emergency meeting of the municipal council about the flies from hell, and she literally ran up the hill to the castle and then along the castle road that led to the military cemetery, located in an artificial ruin built by Prince Schaumburg-Lippe, or maybe it was one of his forebears, in memory of the Austrian soldiers who had died of wounds sustained in the Battle of Kostelec in 1866. Irena's memories of what had happened at the brewery in the final days of the war were still fresh; she had stood watch for a long time outside the brewery gates when Zdenek had gone missing in the uprising and it appeared he might have died a hero's death.

The road, which ran between two rows of trees, was buzzing with blowflies, and as Irena drew closer to the cemetery, they grew thicker and thicker. On the other side of the faux ruins, there was another cemetery, without crosses, nameplates, or markers of any kind, since it was, in fact, a secret burial ground where the bodies of the ss men who had been massacred at the brewery were slowly decaying in shallow graves.

No one knew if they were really ss men; perhaps they were, perhaps they weren't. They had arrived in Kostelec as the rear guard of Marshal Schörner's army,* and many of them could barely speak German. On the town square, these soldiers had turned around the only self-propelled gun they had and, clustered on it like a swarm of wasps, they set off to confront the Russian army, which was, de facto, a Mongolian army, though you weren't allowed to say so. The rank-and-file soldiers were all Asians with huge moustaches; only the officers were Russian.

The ss men clashed with the Russian-Mongolian Red Army at the custom house. The Mongolian anti-tank cannoneers put the self-propelled gun out of action, but many in that cluster of wasps managed to escape into the nearby woods. The last of them was halfway out of the armoured vehicle when an anti-tank projectile took off his head. Berta, at the time a passionate photographer, captured this memorable visual episode in the battle. The picture may still be lying somewhere in the attic over Berta's pub, carefully pasted into an album the way Berta used to do it. I saw the photograph at the time, because Berta showed it to me, and to Marie as well, but it made her feel sick.

Many of the escapees were captured in the woods by the Czech insurgents and taken to the brewery, where I saw them sitting on the floor the night before they were executed—beaten to death. Afterwards, they trundled the corpses away in a cart, though some of them were still moving, and Rosta had said, "Goya? He's shit compared to this."*

The mass grave was quite shallow, and about two weeks before Irena's run along the avenue of trees there had been a heavy rainfall, so when she arrived, partially decayed legs and arms were protruding from the earth. The rain had washed away the thin layer of soil hastily shovelled over the dead ss men, or German soldiers, or whoever they really were. Over at least half the grave, the dead were now visible, almost completely decomposed, like badly wrapped mummies.

Irena's stomach heaved, but love overcame the physical response of her body. She turned on her heels and ran like the wind all the way back to the town hall on the square, a good four kilometres' distance. She was an incredible athlete.

Irena was officially praised by the town, Berta told me, and privately by Dr. Capek. The flies were eliminated by a new discovery called DDT, and volunteers with handkerchiefs tied over their faces reburied what remained of Field Marshal Schörner's rear guard.

Berta was right. It was truly a unique expression of love, if that's what it was. Shortly afterward, Dr. Capek broke up with Irena and married the unlovely daughter of Mr. Lenart, the textile wholesaler. He justified this to Irena by claiming he needed money to set up a private clinic.

Once again, the collapse of a romance failed to break her heart. Irena moved to Prague to study phys. ed., and six months later, she successfully lassoed another medic, Dr. Otto Znenahlo. They had two daughters, and Dr. Znenahlo died before Irena turned forty. What she did after that, as far as love or sex was concerned, Berta didn't know. She played tennis, and for the next thirty years, she continued rock climbing, worked in some office or other, and went to the Krkonose Mountains in northeastern Bohemia for her holidays.

"But it's interesting, Danny: both those guys dumped her for the same reason—the root of all evil," Berta said. "And it really was evil, at least in Zdenek's case. At that time, the clever entrepreneurs were betting that the post-war Republic wouldn't last much longer. Not that they were experts in international politics or familiar with *The History of the Communist Party (Bolshevik)."* Berta knew the title of the book from his compulsory courses in Marxism-Leninism at the technical university, before they dragooned him into the Black Barons. "But they had a good nose for risk," he said, "and they poured as much as they could of that root of all evil into bank accounts in the West. Zdenek wasn't one of the clever ones."

After the Communist coup in February 1948, Berta said, they nationalized the high-end lingerie factory. Zdenek became a mason, and his wealthy bride sank to the social level of the wife of a hod carrier on construction sites, and to the economic level of an office worker on minimum wage in the White Swan department store. And so this married couple, who had never been bound together by anything like love—sex, maybe, though who knows, but certainly by the root of all evil—found themselves bickering constantly, and Zdenek turned out to have a sensitive soul (which surprised me, because he'd always seemed like a big man, a bit of a show-off, and an all-around tough guy). He was ground down by his wife's constant complaining. She would angrily remind him of the many people in a similar situation: small-time capitalists who had failed to move their money to Switzerland in time, but who, on the other hand, had joined the Party, so the very worst that happened to them, as comrades in good standing, was to become bosses in tiny enterprises related to their original expertise, and sometimes even in businesses they had once owned. Zdenek's wife would always end these belated tirades by screaming: "But a lousy good-for-nothing like you would never join the Party, would you? Oh no, you have your precious ideals to protect. And they're not worth shit!"

And so, one day, the former lingerie manufacturer tried to hang himself. It didn't work. The rope broke, and in utter despair, he simply lay in a heap on the ground, where his wife eventually found him. The moment she realized what had happened, she went right at him again: "You can't even hang yourself properly, you useless fool!" So he tried it again, and this time, he succeeded.

Berta made a wry face. He had a shiny metal crown on his left front incisor that looked like iron or steel, the material they used to make crowns and bridges during the war.

"You could blame the suicide on the historical situation," he said.

⚔ ⚔

Knobloch appeared in the doorway. I looked around the room. In the cloud of smoke, which hadn't yet attained meeting-level density, there weren't very many of us. Berta and Pilous were sitting at a table, talking with Kveta, Stazka, and Anka. Nina and I were at the bar. There had been twenty of us in our graduating class half a century ago. Nine were here. Four had not shown up yet.

"And you know what?" I heard Nina say. "He didn't want her to do what guys usually want. He just wanted to earn brownie points in the Party personnel office for seducing another soul, in this case, your Marie. She didn't come across, so he took political revenge for the lost brownie points. He said that since Party members in the Kostelec municipal committee were in a minority, and since everyone in Lesni Mesto was a Communist, he'd transfer one of their Communists to Kostelec and Marie could go to work in Lesni Mesto. That would give the Kostelec Communists in the municipal committee the upper hand, and Marie could represent the non-Communists in Lesni Mesto. So it would sort of balance things out."

I took a deep drink from my Manhattan. For a moment, I thought about the fate of my wise old girlfriend, and of all our fates, or at least those who had stayed in Kostelec. Then I said, "And what about you, Nina? How did Vosahlo justify sentencing you to hours of commuting every day? With four children and only God, in the person of Christian ladies, to help you?"

"Politically, how else?" she said. "It was my husband. Politically, he got up Vosahlo's nose."

I looked at her closely. Her blue eyes were glowing like precious stones. "And the real reason?" I asked.

Nina took a sip from her glass and grinned. "Unlike you, he found me quite attractive," she said. "But like your Marie, I didn't satisfy him in that regard, so I was sent to strengthen the ranks of the Christian community in Nejdalov, such as it was. They were mostly old underground fighters and a couple of collaborators who were now card-carrying Party members."

Unlike me? And was that still the case? Time changes relationships in strange ways. I said nothing.

Knobloch lit up a Havana cigar and offered one to Berta, who shook his head. Stazka, however, reached out and took one. Knobloch lit it for her. Both of them began puffing away, and before long the cloud of smoke had attained meeting-level density.

I turned to Nina. "Nina, I wish you wouldn't keep saying 'your Marie.'"

"Why not? After all, you loved her to kingdom come, didn't you? Even more than that. You wrote a movie for her."

Time changes relationships in unbelievable ways. I looked at those moonlike cheeks with fondness. "You're just as much mine as Marie ever was, Nina. Or Irena."

Nina laughed, and her eyes sparkled like a couple of sapphires. "I know," she said. "Because now it doesn't matter anymore."

Two blowflies landed on the bar and proceeded to get drunk, sucking up tiny puddles of my national drink.

⚓ ⚓

Ruda's suntanned face had long since paled, and in place of the colouring he'd gained on the Caucasian Riviera, he had patches of white, from frostbite. Thoughts, ungovernable thoughts. It was January 1945, the last year of the war, and when he took off his cap in the Beranek, I could see that he had streaks of grey in his hair. His breath came heavily, and sometimes his lungs would rattle. He had frostbite scars on his hands and fingers as well, which he wrapped around the antique glass teacup in the silver holder. In the meantime, I, who was the same age, from the same town and the same school, had spent my time chasing girls, without much success, and playing the saxophone, though not particularly well. I had also stood near the railway station when they sent the Jews off to Terezin, including Erwin Pick and my teacher, Mr. Katz, and it didn't arouse strong emotions in me at the time, perhaps because I did not know, or simply could not imagine, the terror that must have gripped them by the throat. It was only later, a year and a half later, in the winter when we were drilling the cross-bracket machine-gun mounts for the Messerschmitts,[*] that I knew such terror, briefly, and then Nadia came to me and the fear vanished. Back then, on the station platform, they, like me, didn't know much either, but one thing was clear to them: they were moving closer to death, and it would not be the kind of death that comes for you in your bed.

And all that time, my classmate, Ruda, was freezing on the Eastern Front in Stalingrad, where they fought from house to house, and man to man, and death was everywhere among them, except that Ruda was among the elect, and the bullets and the shrapnel, though not the bayonets, missed him, while I, in the meantime ...

"It got me out of Stalingrad, man. It was a piece of luck, but it was luck from hell, which is where I was," he said. "Trapped in the Stalingrad Pocket. We knew very well where we were, though the German broadcasts kept it a secret. But the Russians had their own German-language broadcasts, and they gave it to us full blast. Oh yeah," he went on—and I ordered another shot of rum from Roubicek the moment our glasses were empty—"we knew very well what an awful mess we were in, but we fought like lions, or more like rhinoceroses, Danny, because we knew that if the Ruskies got their mitts on us ..." The very idea made him pause. "What I mean is, our officers were always trying to scare us, but we thought it might have been propaganda. Then, once in a while, someone would manage to escape, and they'd tell us stories ... and then there was what we saw with our own eyes when we managed to break through their lines—they had no time to piss about with prisoners."

He fell silent again. "But I was lucky that day," he went on. "We were trying to take some factory or other, and we were crawling over piles of bricks and crap, and the bullets just seemed to miss me—I wasn't afraid of getting shot anymore—and then there was an open gate in front of us and the Russians come charging out with fixed bayonets, shouting that bloodcurdling battle cry of theirs, which I hope you never get to hear, and I got stabbed in the leg—a bayonet right into the shinbone. I shot the Russian who did it, he fell on top of me, and as his weight come down on his rifle, the bayonet acted like a damned crowbar and broke the bone. We turned back the attack, and the ambulance took me away. And that was my greatest stroke of luck, but I'll bet you can't guess why."

I remembered again how I'd first seen him, bronzed from the high sunlight in the Caucasus, where they marched along mountain paths with magnificent views down into the valleys. The people there welcomed the Germans, so Koba later invented a new ethnic category for them: a "reactionary nation," which, as a scholar of Marxism, he knew from the classic texts, where Engels had used the same expression to describe the Czechs. Then he transported them in railway cars, like Jews, to the Arctic, where most of them died. But Ruda didn't tell me that, because he hadn't witnessed it; I first heard about it after the war. And then, long after the war, when I was no longer in Kostelec, and not even in Prague, I read how, of all those hundreds of thousands of deportees, only a handful returned from Siberia, or wherever they'd been. Now I was sitting in the Beranek, where, besides Ruda and me, there were only two chess players, absorbed in their game, and the clicking of billiard balls around the corner. Ruda continued his story.*

"It was pretty clear the whole thing was a colossal screw-up, just like the war. On the Military Broadcasting Service, they said that Göring promised the Fewer that the Luftwaffe would get us out of there, but nobody in the field hospital believed it. It was in the basement of a huge building that was nothing but rubble above ground. Might have been an opera house, or the Cheka headquarters, for all I know. It was dark because they were giving the generator a rest. They turned the lights on only when the doctors did their rounds and identified the dead and the medics took them away. The field nurses used flashlights when they dressed the wounds. And then it was dark again, and every other guy was screaming in pain because they were trying to save morphine, and there were two or three of us to a bed, sometimes four, lying there in the dark with the weeping

and wailing and gnashing of teeth, as the Venerable Father Meloun would've said — was that his name?"

"That was his name," I said quietly.

"... Meloun—and he never explained what that meant, but there I was in this weeping and wailing and gnashing of teeth, and I'm telling you, man, I was in hell, lying there in the dark. We heard Göring on the radio, promising heaven and earth, and the guys who were still alive made jokes about it. Out loud. You know, when you got nothing to lose, all you got left to lose is fear," Ruda said. "I mean, fear of the Gestapo and other such outfits. Not the fear of death, though. You never stop being afraid of that, because you don't know what it's gonna be like." He coughed. His lungs rattled, and he took a drink of rum from the teacup. "One morning, the lights came on and the doctors showed up on their rounds with a couple of officers in tow. One of the ambulance guys nearby whispered that some planes had landed, and the guy next to me, he had his arm in a cast and he said under his breath, 'So fat boy Hermann came through?' I watched the commission going from bed to bed, ignoring the badly wounded, the amputees, the guys who'd been burned in tank battles or had their guts shot out, but I was still thinking, since the ambulance guy had said the planes had landed, that they were going to evacuate the badly wounded."

Ruda looked at me from under his frostbitten eyelids and started to cough again. It was a while before he caught his breath, and then he said, "Man, was I ever wrong! They took the ones with lighter wounds. And I was one of them, because I only had my leg in a cast and could already hobble about on crutches. The first thought that came into my head was that there wasn't gonna be no airlift, that they were gonna send us straight back to the trenches, stick a gun in our hands so we could provide cover for our buddies who'd be going back on the attack against some other half-ruined factory—there must have been a million of them in Stalingrad. But once we got outside, they loaded us into a truck and drove us through the part of Stalingrad we still held, and it was nothing but stones and ruins and rubble. It took a hell of a long time, because sometimes the driver and the corporal who was riding shotgun had to get out and push a collapsed wall out of the way, but we finally made it out of the city, or what was left of it, and then we started gunning it for the airfield. The guy next to me, the one with his arm in a cast, was talking to himself, or maybe to someone on the other side of him, and he was saying, 'My Lord, fat Hermann meant what he said!' And it sure looked that way. We got closer to the airfield, and it was almost dark, but in the dim light we could see this Gigant *ready for takeoff, with its props ticking over. It looked scary as hell in the dark, but I'm telling you, at that moment, I loved it. The* Gigant. *It was a kind of—"*

"I know what it was," I said. "A six-engine monster for transporting tanks."

⚞ ⚟

Was Nina right about Marie getting in trouble with the Party? I saw Marie's strawberry mouth in the spotlight on the stage of the Dr. Cizek Municipal Theatre while the chorus was rehearsing Dvorak's *Rusalka*, and the lighting technician picked her out, her red lips forming the words to "White Flowers Strewn Along the Path ..." Was Nina right?

If she was, then Hribe took revenge on Marie out of a hatred and malice that was, to me, incomprehensible. His hatred was not that of a dirty old man spurned, but the hatred that belongs to ideologues. The stupidest, most dangerous of human emotions. Our ruin, our ruin, our ruin.[*]

⊰ ⊱

"You know that plane?" said Ruda, surprised. "I thought it was a secret weapon."

"I read Signal," *I said. "They had a picture of it there, with a description."*

"Ah—I never read Signal. *They used to bring it to us at the front, but I was fed up with everything by that time," Ruda said. "Anyway, we drove up to this monster, and these two pilots were just climbing down out of the cockpit. They only had light jackets on, and they barely had time to light up before they had to climb right back up again. The cold was something terrible, because the wind was blowing over the landing strip. The motors were still running; one of the pilots told us later that they were warned not to shut them down after landing because they might not be able to get them started again because of the cold. So the medics loaded us into the belly of the beast, and I looked around and, really and truly, there wasn't a single badly wounded grunt among us. So it was clear as a slap in the face. We got out of it, only to be tossed back* nach Osten *to have another crack at a* Durchbruch—*that's what they call a breakthrough—back into the Stalingrad Pocket again, and not out of it. They reckoned our boys inside would hold out a little bit longer and fight harder because they were scared of what would happen to them if the Russians got their mitts on them."*

Ruda paused to take a sip of his drink. I looked at him, at his frostbitten eyelids. "So we lay down in the belly of the beast, and the guy next to me, the one with his arm in a cast, said to me, 'Thank God it's almost dark. The Ruskies don't fly in the dark. If there was any light, even their Ratas could shoot us down.' The Rata was a—"

"An old Russian fighter. Really slow. Practically useless in the war."

"It could have taken on the Gigant," Ruda said. "Somebody said, 'I don't think we're even armed. Does anyone see a machine gun anywhere?' No one could. It was night, all right, but as the guy with his arm in a cast said— Pinkhausen was his name—'It'd only take one or two Ratas . . .' And so we took off and flew into the night, and it was one big mess of fear, man. Fear. And yet we were stupid, because what else could we have expected once we'd recovered? A Durchbruch back into Stalingrad? Thank you very much."

He was silent, remembering, and I was remembering too. Hannelore, weeping on the stairs coming down from Kleinander's, and Mr. Kleinander telling me she was crying because of Ruda, who was in the Stalingrad Pocket. I imagined Ruda inside that pocket. Ruda from Kostelec. But he had made it out.

"Before they took my cast off, they all surrendered. About a million of them. Now they're somewhere in Siberia. I wonder how many are left?" He fell silent again, then said, "I was saved by my good luck!"

And me? All I could think of was our jazz band, and the girls we chased.

I tried to change the subject. "What about your parents?"

Ruda looked at me uncomprehendingly. It took him a while to bring his mind back to Kostelec and the Sepp family flat, where no one spoke because they were mute with despair at how badly the war was going. He was almost looking forward to leaving the next day and going back to the Eastern Front. Not to Stalingrad this time, but to some-where in East Prussia, or wherever.

"Oh, right, my parents," he said flatly, as if he were talking in his sleep. But a few moments later he left his memories behind and said in a serious tone, "Yesterday, Dad said he'd stick with the Fewer to the bitter end, and when the Fewer fell, he'd do himself and the whole family in."

"Including your mother? And Hannelore?"

"Yeah—even including the nipper, Horst. I'm the only one who'll escape that bitter end, because tomorrow I'm going back to the front. And I think the Fewer will last until tomorrow, God willing," he said, with a sour laugh.

"Don't go back, Ruda!" I shouted. It was almost theatri-cal. "It's crazy! Why don't you go into hiding somewhere?"

"So I can go with the Fewer to the bitter end? And tell me, where would I hide? With a couple of compatriots who live in Kostelec? They'll do what Dad's planning to do, or they'll get caught, and I don't want to be around when ..." He stopped.

"But everyone knows you, Ruda," I said quickly. "Every-one knows—"

"That I'm a Kraut," he interrupted. "Dannyboy, don't be naive. When the war is over in Kostelec—well, I don't want to be here to see it."

He was interrupted by a fit of terrible coughing. Roubicek poured us another couple of rums. I wondered, suddenly, if Roubicek would join in whatever would happen in Kostelec when the war was over, the kind of thing Ruda didn't want to be here to see. Nonsense, I said to myself—very loudly, but to myself. Ruda overcame the coughing fit.

"Anyway," he said, and his voice had somehow changed. "I have to go back. I don't suppose you'd understand that."

"Frontkameradschaft?" I asked.* My voice had changed

also; somehow a tone of mild ridicule had crept into it, against my will.

"Something like that," said Ruda. "You know I've never been a Nazi. But when you live six years like I have—maybe there's a better way of putting it, but I don't know how— six years, Danny!" He waved his hand dismissively. "It's not worth explaining." He looked at his watch. "Time I was going."

And then he added something that sent a cold chill up my spine: "Back to our Begräbniswohnung.*" Our living grave. He meant home.*

He stood up. "Are you good for the tab?"

"Naturally," I said. He turned to leave, and I never saw him again.

◄ ►

"Which of us is still missing?" Pilous looked around. We were all sitting at a round table, and there were only a handful of us. Far fewer than thirty years ago. The barman was standing behind the bar, leaning against the mirror between the bottles, taking a smoke break. But not all of us were here yet.

"Bara's not coming," said Nina.

"Why not?" Pilous asked.

Nina shrugged her shoulders.

"Is she ashamed?" Stazka asked.

"What about?"

"Does it have to be about anything?" I asked. I knew nothing about Bara. I hadn't heard anything after that lousy reunion thirty years ago. Back then, she'd been twice her normal weight. Now maybe she'd tripled it. But she hadn't been ashamed of her size back then. She smelled as though her husband had poured a bottle of perfume over her. *L'esprit de Moscou*. I looked at Nina and suddenly remembered her cold farewell to Bara thirty years before, when she'd said, "My train leaves in fifteen minutes." That midnight hour stuck in my brain like a nail in a coffin. Impossible to pull out.

But Nina turned to me and said, "Are you referring to her husband's stupidity after the Communist putsch?" Her tone was bitter, but not the kind of bitterness that had been in her voice that midnight thirty years ago. Time had softened it with another element—forgiveness, perhaps—or maybe it was just that her wounds had healed. "You're stupid, and you don't know boo," she said to me. "You believe that gossip?"

"Whatever gossip there was never reached me," I said.

"Oh right, I'd forgotten. You're from overseas. Here they used to say she was Werner in a skirt." She turned to address our insignificant little group. "You do remember Werner, don't you?"

"Not me," said Stazka.

"Werner was impossible to forget," said Berta darkly.

"I've forgotten him," said Stazka. "Deliberately. I was afraid he'd show up at the matriculation exams, so I wiped him out of my memory. But, yes, of course, I know who he was."

"What kind of logic is that?" said Pilous.

"There is none," said Stazka.

Nina was silent. Was there something else going on? We all looked at Stazka. She still looked young, but her face was lined. Stazka grimaced.

"Who was Erazim Pokryty, really?" I asked Stazka in the silence.

A faint tinge of crimson rose to her cheeks, but she said nothing.

"Was it just an inappropriate practical joke?" I pressed.

"No!" said Stazka. "He really existed."

Knobloch jumped in. "Less than six months before the matrics," he said tactlessly, "you were engaged to Stejskal. Did you have this Pokryty fellow up your sleeve as a fallback?"

"Knobloch, you're such an ass," Stazka shot back with feeling. It was obvious we'd hit a sore spot. We were silent, remembering the funeral in that pre-spring downpour, though it was still winter, and Stazka in her thin mourning dress and with her broken candle, and how she'd caught the tuberculosis that had killed Stejskal, so that Stejskal had at least managed to dodge Werner and the matriculation exams as well. And life itself, it occurred to me, but that was a cheap thought. Or maybe not entirely. It was just a thought.

We sat in the bar like strange orphans. Three of us had died abroad, in a foreign country, one of us in the modern equivalent of hell. Four hadn't shown up, and they probably wouldn't. Three had died at home, in their own country, which for me was the old country. Franta Jelen, Jebavy—who else? But it doesn't matter where you die. None of that romantic "I shall return" nonsense.* I shall not return. I will die. Ruda cut his own throat.

"I didn't have any fallback." I realized that Stazka was speaking. "But in the print shop where I went to get the invitations done, Mr. Lehm wondered about that name—Erazim Pokryty—so he asked, 'He's not from around here, is he?' 'He's not,' I said. 'Might I ask where he is from?' I had to think fast: not somewhere close by, where Mr. Lehm could ask around, if he was really that curious. So I said the first thing that came into my mind: 'He's from Pardubice.' 'Congratulations,' Mr. Lehm said, as if he knew something I didn't, and at that moment, I knew there was going to be hell to pay."

"People said you did it because of the exams," said Pilous.

"Naturally. Instead of studying, I ..." She paused suddenly. "Well, here's the thing: I couldn't think of anything else. And then, on top of that, there was Werner! His favourite thing was to go from school to school during the leaving exams. He had a captive audience—all the teachers in one place, and he could make their lives miserable all at once."

I knew how Werner could make people's lives miserable. "The thing is," Stazka said, "I hadn't thought it through. I was—dumb. Dumb, dumb, dumb! The TB was what saved me from complications at school, and after the war, they were practically giving high-school diplomas away. So it was all gain, no pain. But before Dr. Eichler told me I had TB, this Erazim Pokryty showed up."

And she told the story about the unreal man, and I remembered plump Mr. Bivoj unsuccessfully trying to get to the bottom of the strange wedding announcement. "Someone rang the doorbell while I was packing my things for the hospital," I heard Stazka continue. "I went to answer it, and there was this great big fellow; he wasn't just huge, he was enormous, and he was staring at me with these big black eyes. 'Can I help you?' I asked, and he said, 'You don't know me?' 'No,' I said. 'Well, unless I'm mistaken, I'm your intended. Erazim Pokryty.' My jaw must have dropped, because he nodded and said, 'There's only one problem. I already have a wife.'"

The materialized Mr. Pokryty was a good man. Stazka invited him in for a coffee, and he listened to her tale of tragic love and fear. At that time, Stazka was a complete orphan, and Mr. Pokryty asked if she had anyone to look after her when she came back from the hospital. When she told him she didn't, he invited her to Pardubice and wouldn't hear any excuses, so his wife looked after Stazka while she was convalescing. She was also a giant of a woman, with no children of her own. They more or less kept Stazka alive until the end of the war. When the war was over, she went to the sanatorium.

"Both of them are dead now," Stazka said. The telephone in the bar rang, and the barman, who had been listening in on our conversation, lowered his voice to answer.

"I'll tell you why Bara isn't coming," said Nina. "Because ... it's almost ... her husband's no longer with us. Delirium tremens. To this day I don't know why they did it, but the fact is that during the Prague Spring, under Dubcek, they actually left the Party. Whether it was a matter of bad conscience, or whether they realised they'd simply jumped on the wrong bandwagon, I don't know. All I know is that there was no right one to jump on after that."

"They could today," said Knobloch ironically. "Today, the Party would welcome them back with open arms." I looked at him. Until recently he had been—and perhaps he still was—a commercial attaché in South Africa, the same position he'd had in Brazil, or somewhere over there.

"But Bara would have had to get back on by herself, and she wouldn't do that," Nina said. "And she doesn't want to talk about it. For twenty years, she scrubbed the stairs in some Prague movie house, and her husband, a former government advisor, worked on the subway, digging tunnels."

"You have that straight from her?" I asked.

The blue eyes gave me the once-over. "Yeah. In the end, we became pals again. As you know, I'm a Christian." Did she smile? As I recalled, she had never been particularly religious, and she explained immediately. "I got it from my husband. I told her she had my husband's death on her conscience, at least in part, and that for Communists there *is* such a thing as collective guilt. At least as I see it. She had no answer to that, but we ended up on good terms anyway. She told me she'd thrown in her lot with the Bolsheviks because her husband wanted her to join. And in the end, they both jumped ship, but she had to drag him off the boat, kicking and screaming."

Silence. I looked around without moving my head. Pilous, Kveta, Knobloch, none of them said a word. They didn't even move. Berta had never held anything against anyone. Nor had Anka. She sat beside Kveta, as still as a statue. Stazka said, "There's one more who should show up, but he won't: Vlasak. What happened to Kulich, I don't know. And where is Erwin?"

No one offered an answer.

There were too few of us at the bar.

Stazka turned to me and said I should tell them about those who had died in exile.

〽 〽

I first heard that Miss Brunnenschatten was still alive in a letter from Berta. God knows when our trans-Atlantic conversations began, but I suspect it was before T.S. Eliot's prediction about the world ending not with a bang but a whimper came true. But only after a fashion, since that particular world hasn't vanished completely, nor has it whimpered its last.

Berta wrote me, and I remember now when that was. His son had died. According to Berta, his son had been a promising architect. He'd already designed a large, modern city hall, I forget where, and then suddenly, he was dead. In his letter, Berta posed the rhetorical question: Why do some die at thirty and others live into their eighties and beyond? To illustrate his point, he mentioned our old German teacher, who was now about ninety.

I could think of no appropriately philosophical answer to his question, so I merely offered my condolences, which is always a mere cliché, always, and in any case, I'd never met his son. Somehow, I managed to slip into the letter another, answerable question, and Berta, though crushed with grief, sent me the address.

I went back to Prague in May 1990, for the first time after that almost inaudible death rattle of Communist power. I did the rounds, visiting old friends, and discovered what many had discovered before me, that the past is the source of everything in man, and then everything is utterly forgotten. And our common past had been brief. Eight, maybe thirteen years at the most, and then our lives began to diverge, and then they ceased to resemble one another— and after the invasion of the country in that sham miraculous year of the Prague Spring, they began to diverge radically. Friendships remained, deeper after all those years than before, but the conversations delved first into the mutually uninteresting years of radical divergence, then focused on the twelve years after matriculation when we each went our own way, and finally came down to the eight or thirteen years we had spent together in school. But by that time that common past had shrunk to become the property of no more than a handful of classmates and a couple of teachers. A lot was eaten, the wives cooked, a lot was drunk, and Lexa gave me Miss Brunnenschatten's address, so now I had it from two sources. Lexa had just gotten over a third heart attack; the fourth one killed him in a pub in Kramolna, a tiny village in the hills above Kostelec where, most Sundays, he would go to play the violin—Lexa the tenor sax player—

with the local fiddlers, the repertoire being mostly folkloric music, or rather "national music," as they preferred to call it, "Gently Flows the Water," that kind of thing. He collapsed and mercifully—gracefully—he passed away.

I got Miss Brunnenschatten's address a third time, this time from Haryk, whom the past—the one that had diverged from mine—had entirely swallowed up. He was now a composer, going to evening classes at the conservatory, though he made a living working in the parts department at a CKD factory. Before that, he'd spent three years behind bars, and before that, he'd started to study chemistry but then never went back to it. Instead, he went back to music, not the kind we'd played during the war, not big-band swing—there were only two remnants of that era left: Vlach and Brom—but just music.* He wrote music for children's TV programs, about which I knew a great big zero. Nothing. Nada.

Finally, after all those visits to friends, classmates, relatives, the thrice-acquired address, plus old memories, brought me to a Prague street with a beautiful name: Jablonova—Appletree Lane. Sure enough, there were apple trees there, and they were in bloom, glowing pink and white in the gardens of family homes that were as alike as brothers and sisters—each one slightly, but only slightly, different. On one of them, beside the buzzer, I found the names Dr. Stepan Ohrenstein, Dr. Ruth Ohrensteinova, and, right at the bottom, Dr. Eva Cvancarova.

I wondered—absurd questions always come to mind first—what the long-dead school inspector Herr Werner would have thought of the relatives and descendants of that one hundred percent German blonde he'd fallen so hard for and then come within an inch of sending to her death when she said no to him and meant it. I drove away these initial thoughts and pressed the buzzer.

The door was opened by a young man in jeans and a T-shirt bearing a Florida Orange Farms logo, with a hint in his face—or perhaps it was only in the shadow of his eyes, his nose—of the narrow, Teutonic face of my old teacher.

"Good day," I said, using a phrase that meant nothing. It was how we greeted each other during the war, during the old regime, always.

"Good day," he replied, a question mark in his voice.

"Is Miss Brunnenschatten in?"

"My grandmother?"

"I used to be—but it's a long time ago—she taught me German..."

"In Kostelec?"

"That's right. We were all terribly fond of her."

"My name is Vilem," said the young man. "Grandma's in her room. Please come in."

My old teacher had a room in the back of the house, with a view into a garden full of apple trees in bloom. She was sitting in a leather armchair, glasses on her nose and a large magnifying glass in her hand, reading a book. I could see that the title on the colourful cover was in German, but before I had a chance to see what it was, she put the book aside and looked at me over her glasses.

"Good day," I said, and then I added: "Miss Brunnen-schatten..."

⚞ ⚟

"The doctor told it to me straight, just like I'm telling you. They'd take my leg off, slice by slice, and then, when there was nothing left, they'd amputate it at the hip. He gave it to me straight. And why wouldn't he?"

Berta looked me in the eye, and I didn't know what to

say. So I said what was probably the most inappropriate remark I could make in the situation. "Wouldn't it be better just to cut it off right away?"

"That's what I thought too. But he said the disease sometimes goes into remission, and when I asked how often that happens, he gave it to me straight again: once in about every hundred thousand cases. It's a great prospect, wouldn't you say, for a contented old age?"

Something glistened in his eyes.

Thoughts, memories, silly things like the little red pedal car that could also run on gas.

"But you know what, Danny?" Berta went on. "When Berta Junior died, and then when my wife, Emila, followed him half a year later, I stopped caring very much about anything. Even this."

Was there anything I could say? Berta still had a daughter. But after that double tragedy, how could a blind girl drive out the dark night of the soul, a girl so obese—in this she took after her mother—that she could scarcely move at all, and whom he and his wife had had to look after at home. Now he was looking after her alone. Without telling her, he had reserved a place for her in an institute for the blind after he died. She hadn't even inherited his somewhat dubious musical talent, but would sit for days on end in a wheelchair, reading books printed in Braille and, more recently, listening to cassettes. "And man," Berta said, "what a great thing that is for the blind! Not music, just novels recorded free of charge by actors, and some of them would bring tears to a blind man's eyes."

Berta was unhappy. I used to think that, like a lot of young men who for many long years had not been able to live a normal human life—who'd gone through the camps, done time in the Black Barons and other prison-like institutions—he'd gone to a village dance and snapped up the first girl he'd laid eyes on. But I later learned that he and Emila had gone out together for a long time before they dragooned him into the Barons, and then I knew that he loved her, though I still didn't understand it. But there were a lot of things I didn't understand, so why not that too? I thought of his old girlfriend Gerta, that night in the woods. God knows where, God knows how she ended up, though I could imagine easily enough.

To change the direction of the conversation, I asked, "What about your department store, Berta? Did you get it back when they started returning people's property?"

Berta looked at his hand; he was wearing two wedding rings. He shrugged his shoulders. "The City of London ..." he said slowly.

"You had a little red pedal car in the window that you never sold. You let me borrow it sometimes for a spin around the square."

Berta laughed. "Someone stole it when they nationalized the store. My father told me, God rest his soul."

I wanted to ask him about that great mystery, why the Communists had allowed the owner of a department store to stay on in his own firm as a sales clerk. Then I thought better of it. My own suspicions disgusted me. It wasn't in my nature; it was my upbringing, my Central European upbringing. In Canada, they would call it "Eastern European" upbringing, because Canadians don't make that distinction; they know nothing about it. It was not innate in me, and it still disgusted me, because even after a long life in a country where such acquired habits were unnecessary, I was still unable to bring my suspicions completely under control. To root them out. To kill them in myself.

"When they started returning people's property after

'89, all they wanted from us was to pay for the goods left on the shelves, the inventory," Berta said. "Then they'd give us back the business. I thought my son, Bertie, might look after it. I—well, what would I do with a department store? My wife encouraged him to go for it. The bank was willing to lend us the money for those shoddy Communist goods. The apartment building they gave back, with no strings attached, so we had collateral for the loan. But Bertie's heart wasn't in it. He'd given us the great pleasure of graduating from architecture school, and his professor had taken him on as a teaching assistant ..."

Berta looked around the room: Knobloch was at the bar with Pilous; the four girls were sitting at the round table. We were a tiny little group. In my mind, I conjured up the two-storey department store. In a small town like Kostelec, it was something unheard of. A neon sign with Mr. Moutelik's name above the entrance, polished brass edges around the counters, the wooden yardsticks they used to measure the fabric for women's dresses, smiling salesgirls in uniforms with the City of London logo proudly emblazoned on them, the bald, mercurial boss—his odd destiny still a mystery to this day—and a flat on the sixth floor of the apartment building with an elevator, the only one in town aside from the one belonging to the industrialist, Mr. Serpon, on the main drag, a long, narrow street that ended at the church. The Mouteliks had a huge four-poster bed with a canopy held up by four gilded posts, an arrangement I'd only ever seen in castles and grand chateaux where they had visiting days and charged admission. And in Berta's room, there had been a school desk made of stained wood, and the little red pedal car.

"I understood my son's position," said Berta. "He was a professional architect, not much of a head for business. And me—at my age, and with a daughter like Kamilka ..." He stopped and tried to master the painful awareness of a life that had been stupidly lost, though the stupidity had not been his own.

⚞ ⚟

"I know you weren't just making it up, Nina," I said to her at the bar. "We're all so goddamned grown-up."

"We are. And Marie wasn't just telling tales to make it sound better. She really did refuse to join the Party. I asked her about it, you know. Just between us girls, as they say. She'd have admitted to me if it was anything else, but she swore to me on the memory of her dead mother that it was true. That other thing—you know he never wanted it from her, even though you probably find that unbelievable." Her eyes were like forget-me-nots, and in them I saw trust, or suspicion, I wasn't sure which. "She wouldn't lie to me. Why should she? And she swore it was true. You know from first-hand experience, after all, how pious she was."

Knobloch headed for the bar.

"The most disgusting reason in the world. Worse than class consciousness ..." I managed to say. The blue eyes flashed a question, and Knobloch sat on the other side of us and honked at the barman, in English: "Scotch on the rocks."

I took a drink of my Manhattan. Two blowflies landed on the bar and proceeded to get drunk on the little puddles of alcohol.

⚞ ⚟

Berta filled me in on the parts of his life I had missed. After the Black Barons, he'd been a warehouse hand in the state tobacco enterprise, then an employee in a strange delivery company that would bring all sorts of goods to your door: the latest Western fashions, veal, oranges, refrigerators— stuff that was usually unavailable in stores, or that you had to stand in long lines for. Berta drove around Prague, wearing a hat with DELIVERY SERVICE on it, dragging parcels up to the fourth floor for a select list of chosen customers who, for some reason, had the privilege of outfitting themselves in clothes from Carnaby Street, preparing veal scaloppinie for dinner, and washing their clothes in American-made General Electric washing machines. He would hand over the parcel in the doorway and be handed back a form on which the privileged customer had ticked off goods from a list of compulsory items (onions, garlic, cauliflower, and other vegetables) for which the unprivileged had to stand in line for hours. That represented 40 percent of the bill. The other 60 percent was products on the optional list, which was the *raison d'être* of this strange delivery service (French *paté de fois gras*, imported oysters, New York steaks, veal, Scotch whisky, bourbon, Mozart balls, etc.), delicacies that were available only in hard-currency stores for diplomats, for the upper ten thousand in the Party, and for the relatives of the so-called traitors, that is, children who had run away to America and then sent back money to buy the special coupons needed to shop in the dollar stores. That was what socialism, finally realized, looked like.*

This company also catered for government and ministerial parties, and Berta, once again in a cap that read DELIVERY SERVICE, would haul plates laden with caviar up long staircases and into the Gothic and rococo halls of the Prague Castle, the Czernin Palace, or the Waldstein Palace, depending on the importance of the honorary guest or the occasion. This was Berta, who had once, long ago, kept a record of personal bests in a notebook and, before that, had lent me his little red pedal car.

He told me how the waiters hired to serve tables at these banquets, and the cleaning women employed to clean up afterwards, would gather up what was left when the guests were finished eating (caviar, Italian salad, cream cakes, smoked salmon, pickled herring, etc.) and stuff it all, holus-bolus, into plastic bags to take home and sort out. If that wasn't possible, then they'd eat the leftovers as is, a mish-mash they called fat-cat food, which they then washed down with beer from the pub around the corner.

Berta talked on. Little Berta, who helped me with Latin at his own school desk in his room, too small by that time for a couple of Fifth Formers. "Some of the fat cats had eaten so much they could scarcely move, and they stayed behind when the guest of honour and all the others had gone and the waiters were going after the leftovers. The only food they never touched were the leftovers on plates within reach of the Party bosses, who would sit there, sometimes till morn-ing, all soused up and singing their tired old sentimental favourites and all the predictable national songs like 'Come to Bed with Me, My Darling Baruska' and that kind of thing. Once, I had my accordion with me and one of them noticed me leaving for home with it slung over my shoulder, so he hollered at me to stay, and I had to play for them while they sang those dreary old songs. It was an awful bore, but in the end, I didn't have a lot to complain about. It turned into the occasional gig, and it always brought in more than my entire monthly wage—just for one late evening. When they would finally break it up, toward morning, they'd pull out hundred-crown notes, occasionally even five-hundred-crown notes, and they'd lick them and stick them to my forehead the way they'd seen it done in those old American films they used to show in the government projection room at the Waldstein Palace. But I got tired of it, and then I saw an ad in a newspaper for a pub-keeper. By that time, I had a pretty good idea of what the job entailed, so I applied and, long story short, twenty thousand under the table landed me the job and I became the pub-keeper in Poloves, near Jaromer."

Berta looked carefully around the bar, then stretched out one leg toward me, in a well-ironed trouser leg and a proper lace-up oxford. "Now Kamilka is taken care of," he said. "I sold our old apartment building, the one they gave back, and the money will be enough for her to spend the rest of her days in an good institute for the blind. And when they start slicing away this leg..." He looked at his leg, with the razor-sharp crease in the trousers, and I looked at him. He'd become a handsome and dignified elderly man, with a carefully groomed moustache, straight out of those old movies that used to be accessible only to fat cats, and for what? Now they were going to start slicing off his leg. He pulled up the cuff a bit, and I could see ugly red bruises on his ankle. "And so I'll be retiring. For a while."

A terrible sadness echoed in the voice of this luckless friend of mine from Kostelec. Many long years ago, he had offered to play his accordion in our band—an accordion in a swing band—but he was no Kamil Behounek,* and he left the Port Arthur pub, sad and defeated. I felt sorry for him then, too, but only for a second, because right after that, a great, wonderful Lunceford-style swing tune boomed out the windows of the Port Arthur and into the darkened wartime streets.*

Gerta, his high-school love, was a puff of ashes, or perhaps a worn handbag that had belonged to an ss woman. Plump Emila, his wife, was also ashes. So was his talented son.

And the thing that was gradually eating him up did not relent or go into remission. Berta died about a month after our fiftieth anniversary party, survived only by his blind daughter, Kamilka, living in her institution. And a character in a novel. Like Nadia. Nada. Nothing.

Nothing?

"Moutelik! Danny!" I heard Stazka shouting. "Enough of this solo drinking. Come and join us. We're trying to remember which of us is already dead, and we can't complete the list."

⚏ ⚏

She may have been eighty-nine or ninety years old, I wasn't sure, but at that age a year is neither here nor there. She didn't recognize me, and then she said that her eyesight was bad and showed me the large magnifying glass with an ivory handle, which she said was a gift from Dr. Ohrenstein. She used it for reading. No optician could make her glasses strong enough to be of any help, she said with a weak little laugh, and she was glad I'd remembered her. Then she rang a little glass bell, a gift from her grandchild Jarmila, and a seventeen-year-old copy of Miss Brunnenschatten's daughter came into the room. The old lady asked her to bring me a cup of coffee. She couldn't drink it herself anymore, she said, but that didn't matter. Then she introduced me to the girl: "This is Jarmila, my granddaughter."

Those names seemed to embody the convoluted, atypical history of one woman's young adulthood. I repeated them to myself like a mantra, or perhaps a curse: Brunhilde, Ruth, Vilem, Jarmila. It felt like a line from the refrain in Karel Macha's famous nineteenth-century romantic poem, "May": an invocation of Hynek, Vilem, Jarmila, but with one name—Hynek—missing.

184

Outside the window, it was indeed the month of May, but my teacher was now elderly, an ancient lady, in fact.

"And what about Canada?" She asked the question in a weak little voice. "Are things good there?"

"They are," I said. "It's a beautiful place."

"And you teach at the university?"

"Yes, I do."

"Just like me," she said, and at first I didn't know what she meant. "And you teach English? To students whose mother tongue is different from yours?"

"Yes," I replied, "but I only teach literature, not the language."

"Ach so," she said.

Jarmila came with the coffee. She was pretty, with large eyes and smooth, dark blond hair—but then I was at an age when every young woman who was not afflicted with some visible misfortune seemed beautiful to me. My old teacher fell silent, and so, to keep the conversation going, I said, "Do you remember Ilse Seligerova?"

Suddenly, she laughed. "Have you forgotten already, Smiricky? Don't you remember how I taught you to say it properly? Not a long 'e'—not 'Sayliger'—but almost an 'i' sound:'Síliger,' Smiricky." She laughed again.

"Do you remember her?" I asked. "She was plumpish then, and she left to attend some German school."

My old teacher nodded, but I could tell she didn't really remember. Still, I went on to tell her how I'd met Ilse, cured by now of her love for the Führer, in a Toronto pub called the Oompahpah, which doesn't exist anymore, and how she had remarked that the world was a crazy place: "Die Welt ist ein toller Platz," she had said. My old teacher kept nodding.

"And do you remember Ruda Sepp?"

"Ruda," she said. "Ach, ja, ja!" And again, I could see

that she'd forgotten about Ruda, so I started to tell her how his parents and sister had jumped under a train, with Hannelore carrying their little brother, Horst, and all at once my old teacher, her almost blind eyes now wide open, said, in an energetic, almost loud voice, "No. Not Hannelore. And not Horst, either."

She paused and took a deep breath, as though she were gathering her strength. Outside the windows, the crowns of the apple trees nodded in the breeze, and the pinkish white reflections of the blossoms came through the window and fell on the elderly lady, to whom I had once written a poem. "Bald kommen Winterstürme mit dem weissen Schneen / Und langsam wird zum Kot ..."

"No, no!" she continued. "Hannelore is still alive. She married a worker from the weaving factory in Jaromer. She once dropped in for a visit. I was astonished."

Then I remembered. The day after the war ended, I had seen a woman marching with Obermeister Uippelt* and Mr. Welzel, who had once owned an auto repair shop, all of them shorn of their hair, in the first line of an array of collaborators who were being marched off to work somewhere. The woman looked like Joan of Arc, but in the lightning flash of memory, I had probably projected onto her shaven head an image from Dreyer's classic film,* which I saw many years later, and in a different country. Could that have been Hannelore, I wondered, that confused, unlovely young girl? At the time, people were afraid of speaking even with old friends just because they were German, and I too had succumbed to that post-war mood and walked right past Mr. Kleinander on the Kostelec main street as though I hadn't seen him, though he stopped, clearly expecting to have a word with me. I knew that Harald and Rheingold had fallen at the front, and that Mr. Kleinander was no Nazi, and that he and my father had a great bond between *them, but I didn't stop. Instead, I pretended, entirely according to the clichéd protocol of all cowards and fools, that I hadn't seen him. For years afterwards, I was ashamed of what I'd done, and then, when I came to Kostelec one Christmas and asked after Mr. Kleinander, my father said he had died, and his wife was dead too. He started telling me about some of the goings-on in Kostelec, but I was no longer paying attention.*

I heard the faint ninety-year-old voice of my old teacher explain how the Sepps' arrangement not to outlive the Führer had turned out, how Hannelore had gone with them to Branka, where there was a narrow pass between two hills through which the railway tracks passed, how they'd picked out the spot in advance, Hilda and Rudolf Sepp, and how Hannelore carried Horst, who wasn't even a year old yet, in her arms ...

⊰ ⊱

Knobloch leaned over toward us. "Hi, Nina. What are you doing, and how are you?"

Nina measured him with her eyes, but what was she trying to see in him? It was Knobloch. This time he had come without his driving gloves.

"I'm not doing anything, and I'm fine," said Nina.

"Hi, Knobloch," I said, so he couldn't ignore me. "And what about you? What have you been doing since the Velvet Revolution?"

Knobloch shrugged his shoulders in his beautifully tailored jacket. "The same thing I did before, but I'm in South Africa now."

"Essential expert?"* said Nina, making a face.

Knobloch shrugged again.

"Have you abandoned the Party?" I asked.

A third time, the well-tailored shoulders shrugged. "Today, in my profession, it's no longer necessary."

"So we're both non-Party members," said Nina. "All three of us."

Instead of shrugging this time, Knobloch polished off his Scotch on the rocks. The barman leaned toward him, and Knobloch raised his empty glass and nodded.

The blowflies were lying on their backs on the bar. Knobloch took a paper napkin out of the holder and swept them to the floor.

⊣ ⊢

But when she heard the train coming, she couldn't bring herself to do it. She saw Hilda and Rudolf jump, and the train roared past, its windows lit because war-time blackouts were over, the surge of air from its passage almost knocking her down. Little Horst wailed, and when the train had passed, she walked back to their house, to the villa that had once belonged to the Karpeles family. She fed little Horst, put him in his crib, sat down beside him and rocked him to sleep. Then she heard an angry pounding on the door.

"What became of Horst?" I blurted out, and my old teacher said, "Became of him? Nothing became of him." And then she started laughing her weak little laugh, that seemed to go on forever. "They merely rechristened him," she said, finally. "They gave him a proper Czech name: Hynek. Hynek Nejezchleba—the name of his brother-in-law, the one who married Hannelore. And it wasn't even a year after the war, Smiricky," she said.

"And what happened to Horst—I mean Hynek—then?"

"He became a locksmith, and I hear, because Ruth told me this—she's his family doctor, and he goes to her for his bronchitis—he's just opened his own business, now that that's allowed."

"And Ruda, his brother. Do you remember him? Ruda?"

"Ruda—ach ja! I hear he's in Vienna." But she didn't know anything more than that about him. Nothing.

Her head sank and her chin rested on her chest, and I was astonished at how things work out. I looked out the windows at the apple trees in bloom. It was May. I got up quietly and walked out of the room. Jarmila was sitting in the kitchen with the young man who had opened the door, her brother, Vilem. "I think she's fallen asleep," I said.

Jarmila got up. "She does that quite often," she said. "Conversation tires her out. It's nothing serious. But…" She looked into my eyes.

"I know," I said. "I think I tired her out a little too much. Well…"

"I'll tell her you said goodbye," said Jarmila.

I walked out into a beautiful May afternoon and down Appletree Lane to the bus stop. In my mind, I repeated the names like a mantra: Brunhilde, Ruth, Jarmila, Horst, Hynek, Vilem. And then that line from my poem, a rough and ready poem, the only one I ever wrote in my old teacher's mother tongue: "In meinem Herze kalte Winde wehen." In my mind, my pronunciation was correct. I hoped my old teacher would be pleased.

⊨   ⊨

Anka shook her head. "My fiancé died. You probably don't remember him. He was three years ahead of us."

"I didn't know that," said Nina. "Were you really engaged to be married?"

"I suppose I was. I don't know if it was official; the

church didn't know about it, and neither did my relatives. Well, I had no relatives anyway. But we did exchange rings." She showed us two rings, with stones that looked like glass, or at least one of them did.

"Who was it?" Stazka asked.

"Janek Samal. He was in Eighth Form when we were in Fifth. After the war, he studied mechanical engineering, and then, after the Communists took over, he had to escape. He'd got mixed up with the People's Party, and he was pretty deeply involved in the struggle to keep the Communists from taking over. But some member of parliament warned him, so he blew the country."

Pilous and Kveta sat there with lowered eyes. Knobloch lit up an English pipe and stared at Anka.

"Why didn't you blow the country with him?" Nina asked.

"I hadn't finished my doctorate yet, but the main reason was, we thought the regime would collapse in a couple of years, or maybe there'd be another war. In any case ..." Anka shrugged her shoulders, "he went by himself."

I knew from Anka that the second ring wasn't the actual engagement ring that her fiancé had worn. They probably turned it into ash along with Janek, or someone in the crematorium nicked it. She bought the ring herself in Boston from her per diems after they told her that Professor Samal had died. She'd barely recovered from that blow when she got another, like a blow to the head with a set of brass knuckles: she suddenly realized why the authorities had kept refusing to give her permission to attend conferences in the West, and then had suddenly allowed her to go—to America, where Janek had lived before he died (though she didn't know he was dead when she boarded the plane, because he had died unexpectedly of a heart attack less than a month before). Professor Samal, her fiancé. Anka tightened her lips and got a hold of herself, but her eyes glistened as she thought of what might have been, but wasn't, because ...

The ungovernable river of thoughts. Looking at Anka's tears, it occurred to me, absurdly, how well informed the security police had been. Maybe they had a mole at the Massachusetts Institute of Technology who also had a fiancée immured somewhere back home, and the mole had tried to prove his reliability by sending them information. They had countless sources like that. I don't know, nor does anyone know for certain, apart from the person involved, and in a few years no one will ever know, unless some records remain somewhere in a top-secret department, which they could well have shredded by now, or else they are still top secret. And all of that is just a drop of the poison they spattered on us, spattered the way someone who has the flu sneezes and spreads invisible droplets to be picked up by everyone around the table, droplets that carry an even more invisible virus that can cripple an organism but will not completely destroy it. Mistrust. Suspicion. Socialism made real.

After a long pause, I asked, "And it was only then that they let you go? Maybe it's just that they weren't afraid anymore that you'd stay in the West."

"I don't know," said Anka. "I kept getting new invitations, but I ignored them. In the end, they practically forced me to go, and now, of course, they wanted me to work for them. So I played the neurotic card. I told them that that one flight over the ocean had been enough to convince me that I was terrified of flying, and that even if I weren't, I was even more terrified that someone from the CIA would get in touch with me and I'd spill the beans—stupid things like that. In the end, they left me alone, and after a while, the invitations stopped coming."

She looked at the ring with the slightly larger stone, the one that didn't look like glass. Per diems, I thought. To pay for this memento of grief, she probably had to spend all the money she'd been able to get from the black market money changers, and from those who sent her on her voyage across the ocean to see her fiancé, only to experience a profound shock, as they knew she would. Perhaps they hoped the shock would break her, make her more malleable. They didn't pass up a single opportunity, no matter how improbable. But she never again set out for America.

"We're only missing Erwin and Kulich," I heard Stazka say. "And Vlasak, of course, but I don't suppose anyone's expecting him to show up."

"He came the last time," said Berta.

"That's because he had comrades here," said Nina. "But just look around now. None of us is in the Party anymore. Or am I wrong about that?"

Three of those sitting here now had still been in the Party at our last meeting, but that was thirty years ago. Now everyone shook their heads; the last to do so was Kveta, in her wheelchair. Out of courtesy, no one had asked why she needed the chair, but she began talking about multiple sclerosis herself. We listened to her out of politeness, but everyone was probably thinking, "That can't happen to me anymore," because most of us were only a few months shy of seventy, and two of us had already crossed that line.

NINA VANISHED FROM THE BAR, and I moved to the little table, beside Knobloch. Fragrant smoke from his pipe wound around me like a sinister veil, and there were little sparks of light in the glass of Scotch sitting in front of the commercial attaché to the Republic of South Africa.

"Ferda," I said to him in a confidential voice, "you don't happen to know what's up with Vlasak, do you?"

The pipe went out, but that happens. I saw no significance in it at all. Even so, there was a pause while Knobloch, with great care, relit his boudoir frankincense until it was ablaze in the bowl of his pipe. The fragrant veil wound around us again, and out of it came Knobloch's flat, indifferent voice. "He remains what he was before," said the voice. "I mean, what he's been since 1945."

The ungovernable flow of wayward memories ... the sounds of Vlasak and Bara making love in the cottage that belonged to Bara's parents, my game of cards ...

"He must have been a very big cheese," I said.

"He was. Starting in February—I mean *that* February, with a capital 'F.'" Knobloch took his fragrant pipe out of his mouth and, quite clearly now—it wasn't just a hint—gave a proper, diabolical, textbook sneer and said, "He never got blood on his hands, if that's what you want to know. He was always too clever for that."

He undoubtedly was. What kind of quality is it, that cleverness? I mean, at a time when the unclever ones—in the exact opposite sense of Vlasak's cleverness—were being re-educated in correctional institutions? Those who never set up resistance groups, the unimportant priests, the former Girl Guides, and others—they were all unclever. And other people, entirely different ones, but also unclever in their own way, got spatters on their hands, their clothes, and their consciences—here and there, at least—spatters of that elixir of life so easily spilled.

"So, he's not coming today?" I said.

"He's much too clever for that," said Knobloch. "He doesn't care to be questioned by anyone."

He looked at me unwaveringly, a gaze certain of its own

matters, the rightness of its cause, cosa nostra. "Mainly because he always was, and is again, a top ranking undercover agent."

"So," I said. I finished my drink, waved at the barman—how often had I already done that this evening?—and returned his steady gaze. "So, Ferda, it's better if you don't mention any of this now. You don't want to spoil the mood."

Nina was just coming back into the bar. I got up to meet her. We sat down at the table where those two girls had been sitting. Anka and Stazka.

I WAS SUDDENLY overwhelmed by indifference, the kind of indifference I had only experienced in Canada when I realized, with a sensation of bliss, that nothing could happen to me there, except that I might die in a plane crash, a quick and, I hope, definitive death. *Indifference, our mother, our saviour, our destruction.* When I wrote that line a long, long time ago, it was an automatic triad, the instinctive impulse of the conscious mind to organize everything into groups of three, a habit that has lasted down through the ages and is said to have its roots in heathen superstition. Today, I'd exclude destruction, and I'm not even sure anymore that indifference is our mother. But it is certainly our saviour.

"Deml. Does anyone know anything about Deml? How did he die?" Stazka asked, looking at me as she said it, because I was the only exile present in the group.

But Berta was the one—the only one—to speak up. "I hear he was an engineer in that chocolate factory, but he had a heart attack. Jarek Pila wrote me about it. Remember? He was a year ahead of us."

"The one Ilse Seligerova was in love with?" Anka asked.

"The last time I saw Ilse was in the Beranek during the war. And she was wearing some kind of uniform," Stazka said.

"The BDM," Berta said. "The *Bund Deutscher Mädl.*"

So I told them the story about the Oompahpah pub in Toronto, where Jindra Bukvice's small orchestra played in artificial lederhosen and Tyrolean hats, though only one member of their quintet was German, the drummer, Sauer. And what Ilse had said by way of farewell: The world is a crazy place.

ONCE AGAIN, I had to play the storyteller, and here I was, up to my neck in this sensation of indifference. I told them how, in California, I had met Vejrazka and his wife, the couple at whose wedding I'd been a witness, and how he told me that my situation—as a brand-new immigrant with no job and, given my unsuitable education, practically no prospects of one—was a tough one, though not entirely hopeless, and how a month later, coming home from his job as an engineer in Silicon Valley, he experienced a classic American death beneath the wheels of a Cadillac driven by a drunk driver.

His wife, Dotty—although only her husband called her that then, everyone else called her Vlasta—had a phenomenal talent for telling stories even back then, in Carlsbad. She spoke, with a velocity that only women seem capable of, about people I didn't know, but even so she held my interest. Perhaps I was hypnotized by her melodious voice, or maybe it was just that she was Vejrazka's sexy bride. According to several witnesses, she turned out to be a faithful wife; that is, if a Czech legend from Los Angeles was true. That was where they lived—in a suburb with a wonderful name, Tarzana—until Vejrazka got the job in Silicon Valley. She worked as a real estate agent, a very successful one, and all the barflies of Czech origin knew her. According to the legend, she turned down all their immoral advances, so they drowned their pique at a bar called Tim's Lounge, and someone, in a fit of that same pique, so the legend goes, starting calling her by her private nickname, Dotty. He meant it as an insult, but the name stuck, and it made her famous in the Czech community, and, paradoxically, underlined her essential smarts.

And I told the story of how she took us to Lake Tahoe, to the casinos, where I saw rows of old crones in hats the Czechs called "little rose gardens" busy pulling the levers of slot machines that were meant to open the doors to fortune, and how they reminded me of the women working the looms in Barton's weaving mills in Kostelec, and how Dotty would chatter on in that rapid-fire, melodious voice of hers, but speaking an American dialect of Czech, just as fast and as hypnotically as she had in Carlsbad, where she spoke in the singsong Prague vernacular. Later, when she bought us tokens for the slots (we'd decided to risk a set amount, I ten dollars, Vejrazka fifty), she chatted just as melodiously (or sexily) to the token vendor, and in the short time it took me to blow my limit, which seemed like an hour but was probably only a minute or two, she regaled him with stories from the real estate business in the kind of English that lower-middle-class Angelinos speak among themselves.

I felt wonderfully indifferent. Someone asked about Ruda. Berta looked at me, I nodded, and Berta told them that Ruda Sepp had survived the war, but as a Russian prisoner. After his escape from Stalingrad in the flying monster, he returned to the front and took a direct hit in the chest, passed out, and came to in a Russian prison, where the freezing air got into his lungs—what kind of pathological process that was, I didn't know—and then he came back and settled in Vienna, where, Berta said, he married a widow who was a little older than he was, and they had two children together before she died. His condition got worse and worse until finally he had to drag a little cart around with an oxygen tank and a plastic tube that went into his nostrils; even so, it was hard for him to breathe, and from then on it was downhill. Berta made the same gesture he had when he told me, drawing his hand across his throat, and Stazka, just to be sure, asked, "He did himself in?"

"Yeah," said Berta. "Poor sonofabitch."

Did that expression apply only to Ruda? They talked about how Franta Jelen, Lexa, and Jebavy had died. They'd all been married, and had left several children behind, as well as a few vague memories. All of them, fortunately, had died mercifully, unexpectedly, and quickly.

Then Erwin Pick appeared in the doorway.

⚞ ⚟

His story was also plain, commonplace, an oft-repeated tale in the century that would soon come to a close. At fourteen, he'd been sent to Terezin, and from there to Auschwitz. He was young, healthy, and exceptionally strong, and rather than putting him to work at the ovens, tossing dead bodies into the fire—a job he would not have survived, no matter how strong he was—they sent him to work digging foundations for new barracks and trenches. The second-rate ss division that ran the camp probably intended to defend that terrible place, proof of their awful deeds, against the Russians. He did various jobs and then, for some reason, they shipped him off to Buchenwald, from which the Americans liberated him in a state of health that, under the circumstances, was almost excellent.

Of course, he was young, and in Buchenwald the well-organized Communists had wound him around their fingers, so when he returned to Prague, where he thought that none of his family had survived (he later discovered that an older sister had come back before him), he went straight to the secretariat of the Party for help. He remained in the Party—in fact, he served with considerable enthusiasm— until the Slansky show trials in the early 1950s, which surprised him in the same way Anka had been surprised in Boston when she was told that her fiancé was dead and she realized why they had let her go to America. He wrote a letter of protest to the Central Committee, and his boss in the Orion chocolate factory, where he was the chief accountant, was ordered to fire him, and—what else could his boss have done in the horror-show atmosphere of the time—he did.

Erwin then spent six years at the address that it was better not to ask about. After that, he went from one manual job to another, as if he'd been born and lived in America, except that in his case it was involuntary, and moreover, he was living in a gradually deteriorating dictatorship of the proletariat, so that at the end of that era—in the 1960s—he found himself working as an accountant again, this time, in a CKD factory. He married a woman who by then was an utter rarity in the country: a pure-blooded Jewish girl. They had three children, all of whom went into exile, and in the final, dying years of that by now terminally ill dictatorship, he and his wife visited the United States twice. Then came the Velvet Revolution.

᚛ ᚜

We greeted him, and he came over to the table, waving a newspaper he had plainly brought along for this occasion, but Stazka managed to ask him, before he started in, what had kept him.

"I missed my train in Prague," And then: "Read this!"

Erwin tossed the newspaper on the table, and Stazka grabbed it. "I've underlined the place," he said.

Stazka read it in silence, and then looked around. "Ladies and gentlemen, hang onto your seats!" She stood up and gave the article a dramatic reading. It was about a meeting of the new, post-'89 Communist Party in a place called Pelc, near Prague (I'd never heard of it before), where Comrade Mirko Kulich was the keynote speaker. There was a long quote from the speech by our old classmate, in preternaturally literary Czech, consisting of preternaturally tried and true—or, given how they turned out, tried and not so true— phrases, mostly using the Russian conjunction "i" instead of the more common Czech "a" for "and."

It was a speech that blithely nullified our past, as though all those years of fear, terror, horror, or whatever it was that had entered our lives, had simply never happened. But I didn't care anymore. Indifference, our—what was it? our saviour?—had settled into my soul like a pleasant, light-weight ballast, keeping me upright.

"Boy, they sure found a live one!" I heard Nina say. "He's a walking textbook of the kind of Czech that teachers used to speak around the turn of the century."

Indifference. It lay on me, pleasantly, like a blanket of ermine.

I WALKED NINA to the door of her room, but I was thinking about her friend. We stopped by her door, and she raised her face to mine, but I asked, "Nina, is it true that Bara's drinking herself to death because of the past?"

"No way," said my potential girlfriend from long ago, had I not been such a goody two-shoes. "It's because she's so fat. That's why she couldn't come to this party. And just so you'll know, Danny, she didn't put on weight from overeating.

She had these agonizing chronic headaches, and they found a tumour on her brain. They really screwed up the operation. She survived, but ..." Nina sighed. "Well, you saw her the last time. Today, she's twice the size she was then."

"Poor Bara," I said.

"So ... good night ..." said Nina. Once again, she raised her face to mine. I wasn't a goody two-shoes any longer, but a lot of good it did me now. I kissed Nina on the lips. Then she turned around and disappeared into her room.

IT WAS ALREADY long past midnight. We were all about to turn seventy, so all of us, except me, tried to practice moderation. But Erwin's news had given us an excuse to drink to excess. The reunion was transformed into an artificially exuberant party, the kind people used to give in Toronto back in the days when alcohol was still cheap and there were always a lot of good Scotches and gins to drink. Later, they turned into wine and cheese parties. Some of my old classmates were not used to drinking wine, so the beverage of philosophers very quickly put them out of action. When I left the bar, I saw Berta sound asleep with his head on the table.

Back in my room, I stepped over to the window and drew aside the curtain. In the light of the moon, I saw the old church, newly renovated. In my head, again, there was a procession of thoughts and memories, even some very fresh ones. I recalled how yesterday—by now it was the day before yesterday—I had gone into that ancient church for evening mass, and afterwards I'd spoken with the new priest, or maybe he was a deacon. It wasn't Father Brejcha; he had long since gone to his reward. The young man spoke Czech pretty well, but he was Polish. "There's a shortage of priests in the Czech Republic," he told me, and I had a sudden vivid memory of the young priest who had, endless years ago, administered the last rites to my mother and then, in the hospital corridor, asked me how many of us had enrolled in the Faculty of Arts. When I told him about the crowds of new students, he sighed and told me sadly how few, how very few theology students there had been in the archbishop's seminar. I didn't know how this priest had fared, or if he too was with the Lord. He didn't look like the kind of priest who could have avoided the fate of the Venerable Father Meloun, or his replacement, the timid, then penitent, Father Brejcha, who was tortured to death by slow degrees. I was willing to bet that not even collaborating with the *Pax in Terris* crowd could have saved him.[*]

I HAD A LONG conversation with the venerable Polish priest, and at one point I asked him if he had ever served mass in Latin, something that could now be done by special request, since the Pope was Polish.

The venerable Polish father—though he was too young to be literally venerable—shook his head sadly and sighed, "Unfortunately, I don't know Latin. In the seminary, we only took Latin pronunciation, and we learned the holy mass as altar boys, from a bilingual missal. I have never served a Latin mass, and I'm afraid I wouldn't know how."

I looked past the church at Cerna Hora, the black mountain looming darkly over the town under a heaven full of stars. Then I pulled the curtains closed, got undressed, lay down on the bed, and tried to sleep. I began to pray: "*Praeceptis salutaribus moniti et divina institucione formati, audemus dicere: Pater noster ...*"[*]

I fell asleep, and had no dreams.

DANNY'S CLASSMATES

Stazka Anastazova: Danny falls in love with her in their first year of high school, but she later becomes engaged to another classmate, who dies of tuberculosis. Stazka contracts the illness from him but recovers.

Deml: A clever classmate. In 1963, he defects to Switzerland, where he lands a respectable job in a chocolate factory.

Bara Innemanova: Nina's best friend. She is forced by her husband to join the Communist Party, with disastrous results for her friendship with Nina.

Antonin Jebavy: A descendant of many generations of working-class families. Although a Party member, he retains his humanity and common sense, and is therefore demoted to teaching at a two-room mountain school.

Franta Jelen: A close friend of Danny's. Although he doesn't join the Party, he is considered reliable because of his working-class pedigree. Therefore, he is drafted back into the army as a lieutenant but eventually becomes station master in Kostelec.

Knobloch: A commercial attaché ready to serve any regime. After the Velvet Revolution in 1989, he retains his diplomatic post in South Africa.

Kulich: A Communist true believer, he speaks grammatically correct Czech, a language long dead as a spoken tongue. He is the only one of Danny's classmates who remains an organized Communist even after Communism's fall.

Lexa: The class jester. He speaks a tongue-in-cheek, super-polite, exaggeratedly elegant Czech. He is a master of sarcasm, irony, and provocation, valuable qualities for a person living under a totalitarian regime. He plays clarinet in Danny's Dixieland band.

Berta Moutelik: One of Danny's best friends. He's a poor athlete and an even poorer accordion player. Because of his bourgeois background, the Communist regime considers him a class enemy, and he serves five or six years in the Army Work battalions, sometimes called the Black Barons.

Nina: Danny's high-school girlfriend. She marries a minister of the Czechoslovak Church, Reverend Novak, who is later arrested by the Communist regime and, after his release, dies of injuries suffered in the prison camp.

Erwin Pick: Like many Auschwitz survivors, he joins the Party but soon becomes disillusioned and joins the crowd on the non-Party-members' side of the reunion table.

Lada Pilous: A communist believer and Party member. When his God fails him, he leaves the Party.

Kveta Pilousova: Lada's wife, who ends up confined to a wheelchair.

Anka Pitasova: A brilliant student. She is the first among her classmates to acquire a Ph.D., and makes several discoveries that are patented. She is not allowed to go to conferences in the U.S., however, because her fiancé has defected there.

Ilse Seligerova: Unlike Ruda and Hannelore Sepp, Ilse is a full-blooded German. She's a nice, normal girl until Czechoslovakia becomes a Nazi Protectorate. Then she becomes an enthusiastic member of the *Bund Deutscher Mädl*, the young German women's league.

Ruda Sepp: His father claimed German nationality, although his original name was Septal, a Czech name. In consequence, Ruda is drafted into the German army, and is wounded in the siege of Stalingrad.

Vejrazka: Another clever classmate. Shortly after his marriage to Milena Cabicarova, nicknamed Dotty, he defects with her to the U.S.

Vlasak: After the war, he joins the state security service (StB) and makes a career as a secret policeman. After the Velvet Revolution he remains in that service. He doesn't dare come to the post-Communism class reunion.

Gerta Woticka: A Jewish girl, and Berta Moutelik's high-school girlfriend. She dies in Auschwitz.

NOTES

PAGE 3
The first sentences of the text are a paraphrase of the opening passage of *The Bass Saxophone*, which takes place in the same hotel, the Hotel Beranek, in Kostelec, where there is also a theatre.

PAGE 4
a pilgrimage to the shrine of Saint Nadia
Nadia is the tragic heroine of *The Engineer of Human Souls*. She's a factory worker from a village on Cerna Hora—Black Mountain—with whom Danny, the narrator and main character in many of my novels, works at a German aircraft factory in Kostelec. Danny's desire to impress her leads him to commit an act of sabotage that gets him in serious trouble but also wins him her affection, and she helps him to lose his virginity (see note for page 8). Shortly after the war, Nadia dies of tuberculosis.

PAGE 4
Sister Udelina
A nurse and a nun of the Franciscan order, and an important character in *The Miracle Game*. She appears soon after the opening of that novel, and then at the very end; she thus frames the action of Danny's dramatic life, a reminder of eternity and of human dedication.

PAGE 5
the Venerable Father Meloun
A Catholic priest who teaches Danny religion at the Kostelec grammar school. He appears in many of Danny's stories, but also in the stories about the melancholy detective, Josef Boruvka.

PAGE 6
My head was full of Irena, Marie, then Lizetka
The first two are the main heroines of *The Cowards* (in which Marie appears only episodically), *The Swell Season, The Engineer of Human Souls, Stories from Paradise Valley*, and several other stories in which Danny tries relentlessly, though unsuccessfully, to win their favour. Lizetka (her full name is Ludmila Neumannova-Hartlova) has a similar role in *Republic of Whores, Tales of a Tenor Saxophonist, The End of the Nylon Age*, and other stories.

PAGE 7
Tonda Kratochvil and *Dasa Sommernitzova*
In "Charleston in a Cage," a story in *The Swell Season*, Father Meloun persuades Danny and his friend, the talented young painter Rosta Pitterman, to help him with a serious problem. He has married Dasa, who is Jewish, to Tonda, an "Aryan," at a time when the Nazi regime has banned "mixed" marriages, and Father Meloun wants to be able to enter their marriage in the register on a date that precedes the ban. His initial attempts to erase the record of an earlier marriage were so obvious that he asks Danny and Rosta to rewrite the entire record book, a task that takes them all night and causes Danny to miss a promising midnight date with one of his girlfriends. But the ruse succeeds, and the newlyweds' lives are saved—for the time being, at least. Father Meloun manages

to put a Gestapo investigator off the scent by getting him drunk on sacramental wine. In the end, however, Father Meloun and the young couple are betrayed by a Gestapo informer called Malina, and sent off to concentration camps. Tonda and Dasa are murdered at Auschwitz, and the priest survives Buchenwald with his health seriously impaired.

PAGE 8

only to see Nadia standing sheepishly in front of my mother
Danny's "deflowering" takes place in his parents' flat in *The Engineer of Human Souls*. He and Nadia are caught practically *in flagrante*, and though they manage to dress in time, Danny's mother can easily see what has happened.

PAGE 9

just before the Nuremberg Laws kicked in
The Nuremberg Laws were passed in Nazi Germany in 1935, establishing a basis in law for racial discrimination against Jewish people. Every citizen of the Reich had to show seven birth certificates: of himself, of both parents, and of all four grandparents. The laws classified people as German if all four of their grandparents were of "German blood," while people were classified as Jews if they descended from four Jewish grandparents, and as *Mischlinge*, persons of mixed race, if they had three, two, or one Jewish grandparent. Their fate, according to Heydrich's decision at the Wannsee Conference on January 20, 1942, was to be specified after the final victory in the war. Thanks to this decision, most of the *Mischlinge* survived the war which, fortunately, did not end with a German *Endsieg*.

PAGE 10

causing the school inspector, Herr Werner, great displeasure
Heinz Dietrich Werner is based on a real person, a government
advisor called Werner who, during the Protectorate period,
was the terror of all Czech secondary schools and had the
blood of several teachers, whom he turned over to the
Gestapo, on his hands. He was hanged after the war.

PAGE 10

Father Urbanec
A Franciscan priest from *The Miracle Game.* At one of the
show trials against the "Vatican spies," he is sentenced to
forced labour in the uranium mines, where he is secretly
photographed by a regular miner. His faithful followers
circulate the photograph, thus helping to create the cult of
Father Urban, the martyr. When the priest is released on an
amnesty, some Catholic widows find him a job in a coopera-
tive farm, where an unofficial and secret order of nuns forms
around him.

PAGE 12

Prema
Prema Skocdopole is a friend of Danny's, though not a classmate. He first appears in *The Cowards*, in which he manages
to destroy a German tank using a heavy machine gun that
had been hidden for the entire war. In *The Engineer of
Human Souls*, his involvement in the anti-Communist underground ends with his escape abroad. After many adventures,
including a stint with the French Foreign Legion, from which
he escapes, he ends up in Australia. He returns to Czechoslovakia just after the Soviet invasion of 1968, because
Danny assures him that the records of his trial for resisting
the Communist regime have been destroyed, and that there-

fore his return to Czechoslovakia, though risky, would be feasible. At the same time, after the Soviet invasion, Danny flees to Canada—so that the two friends do something that resembles "castling" in chess. In the end, the Communist officials expel Prema from Czechoslovakia, and he returns to Australia, where he dies of encephalitis from a tick bite incurred while he's working on the railroad.

PAGE 12

She showed up in her blue coat, the white hood that normally hung down like a V for Victory covering her head
The hood on Marie's coat is fringed with white fur that forms a "V" on her back when it hangs down. The British prime minister Winston Churchill popularized the "V" sign during the Second World War, when he used it at the beginning of his speeches. The Nazi minister of propaganda, Josef Goebbels, ordered a large "V" to be placed on public buildings, and even on the boilers of locomotives; it was intended to stand for the slogan "*V für Victoria*," but whether this was meant as a riposte to Churchill's gesture, I don't know. The symbol made sense in English, where it stood for "victory," but in German, Goebbels had to use the Latin word "*victoria*," because the German word for "victory" is "*Seig.*"

PAGE 13

Slansky gang
Rudolf Slansky was the Czech Communist party's general secretary. He became a victim of Stalin's paranoia, which peaked shortly before the Soviet dictator's death in 1953. According to Stalin, there were counterrevolutionary groups in the leaderships of all postwar Communist states, whom he personally indicted. Show trials followed, which ended in one or more death sentences. Slansky was executed with ten

other top-ranking Communists, nine of whom were Jews; a circumstance duly stressed at their sentencing. Years later all of them were rehabilitated.

PAGE 15
Ruda Sepp
Ruda first appears in "The Cuckoo," from *The Menorah*, where he is called Ruda Husa. When his father declares himself a German and alters his name to the more German-sounding Hüsse, Ruda refuses to accept it. As a result, his parents send him away to school in Munich, and from there, he is drafted into the German army. In the war, he is seriously wounded on the Eastern Front.

PAGE 15
Lexa
In *The Cowards, The Swell Season,* and *The Engineer of Human Souls,* Lexa is the ironic commentator on everything that goes on around Danny's jazz band. (See also note for page 97.)

PAGE 15
Der Fewer
During the war, Czech young people sometimes referred to Hitler as the "fuja" (pronounced "fuia"), which is how Hitler's title, Der Führer (The Leader) sounded to Czech ears. The translator has rendered this in a way that suggests how English ears might hear the word. There were other such distortions in Czech during the war. In *The Swell Season,* for instance, one of the characters uses the expression "Hait-la" which is phonetically close to the way many Germans pronounced the official Nazi greeting, "Heil Hitler."

PAGE 17
Berta Moutelik was still in the army.
Berta makes his first appearance in *The Cowards*, as a passionate photographer who displays his work in the windows of his father's business, a store called The City of London, the only department store in Kostelec. Berta provides his photographs with embarrassing captions, and in *The Cowards*, he's largely a comic figure. But as I recount in this novel, as he goes through the experience of being on the wrong side of the totalitarian regime and grows older, he is transformed into an appealing character, a handsome, well-dressed man. At the time of this first class reunion, Berta is enlisted in a special unit of the army for politically unreliable men, popularly called the Black Barons, after their black epaulettes.

PAGE 18
Ilse Seligerova
Unlike Ruda Sepp, Ilse is a real German, and before the arrival of the Nazis in Bohemia, she's a normal girl, in no way different from the rest of the girls in Danny's class. But the moment the Czech lands become the *Protektorat Böhmen und Mähren* in 1939, Ilse becomes a zealous member of the *Bund Deutscher Mädl*, the female equivalent of the all-male *Hitlerjugend*. In *The Engineer of Human Souls*, she meets Danny by chance on a train, and behaves like a disgusting anti-Semite, which she had never been before, and when an ss officer enters the compartment, she ignores Danny and spends the rest of the trip talking with the ss man.

PAGE 19
Fest steht und treu die Wacht am Rhein
"The guard on the Rhine stands strong and true." A German

chauvinist anthem that was particularly popular during the Franco-Prussian War and the First World War.

PAGE 19
Gerta Woticka
A Jewish girl who figures in the collection of stories called *The Menorah*, in "Mifinka and Bob Zabijak." In that story, she's called Mifinka, and she has a sweetheart called Arnostek Liehm, whose father owns a large department store in Kostelec. When the occupation begins, Mr. Liehm forbids Arnostek to go out with Mifinka, and gets into an argument about it with Father Meloun, who wants to marry the couple secretly. In response to Mr. Liehm's objection that the marriage would be a fraud, Father Meloun replies, "A fraud, my dear man, can in certain circumstances become an act of Christian charity." Gerta appears again, this time as Woticka, in the story "Feminine Mystique," in which the members of Prema Skocdopole's resistance group (Danny, Lexa, etc.) try to get her to join the resistance.

PAGE 24
Wie eine Glocke. Sehr traurig.
In the novella *The Bass Saxophone*, the Lothar Kinze Orchestra, a wretched German ensemble made up of invalid musicians and other marginal characters, tours the small German communities in the Protectorate of Bohemia and Moravia. In Kostelec, the orchestra's bass saxophonist tries to commit suicide, and the bandmaster tempts Danny into taking his place by showing him the enormous instrument. Danny has heard of the bass saxophone but has never seen one, and the instrument casts a spell over him. Suddenly, during a performance that consists mainly of sentimental German dance-hall favourites, the failed suicide appears

on stage, pushes Danny aside, takes the bass saxophone, and begins to play a solo that transforms the corny music-hall tune into a grand, futuristic bass sax solo that anticipates the music of Charlie Parker and other classic bebop artists.

PAGE 25

Zdenek Pivonka

The lover of Irena, the alderman's daughter, Zdenek is therefore Danny's rival. In *The Cowards*, he disappears for a while during the battle near the customs house, and Danny has a faint hope that he will be rid of his rival should Zdenek die a "heroic death." In *The Swell Season*, Danny manages to convince Irena that Zdenek is an unfaithful womanizer, but in the end, it doesn't make her any more inclined to favour him. His hopes are revived in the last story in the book, "Sad Autumn Blues," but this time with Marie, who promises to go with him to a secret dance. But Zdenek shows up at the dance—Marie having stolen him, for a time, away from Irena—and Irena shows up with Kocandrle, Marie's boyfriend. Thus, Danny's hope of getting either girl is extinguished to the tune of "I'll Lock Up Today," an arrangement written secretly by Bedrich "Fricek" Weiss, who later died in the gas chamber in Auschwitz.

PAGE 26

some Protectorate bureaucrat

After the Munich Agreement among Hitler, Chamberlain, and Mussolini in 1938, the border regions of Bohemia and Moravia, called the Sudetenland, were seceded to the German Reich. When, with Hitler's approval, Slovakia, the eastern part of Czechoslovakia, proclaimed its independence as The Slovak State, Hitler occupied the western parts of

Czechoslovakia, Bohemia and Moravia and annexed them to the Reich as the *Protektorat Böhmen und Mähren*.

PAGE 26

Turnverein

A German sports and gymnastic organization.

PAGE 28

Kaltenbrunne

This is Ruda's subtle reference to Ernst Kaltenbrunner (1903–46), a fanatical Austrian Nazi who rose to become Chief of the Reich's Main Security Office. He was hanged in Nuremberg prison in 1946.

PAGE 29

Your students might think he was a Czech corporal.

A reference to a mistake made by the German Chancellor, Hindenburg, who, shortly before his death, confused Hitler's birthplace, Braunau am Inn, in Austria, with Braunau (which Czechs call Broumov), in Bohemia. Because he despised Hitler, Hindenburg spoke of him disparagingly as a "Bohemian corporal." So, at least, the story goes.

PAGE 32

an amendment officer

After the February 1948 putsch, the new Communist authorities tossed a lot of "bourgeois" officers out of the army. Because they couldn't replace them immediately, the puppet parliament passed a new amendment of the law on conscription, recalling discharged officers from politically reliable backgrounds back into the army. Because these officers had the new amendment to thank for their redrafting, they started calling themselves "amendment officers."

Thus, Franta Jelen becomes an "amendment officer." Although he isn't a Party member, he is of working-class origin and an employee of the railway, and is therefore considered politically reliable.

PAGE 35
Dr. Strass
A dedicated, hard-working Jewish doctor in Kostelec who saves Danny's life when Danny is a child with a medicine he brings back from a conference in London, which may have been penicillin, a drug that had just been discovered. He is transported to Auschwitz via Terezin (Teresienstadt). He survives, but when he is on his way back to Kostelec by foot, he steps on a mine and is killed. I tell his story in *The Menorah*.

PAGE 35
nor did he have a weakness for the communion wine Father Meloun offered him
The ruse with the parish register (see note for page 7) works the first time because Father Meloun manages to get the Gestapo man who comes to check on the register drunk on communion wine.

PAGE 38
Onkel Otto's German-speaking camp
A holiday retreat from the story "The Great Catholic Water Fast," which was originally part of *The Menorah*. At the camp, speaking German is mandatory, so that the boys and girls whose parents send them there will improve their command of that language. Danny gets to know Alex Karpeles and Paul Pollack there, and he also learns to play a game that in Bohemia is called Business but in the West is known as Monopoly. The children play the game passionately, for most

of them are the sons and daughters of Jewish businessmen, among whom "Aryans" like Danny and Berta Moutelik (who, of course, is also the son of a businessman) are anomalies. Both Danny and Berta become hopelessly addicted to this purely capitalist game. Onkel Otto, in whose camp I enjoyed some of the happiest times of my youth, died in a concentration camp.

PAGE 38
Mr. Katz, the cantor in the Kostelec synagogue
Mr. Katz supplements his inadequate cantor's salary by giving private lessons in German and, if his students are Jewish, Hebrew. He is the hero of the story "My Teacher, Mr. Katz," in *When Eve Was Naked*, in which his daughter marries a factory owner. She has a daughter, Hannerle, whom Mr. Katz loves with all his heart. All of them—Mr. Katz, his wife, his daughter, her husband, and little Hannerle—die in a concentration camp.

PAGE 40
the Messerschmitt factory
A Kostelec factory that produced parts for German military aircraft like the Stuka, the Messerschmitt 109, the Focke-Wulff, and finally the "secret weapon": the v-1. Danny is forced to work there by the Nazi labour policies—the *Totaleinsatz* program. There is a reference to it in *The Cowards*, but it has a central place in *The Engineer of Human Souls*. Danny meets Nadia there, and attempts to commit sabotage to impress her.

PAGE 44
Nosek
A friend of Danny's from the group around the band. In *The*

Engineer of Human Souls, he works in the Messerschmitt factory on the ferroflux, a device that determines if there are any cracks in welded joints. The ferroflux is in a room of its own, and Nosek lets Nadia and Danny use the room, though not to find flaws in welded joints. Nosek puts in a brief appearance as Vlada Nosal in the story "My Teacher, Mr. Katz" when the pharmacist, Mr. Hess, despite the ban on selling insulin to Jews, gives the medication to Mr. Katz and then orders Vlada to record that the insulin went to an Aryan customer.

PAGE 46
Milada Horakova
Milada Horakova was a Czech socialist politician who spent the Second World War in the Ravensbrück concentration camp, and after the Communist coup in 1948 was arrested again. Her trial was the first of a series of show trials which culminated in 1952 with the anti-state conspiracy centred around Rudolf Slansky. Horakova was accused of the usual assortment of anti-Communist "crimes" and hanged—the first woman in Czech history to be executed for political reasons.

PAGE 46
a celebratory mass in St. Vitus's Cathedral
Traditionally, Czech kings and, later, presidents, inaugurated their official duties with a ceremonial mass in the cathedral in Prague Castle. For tactical reasons, the first Communist president, Klement Gottwald, who was duty bound to be an atheist, did the same thing. Because he had clearly never been in a Catholic church before, and because they sat him and his wife, Marta, on a special honorary pew directly in front of the altar, he became confused when he heard people

behind him standing or kneeling, and sometimes he got it wrong, so that while the congregation was kneeling, he and his wife were standing, and vice versa.

PAGE 48
if the gentleman here ... would adopt German nationality
Oddly enough, adopting German nationality was not that difficult for Czechs if they had any German ancestors, and sometimes even that wasn't an absolute condition. I don't know what laws the Germans were guided by in this instance, except that in a total dictatorship, anything is possible. For instance, the Air Marshall of the Nazi Luftwaffe, Erhard Milch, who did such an outstanding job organizing the invasion of Norway, was half Jewish—or even a pure-blooded Jew, according to some researchers—in spite of which the Führer himself declared him indispensable for the Luftwaffe.

PAGE 50
the operetta that, out of ignorance, I referred to as a musical
In those novels of mine that are narrated by Danny Smiricky, Danny is not a novelist but writes librettos for operettas. He tries his hand at fiction only once, a novel called *The Tank Brigade* (published in English as *The Republic of Whores*), which remains in manuscript form but gets him into serious trouble when it falls into the hands of Ludmila Neumannova-Hartlova—Lizetka—who uses it as erotic blackmail against Danny.

PAGE 50
L'esprit de Moscou
A penetrating perfume that was popular in the Soviet Union at the time. Consequently, it was also popular with some Communist Czech women.

PAGE 51
The Golden City, *Kristina Söderbaum*, The Jew Süss
I didn't see *The Golden City* or *The Jew Süss* until after the war, in Canada and on video. I took the information about Söderbaum's nickname (she was the wife of Veit Harlan, the director of *The Jew Süss*), and about why they banned *The Golden City* during the Protectorate period, from Harlan's memoirs, *Im Schatten Meiner Filme*, and from the memoirs of actress Lida Baarova's lover, Gustav Fröhlich, *Waren das Zeiten*. Anyone who wanted to see *The Golden City* during the war had to go to Vienna, as Babocka did.

PAGE 55
Dotty
Dotty first appears in *A Tall Tale About America*, where I call her Milenka. Only later, in *The Engineer of Human Souls* and then in a farce I wrote for the theatre called *Our Guest Is Our God*, does she appear as Dotty, whose proper name is Milena Cabicarova. In *A Tall Tale About America*, she takes Danny on a breakneck trip to the casinos of Lake Tahoe, Nevada, in a small private airplane.

PAGE 56
Mr. Puchwein
Although this German teacher didn't have an exemplary Aryan name, he was not Jewish. At the end of the First Republic (1918–1938), he published a novel, *People from Pol-jana*, in a magazine called *National Politics*. During the war, he published a collection of sentimental stories (which he later left out of his bibliography), and after the war, he dedicated himself to writing in the socialist realist vein under the pen name Jiri Marek, and serving in various high offices. Later, he switched to crime fiction, from which a series of

movies was created called *Sinners from the City of Prague*. This finally made him popular.

PAGE 58
Ernst Udet
An ace pilot from the First World War (sixty-two kills), and later, a designer of fighter planes like the Messerschmitt 109 (on which Danny works in *The Engineer of Human Souls*, and which he tries to sabotage to impress Nadia). After the defeat of the Luftwaffe in the Battle of Britain in the fall of 1940, and after he got mixed up with Rudolf Hess, whose plane he was supposed to have piloted for Hess's secret flight to England, he lost favour with Hitler, had a falling out with Goering, and, in 1941, committed suicide. The Nazis kept this a secret because they had already made of him a model of behaviour for young people, so the official version was that Udet had died a hero's death test-piloting a new kind of military aircraft.

PAGE 59
the one-armed legionnaire Mr. Skocdopole
Here, Danny is thinking of the scene from *The Engineer of Human Souls* in which Prema's father, while getting him drunk on slivovitz, tells him about a famous battle he fought as a legionnaire in Russia at the end of the First World War.

PAGE 64
where I had once carried the slender Nadia
A reference to a scene in *The Engineer of Human Souls* in which Nadia, who is suffering from tuberculosis, collapses on her way home to Cerna Hora and Danny has to carry her to her village on his back.

JOSEF SKVORECKY

PAGE 69

Nunc est bibendum; Gaudeamus igitur
From his fragmentary recollection of Latin, Berta is con-
necting quotations from two different sources. The line about
drinking is from Horace's Ode 1.37: 1, *"Nunc est bibendum,
nunc pede libero pulsanda tellus."* Freely translated, it
means, "Now is the time to drink and stomp on the ground
with abandon."

"Gaudeamus Igitur" is an ancient student song, the modern version of which probably crystallized around the end of
the eighteenth century. The words translate roughly as: "Let
us rejoice, friends, while we are young. When joys depart and
we feel age in our bones, that will be the end of us."

PAGE 78

my cousin Danica, whom I'd always called Dinah
Danny, who is an anglophile, doesn't much like the Southern
Slav name Danica, or the Czech derivative, Dana. So he calls
the young woman Dinah, a name from the old jazz number
by Harry Akst from 1928. He knows it from a version by the
Boswell Sisters, a recording of which was available in
Czechoslovakia until the Americans entered the war after
the Japanese attack on Pearl Harbor.

PAGE 79

*Ich spreche Goethes Deutsch, nicht Schweindeutsch, Herr
Inspector!*
Professor Propilek (1911–1976) was a specialist in Balto-
Slavic languages, which, naturally, were not taught during
the war. Like many who had no outlet for their specialities
during the war, Propilek had to teach German. Both the
Nazis and the Communists contributed to shortening his
teaching career. His statement, that he speaks Goethe's

221

German, not pig German, is taken from *The Bass Saxo-phone*. His riposte to the inspector is probably student folk-lore, but in any case, it perfectly captures the man's courage and integrity.

PAGE 84
Lexa blew a sour note on the clarinet
This passage is taken verbatim from *The Cowards*.

PAGE 85
a female suicide pilot
Her name was Hanna Reitsch, and she began her career as a glider pilot. She broke the world record for women when she flew 305 kilometres in 1933, and again when she reached a height of 2,800 metres in 1934. During the war, she became the first female test pilot, flying the monster transport plane, the Messerschmitt Gigant (which evacuates Ruda Sepp from Stalingrad; see page 164), and the first rocket-propelled fighter, the Henschel 293 (which existed only in prototype; it was never mass-produced). She even undertook several test flights in the prototype of the v-1, which was later used as a pilotless jet bomb in air attacks on London. In April 1945, she managed to fly through Soviet anti-aircraft fire around Berlin and reach Hitler's bunker, intending to die by the Führer's side. But the Führer ordered her to fly to the headquarters of Admiral Doenitz, whom he had just named the new Führer, where she was to have gathered together the remnants of the German air force. Once again, she flew through Soviet anti-aircraft fire, but in the end, she was captured by the Americans, who released her a year later. She went on devoting herself to aeronautics. Among many other achievements, she founded the National School of Gliding in Ghana. She died in 1979 as the holder of at least forty world gliding records.

Though a colourful personality, she was an archetypical political naïf with a head full of flying and not much else.

PAGE 89

The enemy ... would have a field day with that.
Jebavy doesn't have the courage to vote against the death penalty. This was a time when it was expected that people would vote unanimously, and en masse, for the "hard but just" punishment of the gallows, and to abstain would have meant an immediate sacking, and probably something a lot worse (which, in turn, would depend on the daring and character of the local Party functionaries). That is why he chooses to justify his behaviour with this hypocritical "warning."

PAGE 92

in accordance with the laws as they applied at the time
This nonsensical appeal to the laws "as they applied at the time" was used once again by Communist Party "lawyers" after 1989 in defence of the phony monster trials of the 1950s. The legal and, above all, the moral untenability of this argument shines through when you consider the Nuremberg race laws, according to which people were ultimately sent to the gas chambers. These laws also "applied at the time."

PAGE 95

a church that changed its name according to the political situation
The Czechoslovak Church, which was founded as a result of the revolt of a large group of Catholic priests after 1918, had to change its name to the Czecho-Moravian Church during the Protectorate period. After the war, as far as I know, it reverted to its original name, and now, after the collapse of

Czechoslovakia, it still stubbornly calls itself the Czechoslovak Hussite Church.

PAGE 96
angels on the head of a pin
It is traditionally believed that the debates between medieval
scholars had to do with nonsensical questions, such as how
many angels could dance on the head of a pin. Such debates
led to the undermining of medieval dogmatism and, ultimately,
to modern thinking, the basis of true science. I don't know
whether scholars actually did argue about angels dancing on
the head of a pin, or whether the example was made up in
order to satirize questions that today seem to us, not always
justifiably, to be pseudo-problems. Be that as it may, the idea
of arguing about angels on the head of a pin always strongly
reminds me of aspects of Communist Party debates about
socialist realism, about how there is essentially no contra-
diction in the notion that democracy can exist in a one-party
state, about correct, constructive criticism versus bad, destruc-
tive criticism, about the role of Marxism in astronomy, and
so on.

PAGE 97
Putych, Haryk
Putych is a cynical, socialist snob; all his apparel is tailor-
made, from his hat down to his shoes. But politically he is
very clever. He appears in the story "As Did the Ancient
Egyptians," from the collection *Bitter World* (which has not
been translated into English).

Haryk is one of the heroes of *The Cowards*. He's the gui-
tarist in the Bob Crosby–esque Dixieland band in which
Danny plays the tenor saxophone. Of the other members of
the band—Fonda (piano), Benno (trumpet), Lexa (clarinet),

and Venca Stern (trombone)—only Lexa appears in *Ordinary Lives*, though there is a glancing reference to Benno.

PAGE 97
Comrade Kral
In *Miss Silver's Past*, Kral is a kind of grey eminence, the head honcho over culture. He never directly appears in the novel, but his name alone is enough to inspire fear.

PAGE 106
Krista from Myto, Karla-Marie and Marie-Karla
Girls that Danny unsuccessfully but determinedly tries to woo in *The Swell Season*.

PAGE 107
the Prague Spring was going on outside
The Prague Spring is the term for the period from January 1968, when Alexander Dubcek replaced the Stalinist Antonin Novotny as the Communist Party chairman, until August 1968, when Czechoslovakia was invaded by the Soviet forces and their allies. Dubcek abolished censorship so that for the first time in twenty years newspapers and magazines were free to publish truthful reports about events; he also promised a multi-party democratic system within which, however, the Communist Party would retain its "leading role," a euphemism for Party dictatorship. In other words, he promised to square the political circle—an experiment which was doomed to failure, as every impossibility is.

The term Prague Spring applies also to a May festival of classical music which was held annually for several years before the invasion. This old meaning of the term was overshadowed by the new one.

PAGE 108

Once, long ago, Benno ... had caused me to waver
A reference to the story "Conversations with Oktyabrina,"
in which Danny shares digs with Benno, the trumpeter
(from *The Cowards, The Swell Season,* and *The Engineer of
Human Souls*) who becomes a Communist through a merger
between the Communist Party and the Social Democrats.

Ivana Hrozna is the well-meaning principal of the voca-
tional school in *The Miracle Game* who loves Stalin. Zdena
Prochazkova, the wife of the "benevolent tutor" for the indoc-
trination of high-school teachers in Vyhlidka, is a sworn,
though secret, enemy of Lenin.

These characters, along with the heroine of "Conversations with Oktyabrina" and the heroine of *The Miracle
Game*, Vlasta Koziskova, called Vixi, were Danny's real political instructors, who, consciously or not, guided him through
the jungle of Communist absurdities.

PAGE 110

*that evil day in February 1948 when the Communists took
power*
The democratic Czechoslovak republic ended with the
Munich decree of 1938 (see note for page 26). After the
Second World War it was restored, but its democracy, right
from the beginning, was limited. Only four political parties
were permitted: Communist, social democratic, socialist, and
the Catholic "Peoples party"). In February 1948, ministers of
the three non-Communist parties resigned, hoping that
president Benes would nominate a non-political caretaker
government which would order new elections. Since the
mood of the country was already largely anti-Communist,
the ministers felt sure that in this election, the Communists
would lose. But Benes, weakened by a fatal ilness and under

pressure from the Communist chairman Gottwald, accepted the resignations and asked Gottwald to name a new government. This new government was composed of Communists and a few fellow travellers, and it soon turned Czechoslovakia into a totalitarian dictatorship modelled on the Soviet system. What followed was the arrest of thousands of non-Communists (their number eventually reached more than 100,000), show trials and executions (officially two hundred, but in reality there were many more), an absolute censorship of the press and of all publication activities, and a wide-spread system of police informers.

PAGE 112

"The Devil!" she had said

In *The Miracle Game*, during a discussion with Danny, who has been infected by "university Marxism," Zdena Prochazkova declares that Lenin is the devil incarnate.

PAGE 112

an evil mafia and its hit man, Ponykl, in that beautiful year—1949—of the miracle in the rocks near the church of the Virgin Mary under Mare's Head

All of this appears in *The Miracle Game*. In the chapel of the Virgin Mary under Mare's Head, a miracle occurs and is witnessed by Danny, who is there with Vixi. That leads, through Ponykl's Communist Party "mafia," to the murder of the priest, Father Doufal, who was delivering a sermon in the church when the miracle occurred.

PAGE 113

Lester

A characteristic figure in the "grey zone": that is, he is neither a dissident nor a member of the establishment. He's an academically educated connoisseur of jazz who defends this music and other cultural phenomena against Party authorities, using the method of "nodding and baffling." He appears to agree with the comrades, but then he so completely confuses them with erudite talk about the subject they are thinking of banning that, instead of issuing the ban, they permit it. He appears in this role in *The Miracle Game*, in *Two Murders in My Double Life*, and in the film script for *The Little Mata Hari of Prague*.

PAGE 124
Luis Trenker–style wind
Luis Trenker was a Tyrolean Italian, originally an actor and then a director of "Alpine films." His heroes were windblown Alpine skiers, often played by Trenker himself. He became quite popular, even in America, and some rather uninitiated post-war critics saw in him a kind of precursor, if not a propagator, of Nazism. In reality, Trenker was something like a Tyrolean John Wayne. When he shot most of *The Prodigal Son* (1934) in the United States, he fell afoul of Goebbels, and from that time on, he began to trip over the censors. His movie *Condottieri* (1937), about the revolt of the Condottieri against Cesare Borgia, played for only a week because Goebbels recognized in it an undisguised criticism of conditions in Nazi Germany. Finally, with *The Fire-Devil* (1940), Trenker's directorial career among the Nazis came to an end—the film contained parallels between Napoleon's role as the suppressor of a popular uprising and Hitler.

PAGE 131
Auschwitz, Majdanek, Treblinka
The refrain of a song by a Bucharest cantor called Katz (not Danny's teacher of the same name), who became famous in

Prague when one of his recordings was the first to come out right after the war. Katz was a marvellous singer in the cantor-style tradition, and his song was a lament for those murdered in Auschwitz and nearby camps.

PAGE 145
Marie's favourite way of addressing me
When Marie is angry with Danny, in *The Swell Season* and elsewhere, or when she's teasing him or making fun of him, she is fond of saying, "You know what I mean, Dannyboy?"

PAGE 148
"Ich werde Stalingrad errobern!"
"I will conquer Stalingrad!" The Führer's overhasty declaration was made before the Battle of Stalingrad. It stuck in my memory when I heard it coming out of our family radio one day at the end of summer.

PAGE 149
Ruda is right there in the pocket. At Stalingrad.
In early fall 1942, German armies reached Stalingrad, an important industrial city on the Volga river. After months of bitter fighting they managed to conquer most of the city, largely in ruins by now, on the western bank on the river. Eventually the Soviet armies crossed the river north and south of the German salient, cut it off, and completely encircled Stalingrad. Then they formed their forces into a two-sided defence—one facing inwards, to keep the Germans from breaking out, and the other facing outward, to keep relief forces from breaking through from the outside. Inside this huge "pocket" a German army of about a million men fought desperately, hoping for a *Durchbruch*, or break-through. This never happened. Goering, the commander of

the German air force at the time, bragged that he would keep the German forces well supplied with food and other necessities, but the success of this effort was extremely limited. Eventually the Soviets conquered the only airport that remained in German hands, and soon afterwards the German commander Marshall Paulus surrendered. Of the nearly one million men who spent long years in Siberia as POWs, only a pitiful few survivors ever returned to Germany.

PAGE 150
"... Ich hatte einen Kameraden ..."
This very old, famous German army song is a lament for a fallen friend.

PAGE 155
Marshal Schörner
Ferdinand Schörner sympathized with the Nazis from the very beginning. He ended the First World War as a mere lieutenant, though he distinguished himself at Caporetto (where Hemingway was in the retreating Italian army—see *A Farewell to Arms*). Even so, the Nazis ignored him for a long time, and he was given command of a full division only after the start of the Second World War. He displayed exemplary brutality not just to the enemy, but to his own soldiers, and he executed both ordinary soldiers and colonels with equal relish, so that he came to the attention of the Führer himself, and in his final days in his Berlin bunker, Hitler promoted Schörner to the rank of field marshal and entrusted him with full command of the Silesian front, where he led an army that had been thus far relatively unscathed in battle. With this division, Schörner was to liberate besieged Berlin, which he did not do; instead, he took a substantial part of his army into American captivity, where he sought refuge him-

self. But the Americans sent him back to the Soviets, and he spent ten years in a Soviet prison. He then returned to Germany, where he was immediately made to stand trial for killing his own soldiers. He spent a further four and a half years in prison, and died in 1973 at the age of eighty-one.

PAGE 155
"Goya? He's shit compared to this."
Rosta's comment also appears in *The Cowards*. Seeing the ss men who have been tortured to death reminds Rosta of Goya's famous series of etchings, *Disasters of War*.

PAGE 160
cross-bracket machine-gun mounts for the Messerschmitts
The object of Danny's sabotage in *The Engineer of Human Souls*. The cross-brackets were used to attach the ammunition drum to the wings of the Messerschmitt 109.

PAGE 162
Koba
Stalin's unflattering nickname, which was embraced by him, but used disparagingly by his detractors.

PAGE 165
Our ruin, our ruin, our ruin
An echo of the invocation of indifference at the end of "The Legend of Emöke." The passage runs: "And in time, very quickly, I was permeated with an indifference toward the legend, the indifference that allows us to live in a world where creatures of our own blood are dying every day of tuberculosis and cancer, in prisons and concentration camps, in distant tropics and on the cruel and insane battlefields of an Old World drunk on blood, in the lunacy of disappointed love,

under the burden of ludicrously negligible worries, that in-difference that is our mother, our salvation, our ruin."

PAGE 167
Frontkameradschaft
A soldier's term. It assumes that friendships formed between soldiers who fight together at the front last until death.

PAGE 170
None of that romantic "I shall return" nonsense
A reference to a lyrical essay in which the celebrated Czech poet Frantisek Halas promises his native soil that he will return to it—that is, that he will be buried in it.

PAGE 175
Vlach and Brom
Two leading Czech swing and jazz orchestra leaders. Karel Vlach founded his swing band shortly before the Second World War, survived both the attempts of the Party to liquidate him and the coming of rock 'n roll, and died in 1986. The band, bearing his name, continues to perform under a new bandleader. It was and is a traditional big band of the swing era. Gustav Brom came later, also survived rock 'n roll, and never ceased to be popular.

PAGE 181
That was what socialism, finally realized, looked like
Sometime in the late 1950s, when the Party and the govern-ment decided that socialism in Czechoslovakia had finally been realized, they changed the country's name from the Czechoslovak Republic to the Czechoslovak Socialist Republic.

PAGE 183

he was no Kamil Behounek

Kamil Behounek was one of the most important figures of the Czech swing era (roughly 1939 to the end of the 1950s). He was a composer and a tenor saxophonist, and he also played the button accordion, an instrument that almost never appears in a jazz ensemble. Nevertheless, he wrote solos for it, and scored it for big band ensembles as well, thus demonstrating its surprising potential as a swing instrument. He died in exile in Germany.

PAGE 183

a great, wonderful Lunceford-style swing tune

Jimmie Lunceford was the leader of one of the best swing bands. With his own orchestra, he recorded many hits that are considered swing classics ("Margie," "Annie Laurie," "Organ Grinder's Swing," etc.) During the war, I was always enchanted by his swinging, singing battery of saxophones in numbers such as "Sweet Sue" and "My Melancholy Baby"— those "honey-comb saxes."

PAGE 184

Karel Macha's famous nineteenth-century romantic poem, "May"

Karel Hynek Macha (1810–1836) was a romantic poet whose poem "May" is the first modern Czech poem. It is essentially the story of Vilem, who is executed for the murder of his own father, the seducer of Vilem's lover Jarmila. A wildly romantic tale, but written in beautiful rhymed verses which were something entirely new in nineteenth-century Czech poetry.

PAGE 186
Obermeister Uippelt
The chief technical inspector in the Messerschmitt plant, and an important character in *The Engineer of Human Souls*. He's an American-born German who was drawn by Nazi propaganda into "returning" to Germany. He later comes to regret this, and it appears that he has some connections to the Czech resistance movement. Nevertheless, Comrade Pytlik, a very active Communist, murders Otta Uippelt during the May uprising in 1945.

PAGE 186
Dreyer's classic film
The Passion of Joan of Arc (1928) by the Danish director Carl Theodor Dreyer was one of the top films of the silent era. The warlike St. Joan, who is ultimately burned at the stake, appears in the film with her hair cut short, military-style, which reminds Danny of the shorn heads of the female collaborators.

PAGE 187
Essential expert
Nina, once again, is making an ironic comment about a Communist Party phrase, this time one that describes the practice of making exceptions for people of clearly bourgeois background if they were specialists in a profession where there were not enough politically reliable people of working-class origin, such as mechanical engineers, medical doctors, or people who could speak foreign languages. Such individuals survived all the purges and political somersaults of the Communist era without even having to pretend that their thinking was politically correct.

PAGE 201

the Pax in Terris *crowd*

A reference to the organization of Catholic priests called *Pacem in Terris* (Peace on Earth, after the opening words of a papal encyclical), which collaborated with the Communist regime.

PAGE 201

Praeceptis salutaribus moniti et divina institucione formati, audemus dicere

The words sung by the priest during the celebration of high mass. Since the second Vatican Consilium, it can be quietly said in the vernacular. Roughly translated, the words mean: "Mindful of His worthy precepts and instructed by His divine wisdom, let us pray with confidence to the Father in the words our Saviour gave us."

ACKNOWLEDGEMENTS

My thanks to Paul Wilson, my translator, and to Jane Warren, my editor, for their efforts to make my Czech read like an English novel.

—Josef Skvorecky

The publication of this book is a multiple milestone. For Josef Skvorecky, it marks the fiftieth anniversary of the publication of his first major novel, *The Cowards*. It marks the fortieth anniversary of my first encounter with Josef's writing, and my first awkward attempts to master Czech by translating some of his short texts into English. And it was thirty years ago that a young editor and publisher, Louise Dennys, hired me to translate Skvorecky's magnum opus, *The Engineer of Human Souls*. That was the real beginning of a relationship with Skvorecky's work that has lasted through three decades and many books.

For all of these reasons, I would like to thank Josef Skvorecky, in gratitude for the privilege of rendering his words into the language of his second homeland.

I'd also like to thank Jane Warren, my editor at Key Porter, for her enthusiasm for the book, her sensitive reading of the text, and her elegant editorial suggestions.

Finally, my thanks and love to my wife and editorial assistant, Patricia Grant, for the hours she spent reading the different drafts of this translation, for her keen eye for false notes, and her suggestions for improvement. Patricia does not read Czech, but she loves Josef's work with the same passion that Josef's Czech fans do. Her responses encourage me to believe that something of the magical qualities of Josef's storytelling, which make him the most beloved author in the Czech Republic, have survived into English.

—Paul Wilson